Robert Muchamore

Hodder
Children's
Books

A division of Hachette Children's Group

HODDER CHILDREN'S BOOKS

First published in Great Britain in 2015 by Hodder and Stoughton

This paperback edition published in 2016

1 3 5 7 9 10 8 6 4 2

A CIP catalogue record for this book is available from the British Library

ISBN 978 1 444 91457 3

Typeset in Goudy by Avon DataSet Ltd, Bidford-on-Avon, Warwickshire

Printed and bound in Great Britain by Clays Ltd, St Ives plc

The paper and board used in this book are made from wood
from responsible sources.

MIX
Paper from
responsible sources
FSC
www.fsc.org   FSC® C104740

Hodder Children's Books
An imprint of Hachette Children's Group
Part of Hodder and Stoughton
Carmelite House
50 Victoria Embankment
London EC4Y 0DZ

An Hachette UK Company
www.hachette.co.uk

www.hachettechildrens.co.uk

Robert Muchamore worked as a private investigator before starting to write a story for his nephew, who couldn't find anything to read. Since then, over twelve million copies of his books have been sold worldwide, and he has won numerous awards for his writing, including the Red House Children's Book Award.

Robert lives in London, supports Arsenal football club and loves modern art and watching people fall down holes.

For more information on Robert and his work, visit **www.muchamore.com**, where you can sign up to receive updates on exclusive competitions, giveaways and news.

BY ROBERT MUCHAMORE

The Rock War series:

Rock War
Boot Camp

and coming soon:

Battle Zone

The CHERUB series:

Start reading with *The Recruit*

The Henderson's Boys series:

Start reading with *The Escape*

1. Forbidden Fat

July 2014
Camden, North London

The chip shop closed at one thirty on Friday mornings. By daybreak, the oil in the deep-fat fryers had a solid white crust, but still retained enough heat to gently warm Jay Thomas's outstretched palm.

In younger days, Jay had been fascinated by the way bubbling oil cooled to solid white fat, delving into the warm crust with a finger before making a half-baked attempt to smooth out the evidence. The oil beneath the white crust stayed hot and he'd have been yelled at for going near it.

Jay got yanked out of Memory Lane by a thump on the floor above. He shared the flat over the chip shop with his mum, stepdad and six siblings. The place was rarely quiet, but he'd learned to tune out noise, like his little siblings chasing around, or brother Kai cursing at FIFA 14.

But the floor-shaking crash of a case packed with studio

lamps wasn't familiar, and nor was the shouting that followed it.

'Get the leads first, Damien!' a cameraman yelled. 'Then I can start wiring up while you're carrying all this gear in.'

Jay heard Damien grunt, then the twenty-something runner bolted downstairs and out the rear door to one of three vans the TV crew had parked in the courtyard out the back. Jay caught a glance, as Damien and a pretty runner called Lorrie exchanged words.

I already told you there's no leads in this van . . .

Well if they're not here we must have left them when we picked up the gear at ProMedia . . .

John's gonna blow his stack if . . .

As Damien headed up to break the bad news to his boss, Jay felt a nervous ache in his belly. His heart was thumping, he'd barely slept and his mum had given him a couple of Imodium to settle a rebellious stomach.

Getting picked for *Rock War* was the most exciting thing that had ever happened to Jay, but right now a chunk of him craved simpler days, driving his Lego trucks between chip-shop tables and standing up with salt stuck to his knees.

'Are you Jay?' a woman shouted.

Jay spotted her squinting through the letterbox opening, halfway up the shop's metal grille.

Someone else yelled from a top-floor window, 'Can we have some quiet on set, *pl-eeeease*? We're trying to shoot an interview.'

Rather than shout back at the woman, Jay made a 'go

around' gesture and headed out the rear door into warm air and breaking sun. It was Friday rush hour on the main road out front and a truckload of rubble rumbled by as the woman offered a slender hand attached to a wrist festooned with fluorescent wristbands.

'I'm Angie, director camera-unit B. Can you spare us ten for an interview?'

Jay ran a hand through his scruffy hair and shrugged. 'I kinda look like shit, and I'm still in my night shorts.'

'No worries,' Angie said, as Jay picked up an Aussie accent. 'The just-out-of-bed vibe is exactly what we're going for in this segment. It's the first day of summer holidays. You're heading off to *Rock War* boot camp. You're excited and a bit overawed, which is exactly what we want to capture on camera.'

Jay liked hearing that he was *supposed* to be excited and overawed. He didn't exactly agree to be interviewed, but Angie's arm guided him towards the pub next door anyway.

The White Horse pub and the adjoining chip shop had been owned by Jay's family for more than fifty years. The pub was run by Jay's auntie, Rachel. She lived over the pub, with her four daughters, a granddaughter and a few hangers-on. As Jay followed Angie through the White Horse's swinging saloon doors, he was surprised to see black sheeting taped over all the windows. Lights and cameras were set up to film interviews, with the pub's dartboard as a backdrop.

'I've captured one from next door,' Angie said, smiling triumphantly at her crew as she led Jay inside.

The crew comprised a camerawoman, a sound man and a runner, plus Angie the director. Jay's cousin Erin stood at the bar, looking fit in tight denim shorts and a lime vest. She was tanned and athletic, and Jay felt really awkward. He usually only wore shorts in bed and was self-conscious about being skinny, hating the idea of his bare legs getting on TV.

'Do you think I could nip back and get some jeans?' Jay asked, as the runner swooped with a make-up kit and started dabbing foundation on his forehead.

'It's just so you don't look greasy under the lights,' the guy explained.

Nobody answered Jay's question about the jeans and he was too intimidated by all the fussing to ask again.

Two minutes later, he was on a bar stool in front of the dartboard, with a wireless microphone taped under his shirt, two cameras aimed his way and his cousin Erin on another stool next to him.

'All set?' Angie asked, as the cameraman let her take a look at his framing. Then she turned towards the two teenagers and tried to sound soothing. 'Try and relax, I'm going to ask a few questions about your bands. If you fluff your answer or say something you don't like, just start the answer again and we'll patch things up in the edit suite . . . Camera? Sound? OK, Bob . . .? Action!'

Angie put on the glasses around her neck, grabbed a question sheet from a tabletop and stepped close to Jay and Erin.

'I'll start you off gently,' she began. 'I want you both to

say your name, your age, the name of your band and what your role in the band is. OK?'

The two teenagers both nodded as Angie pointed at Jay.

Jay froze. It felt like he was seeing a hundred things at once: heat from the lights, sandbags holding the equipment stands down, two dozen cables sprawling over cigarette-burned carpet. Millions of people would see him this way for the first time – with slim white legs and hand-me-down Superdry shorts.

'Loosen up around your shoulders,' Angie said soothingly. 'Imagine it's just you and me, over a nice cup of coffee.'

'Err . . .' Jay began, feeling like all the moisture had been sucked from his mouth. 'My name is Jay Thomas. I'm thirteen years old and I'm the lead guitarist with Jet . . . Was that OK?'

Angie gave Jay a double thumbs-up. 'You're a natural,' she lied, before pointing at Erin.

'I'm Erin,' she said, looking coy as she flicked hair off her face. 'I'm thirteen years old and I sing vocals and play guitar for Brontobyte.'

'And how do you two know each other?'

'We're cousins,' Erin said, smiling again. 'We're only two months apart in age and we live next door to each other. So when we were little, we were like that.'

Erin held up her hands and placed one on top of the other, before continuing. 'In all my earliest memories, Jay is with me. Just rolling around the floor, playing tag. Wrestling and stuff.'

'Cute,' Angie said. 'But if you're so close, how did you end up playing in different bands?'

Erin shrugged and smiled. 'We're still mates, but I don't think we've been like, *mega* close, since . . .'

Jay spoke. 'Probably year four or five at school. We started getting more into our own mates. And boys and girls are into different stuff.'

'Sounds about right,' Erin agreed.

Jay drew some relief from the fact that his cousin sounded as nervous as he felt.

'As I understand, Jay, you used to be a member of Brontobyte,' Angie said. 'Can you tell me a little bit about that?'

'I guess,' Jay said warily, as he turned slightly on the bar stool. The camera operator silently gestured for him to move back to face the lens. 'I started Brontobyte with two of my mates, Tristan and Salman, plus Tristan's little brother Alfie. We played together for a couple of years, but there were a lot of musical differences and in the end I walked away.'

Erin scoffed. 'That's not *exactly* how I heard it!'

Jay turned towards her accusingly. 'Well, I left, didn't I?'

Erin seized the opportunity. 'Jay gave his bandmates an ultimatum,' she explained. 'Either they replace Tristan as drummer, or he walks. Jay lost the vote.'

Jay scowled at Erin, angry that she'd chosen to dig up his humiliation. On the other hand, Angie looked pleased. She'd clearly been going for this angle all along.

'It was hardly a fair vote,' Jay explained. 'Tristan voted for himself, and Alfie knew he'd get his arse kicked if he voted against his big brother.'

Erin smirked. 'If you say so, cuz.'

'You weren't there,' Jay spat. 'And you would take Tristan's side now because the idiot's your boyfriend.'

There was a lull. Jay *was* angry, but he didn't want to fall out with Erin, or look petty in front of the camera. He shrugged and gave Erin a smile to indicate that he wasn't taking this too seriously.

Erin understood Jay's gesture, raising her hands and giving a false laugh. 'You say Tristan's an idiot, but wasn't he your best friend for like, seven years, or something?'

Erin's question stumped Jay, so he changed tack. 'I happen to take my music seriously. Whatever you think of Tristan as a person, he can't play drums to save his life.'

Jay realised that *I happen to take my music seriously* sounded pompous, and cringed.

'In case you haven't noticed, Jay*den*, your lead singer ain't exactly about to sell out the Sydney Opera House. And Tristan's drumming wasn't so bad that it stopped the judges from picking us for *Rock War*.'

'Who needs a great singer?' Jay said, needled but keeping up the smile for the cameras. 'Were Kurt Cobain or Elvis great singers? Is Bob Dylan a great singer? It's stage presence that counts. And as for the real reason Brontobyte got into *Rock War* . . .'

Now Erin's face flashed with proper anger. 'What?'

Jay shrugged, and put a hand over his face, as if to indicate that he didn't want to say it on air.

'No,' Erin said, leaning forwards and placing one hand on a hip. 'Brontobyte got into *Rock War* because what?'

'Fine, let's air *all* our dirty linen in public,' Jay spat. 'Jet got into *Rock War* because we won Rock the Lock and put a great three-track demo online. Brontobyte only got in because of your rivalry with us. Having two bands that hate each other makes for good TV.'

'Listen to yourself,' Erin sneered. 'You're just jealous because your band kicked you out and me and Trissie got together.'

Jay ignored his cousin and kept going. 'You're a novelty act. Brontobyte is like the old granny contestant. The one who keeps falling on her arse on that ballroom dancing show, or the four-eyed kid who can't juggle on *Starmaker.*'

Erin didn't reply straight away, and Jay felt anxious as her eyes drilled him.

'You're so full of it!' Erin snapped, as she aimed a slap at his cheek.

Jay ducked the slap, but there was no avoiding a powerful two-handed shove that sent him sprawling sideways off his stool.

'Chicken-necked geek!' Erin shouted, knocking a studio light flying as she stormed out of shot.

Jay spent a couple of seconds reeling on grungy pub carpet, before using the stool as a prop to get up. Once he was vertical and had straightened out his T-shirt, he realised that the camera was still running.

Angie lunged with an off-the-cuff question.

'Jay, Brontobyte and Jet are going to be spending the next six weeks in close proximity at the *Rock War* boot camp. With all this tension between the two groups, how do you think that's going to pan out?'

Jay realised he'd been manipulated by Angie's questions and decided not to give her anything more to fuel the fire.

'It'll be peachy,' he growled. 'Fine and bloody dandy.'

2. Best Summer Ever

Dudley, West Midlands

'Hi! My name's Summer Smith. I'm fourteen years old and I'm the lead singer with Industrial Scale Slaughter . . . Sorry, can I do that again?'

'What for?' Joseph, the director, asked. The little man wore a spotted cravat, a grey Father Christmas beard and gave the impression that he was directing next year's Best Picture winner, rather than filming a reality TV contestant on a council estate in Dudley.

'I dunno. Didn't my voice seem funny?'

'Your voice was perfection,' Joseph said, before turning to the cameraman. 'That's a wrap.'

'Can I finish packing my clothes now?' Summer asked.

Joseph ignored Summer, and kept speaking to his cameraman. His toff's accent wasn't something you heard much around here. 'I need establishing shots from this room,' Joseph said. 'Get some books, clothes on the floor.

The swimming medals are a must, and the photo of the mother on the radiator.'

Summer's bedroom was only a metre wider than her single bed, and even though she didn't have many clothes, the room never looked tidy because she had more stuff than fitted in her pink-doored wardrobe.

'I'd prefer to film out on the balcony,' Summer said. 'I'm sweating under these lights.'

Joseph put a hand on Summer's shoulder, and stood close. Maybe it was just because there wasn't much space with camera and lights set up in her titchy bedroom, but she felt creeped out having two strange blokes invading her most personal space.

'I'm painting a portrait of you, sweetheart,' Joseph explained. 'This room. Your clothes, music, posters. In the hands of a skilful editor, a few brief shots paint a better picture than a five-minute speech.'

Summer didn't like the idea of a picture painted by the contents of her drab bedroom, but she didn't have the courage to argue with a director on the first morning of shooting. And she had more important stuff to worry about.

While the director headed out to set up the next shot in the living-room, Summer did an awkward dance with the cameraman, snatching up her clothes while he took the camera off tripod and filmed a few establishing shots and close-ups.

Summer didn't have proper luggage, so she grabbed stuff and pushed it into a pair of Lidl bags-for-life.

'You're not filming my dirty bras, are you?' Summer asked.

The young camera operator was momentarily flustered, and Summer used his discomfort as an opportunity to take the framed photo of her mother off the radiator and drop it through the gap between her bed and the wall. The last thing she wanted to do was give someone an excuse to start asking questions about her mum.

'Summer, darling,' Joseph called airily. 'Could you be a petal and come through to the drawing-room?'

Summer wasn't exactly sure what a drawing-room was, but she found Joe in the living-room. Summer's nan, Eileen, sat in her usual armchair with her oxygen mask dangling around her bust, and two old-skool hard-sided suitcases packed and ready on the sofa.

'Your grandmother's been telling me how hard you work looking after her,' Joseph said, sounding genuinely impressed.

'Washing, cooking, shopping,' Eileen said. 'Without Summer's help, I'd be six feet under for sure.'

'Don't be daft, Nan,' Summer said.

Eileen wagged her finger. 'How many times have you called the ambulance when my lungs are bad? First time she called 999 she were barely six years old.'

'Phenomenal,' Joseph said, as he gave Summer a broad smile. 'You're a hero. So, Eileen, are you off to stay with relatives while Summer's at boot camp?'

Eileen shook her head. 'There's no extended family, but

– Lord be praised – Mr Wei kindly agreed to pay for me to spend six weeks in a respite home.'

Joseph scratched his beard. 'And Mr Wei is . . .?'

'My two band mates' dad,' Summer explained. 'Michelle and Lucy Wei. I feel really guilty taking his money, and putting my nan in a home while I'm off enjoying myself. But I've told her, if she doesn't like it, I'll leave boot camp and come straight back here to look after her.'

Eileen spoke firmly. 'I've told you *not* to worry about me, Summer. You've done more than your share and I'm sure there'll be nothing I can't put up with for a few weeks. Now get over here and plant one on your grandma.'

'I'll always worry about you,' Summer said, as she leaned forwards and kissed her nan on the cheek. 'Don't ever try and stop me.'

Joseph was touched by the kiss, and wished he'd had a camera rolling.

As Summer backed away, the cameraman came into the room and spoke like a foghorn. 'All done in there, guv.'

'Perfection!' Joseph said. 'So, we've got our little intro in Summer's bedroom. Now I want to film Eileen here telling us all about her granddaughter, and we'll wrap up on the doorstep with Summer and a tearful goodbye.'

'My nan's actually coming with us to the Weis' house. Their dad will take her to the care home later.'

'Yes, yes,' Joseph said. 'But we've got a wonderful story here with your difficult background and the way you've looked after your grandmother. If I have my way, this segment about you will open the show.'

'I've seen the videos of you singing,' the cameraman said. 'You're beautiful, you've got a great voice and a gut-wrenching back story. You'll be going a long way in *Rock War*.'

Eileen cracked a huge smile. 'You hear that, my love? You're a red-hot favourite.'

Summer laughed. 'That's *not* what he said.'

'And you'll have to be careful,' Eileen teased. 'All the boys will be trying to get down your knickers.'

'Nan!' Summer gasped.

Joseph and the cameraman both laughed at Summer's red cheeks, as Joseph started giving instructions on how to set up lights for the interview with Eileen.

The upbeat mood broke when a breathless runner charged into the apartment. He was a uni student doing work experience. Quite beaky-looking, but he seemed really nice.

'There's three . . .' the runner gasped, before pausing to suck up all the air in the room. 'Three guys downstairs. I tried to get a fresh camera battery out of the van, like you asked. But they want to know why we're filming on their *turf*. Then one of them said he wanted fifty quid, and when I tried to open the back doors, he smashed the door mirror.'

'Little buggers,' Joseph said, as he straightened up purposefully.

'A satellite channel filmed a documentary about this estate a few years back,' Summer said. 'A lot of people got pissed off, saying it made us look like we were all dole bludgers and chavs.'

'Well, let's go see if they can be reasoned with, shall we?' Joseph said.

The cameraman was forty centimetres taller than Joseph and blocked his path. 'What if it gets hairy? Why don't we call the cops?'

Joseph squinted at the cameraman. 'I've been in this game for thirty years, and I'm at where I'm at because Joseph Tucker *always* keeps on schedule. If we call the cops, it'll take half an hour for them to arrive, by which time the bad guys will have run off. Then we'll waste the rest of the morning giving pointless statements.'

Joseph barged past his cameraman, grabbing his white-handled cane from a coat hook as he charged out. Summer followed the cameraman and runner, with Eileen shouting 'You be careful,' after them.

Summer hoped that she might know the lads by the van, but after eight flights of stairs, she emerged cautiously out of the stairwell and saw unfamiliar young men in trainers and tracksuits.

'So what's this, a blasted shakedown?' Joseph demanded, as he closed on the three men, extravagantly twirling his cane.

'We don't like people from outside filming here,' the smallest of the three lads said, in an accent from somewhere out of Eastern Europe.

Joseph ignored him, and went straight to the biggest lad. He had a bull neck and skinhead. Clearly the leader, he stood blocking the hired van's rear doors.

'Time is money,' Joseph said, as he fearlessly faced down the huge man. 'Back off now, lad, before you make a fool of yourself.'

Summer couldn't believe what she was seeing. Joseph was at least sixty and not particularly well built. He wore old-man trousers that almost went up to his armpits, and suede moccasins half a step removed from carpet slippers.

'Fifty quid, Santa Claus,' the big guy said, as Joseph stopped less than a metre away.

'Very amusing,' Joseph said, as he tapped his pockets, rattling some small change. 'You're not getting fifty pence. Now let me in my damned van.'

As Joseph took a half-step towards the white doors, the thug made a lunge to push him away. As soon as the big lad was off balance, Joseph crouched, hooked his opponent's ankle with his cane and sent him sprawling to the ground. Summer was shocked, not just by the way Joseph had knocked down a much larger opponent, but by the way he'd made it seem effortless. More like a dance step than an act of violence.

'You old shit,' the thug roared as he rolled on to his bum, before springing up and making another charge.

Joseph became a matador, sidestepping the charging bull, before delivering a neat karate chop to the back of his neck. The pain from this blow made the thug land hard on his kneecaps. Joseph took a step back and raised his walking cane.

'Still game, sport?' Joseph asked confidently, as the thug

spluttered. His two pals didn't fancy their chances either, and after a tense moment the trio skulked off, hands in hoodies, expressions like little boys told off by their dad.

'God help me if I forget to back up the SD cards,' the cameraman joked. 'Where'd you learn that, Joseph?'

'Royal military police,' Joseph explained, as he puffed out his chest and swung his cane under his arm. 'I might be light on the scales, but I've seen off a few like him in my time.'

Joseph seemed a much grander figure to Summer as he theatrically threw open the van's rear doors.

'Voilà,' he said. 'Now, get your spare batteries, set up in the living-room. Let's interview Grandma and leave this tiresome place before anyone else tries it on.'

3. Hoop Dee Doo

The limo stopped on the street outside Richardson's fish and chip shop, two wheels on the pavement and ignoring double red lines. The gaggle of people and cameras on the pavement drew some curious glances, but mostly it was horn blasts and two-fingered salutes as the parked car cut rush-hour traffic to a single lane.

Jay got in first, entering roadside and sliding across quilted leather to the opposite end of the rear bench. The blacked-out windows made things gloomy. The seat was a beast, with buttons to recline, heat and massage. Inside the roof, hundreds of LEDs subtly changed from gold to blue, and a zebrawood and chrome drinks console was stocked with ice cubes and glassware branded with the Rage Cola logo.

Adam, fourteen, and Theo, who'd just turned seventeen, climbed in after him.

'Budge up, fatty,' Theo said, squishing Adam, even though there was a ton of room. 'Driver, where's the booze?'

There was enough resemblance to tell that Theo and Adam were Jay's half-brothers, but the pair were blond and muscled in a way that got the opposite sex excited and made Jay jealous.

The limo stretched on to a second row of passenger seats facing the other way, and it was only after Jay had finished messing with his seat belt that he realised there was a little person down there filming him.

The dude was short enough that he could stand erect inside the limo.

'Looks like you've found your niche,' Theo said. 'What's your name, titch?'

Jay cringed. Theo was a bad boy, and he liked winding people up.

'They call me Shorty, for some reason,' the cameraman said. 'You're supposed to be acting natural, like I'm not here.'

The driver hit the gas, but got less than two metres before Angie started knocking on the window. She opened the back door. 'We'll have to take that again. Back up, please.'

The driver sounded furious. 'I can't keep sitting here. I've got fifty cars stuck behind me.'

Angie gave the three brothers a slightly irritated look. 'I know it's your first day and all,' she told them, 'but remember, you've got to act like the camera operator isn't there. Have you ever seen a show where they start talking to the cameraman?'

'I saw a porno once where the cameraman came and

joined in,' Theo said.

Adam started to laugh, but Angie just looked more irritated.

'OK, get out,' she said. 'We'll do the leaving shot later.'

'You need to calm down, love,' Theo said, as the driver unleashed a stream of curses and said something about *taking the piss*. 'I'll give you a massage that'll rub that tension right out.'

Angie correctly sensed that Theo would cause mayhem if you gave him a millimetre and decided to shut him down.

'I date *men*, Theo,' she said curtly. 'Not schoolboys.'

'Burn!' Adam yelled, slapping his thigh as he and Jay stumbled out of the car howling with laughter.

Jay's mum, siblings and stepdad were all lined up outside the shop waiting to film a wave-goodbye shot, and Jay stopped laughing when he saw that his six-year-old brother Hank was in tears.

'Hey,' Jay said, going down on one knee as the youngster clutched his dad's leg. 'Don't be sad. We'll be back before you know it.'

'You'll be doing loads of cool stuff while I'm stuck here,' Hank moaned.

Much to Jay's irritation, one of the cameramen had spotted the tearful scene. Hank didn't like being filmed crying, so he put one hand over his face and backed up behind his dad.

'Cheers, mate,' Jay said, as he stood up, glowering at the cameraman. 'Can't you see he's upset?'

The cameraman backed off without saying anything, and Jay's stepdad, Len, put a reassuring hand on Jay's shoulder.

'Hank'll be fine,' Len said. 'Once we get down to the coast he'll be building sandcastles, happy as a pig in shite.'

'No I won't,' Hank insisted, before his face lit up. 'You said a word! Mum! Dad said a rude word!'

Jay couldn't do any more to soothe his little brother, because the cameras were running and Angie was yelling at him to get back in the car. A woman in a Mini convertible kept blasting her horn and yelling at the crew, so they had to wait for her to drive past before they could resume shooting.

The second take went much better, with Shorty filming in the limo, another camera on the departing car and a third facing the other way at the waving relatives. Jay's obnoxious brother Kai held up a placard that said, *Hope you loose.*

'God, I hope they show him holding that,' Jay said, as he waved back.

'Why?' Theo asked.

Adam and Jay smirked at one another. 'Spelling not your strong suit either, Theo?'

Theo grunted. 'No, but kicking you two's teeth out might be.'

The limo drove three hundred metres and took a left into a turning that ran up towards one of the housing blocks behind the chip shop.

'Out you get, boys,' Shorty said.

'What's going on?' Adam asked from the middle seat, as his brothers followed Shorty out into the sun.

Shorty produced a set of magnetic number plates from his backpack and began switching RW3 for RW2.

'You can't just swap plates,' Jay said incredulously. 'That's gotta be illegal.'

Shorty laughed. 'It's only for a few minutes. We're taking the limo back for Erin to give her the send-off treatment.'

'And then the limo comes back and takes us to the *Rock War* house?' Jay asked.

'You hire limos by the hour and they're not cheap,' Shorty said, as the RW3 plate pinged off in his hand, hitting the tarmac and revealing a more mundane KZ13 PPH beneath it. 'The van you put your luggage in has gone off to pick up your band mate, Babatunde. He should be here in about fifteen minutes.'

'That was some crappy school minibus,' Jay said. 'It was all muddy inside.'

'Probably spent all year ferrying kids to and from the playing fields,' Shorty said, as he grinned knowingly. 'But schools don't use minibuses in the summer holidays, which means our beloved producer Mr Allen has been able to hire half a dozen of them on the cheap to ferry you brats around.'

'And let me guess,' Jay said. 'There'll be another limo waiting when we arrive at Rock War Manor.'

Shorty pointed, and made a kind of *click-click* sound. 'You learn fast, kiddo.'

*

After the limo fiasco, then a three-hour drive broken up by a service station Burger King, Jay was half expecting to find that he'd be spending summer hols in the dorm of some grim boarding school. But the first signs weren't bad. The minibus dropped them at the gates of a grand house, with a white gravel driveway leading up to a rambling country estate with a jarring modernist extension at the far end.

Babatunde and the three brothers had to wait to learn more, because they were dropped at the main gates and told to wait. Within fifteen minutes, a band called Dead Cat Bounce joined them and a production assistant came down with clingfilm-wrapped sandwiches and warm cans of Rage Cola. She announced that all the bands were going to be let into the house at the same time, to *maximise impact*.

The sun burned bright and as more young contestants arrived, Jay found shade under a tree and lay back on a grass verge using his backpack as a pillow. Meanwhile, Theo kicked up a storm. He didn't like being told what to do, and the idea that his schedule was now at the mercy of a bunch of TV folk pissed him off mightily.

Jet were first, but eight more bands arrived within the hour. Erin and her band mates in Brontobyte kept their distance, but Jay was delighted to see Summer, Michelle, Lucy and Coco from Industrial Scale Slaughter, who he'd met at Rock the Lock battle of bands competition back in the spring.

'I was all made up when I saw that you'd got into *Rock War*,' Jay said, feeling even better as Summer gave him a monster smile and hug. He fancied her to bits, though she was older and probably out of his league.

Frosty Vader were another band that had played Rock the Lock, but they had a new line-up, with two kids from Belfast. There was a girl called Sadie and a kid called Noah, who was in a wheelchair.

'I bet they put him in the band so he could drool on camera and win sympathy votes,' Theo moaned, when only his band mates were in earshot.

Jay got on OK with Theo, but still didn't have the bottle to criticise his off-colour remarks.

Jet's drummer Babatunde took exception.

'There's a fine line between being a rebel and being a dick,' Babatunde hissed.

For a moment Babatunde and Theo eyed each other up. Babatunde was a mystery man, dressed in dark glasses and a permanently raised hoodie, even in high summer. He was no weakling, but Theo was older, with a shelf of boxing trophies and an aggressive reputation.

'Guys,' Jay said, desperate to avoid having two band mates kick off before they'd even reached the house.

But for once Theo managed to accept that he was wrong and took a step back. 'Just saying,' he mumbled defensively. 'A kid in a wheelchair will get sympathy votes.'

Adam laughed. 'Maybe we'll get sympathy votes because Theo's such a dumbass.'

Theo didn't seem to like that, but luckily a couple more female production assistants came down to the gate and started calling out band names.

'Crafty Canard?' the first woman shouted. 'Delayed Gratification?'

The other woman called out Jet, and the four lads joined a queue. Jay was impressed to be handed a navy blue T-shirt with his band's logo on it. He'd designed a primitive version himself when he uploaded Jet's profile to the *Rock War* website, but the show's design team had given the logo a professional makeover, and seeing it on a T-shirt made his band seem much more real.

The show's wardrobe team had clearly put a lot of thought in. Babatunde got a Jet-branded hoodie, while Adam and Theo got snug-fitting Jet tank tops to show off their physiques. The four boys were less impressed by baseball caps bearing the logo of show sponsors, Rage Cola.

With the focus on his T-shirt, and one of the assistants barking that everyone had to wear their Rage Cola hats for their walk to the house, Jay missed the arrival of Meg Hornby.

Meg's career had been founded with a flash-in-the-pan solo TV hit called 'The Beater'. She'd gone on to make a fortune as a punkish fashion model in the nineties, getting tattoos and body piercings when they were still radical enough to get you noticed.

Now that her looks had faded, hosting *Rock War* was a step up from her staple work on celebrity panel games and occasional appearances on breakfast TV as a kind of self-appointed music and fashion expert.

But while Meg was hardly a megastar, Jay was still excited seeing someone moderately famous less than ten metres away. Meg took three takes to say, 'Welcome to the *Rock War* house, let's see what we've got waiting for you,' and Angie the director still didn't seem wildly enthused with her performance.

Two hours after being dropped at the gates, Jay got through them. Several cameras filmed as forty-four young musicians dragged their luggage and an occasional guitar over the white gravel driveway leading up towards the house.

Summer was the only one of the few contestants who didn't have wheeled luggage, and Adam swooped in to grab one of her supermarket bags.

'Oh, you're a gentleman,' Summer said brightly, giving Adam a smile that made Jay dead jealous.

Jay found himself at the back of the group, where he was surprised to discover Theo pushing Noah's wheelchair, possibly out of guilt at the idiotic comment he'd made earlier. Noah was fiercely independent and hated being pushed, but luggage and wheels that bedded in the gravel gave him little choice.

'So I'm Jay,' Jay told Noah. 'I saw the video Frosty Vader uploaded on the *Rock War* website. Pretty neat, with all the samples and stuff.'

Noah's best friend and fellow Frosty Vader member, Sadie, was keeping pace with the wheelchair.

'It was OK, but not our best,' Sadie said. 'But you guys are Jet, right? Your drummer – the black dude? He's *unbelievable*.'

'His name's Babatunde,' Jay said. 'I didn't catch your name.'

'That's because I didn't say it,' Sadie said bluntly. 'I'm Sadie, this is Noah.'

'Howdy-ho,' Noah said, giving a wave and then feeling dumb for not just saying *hi*.

'So is Sadie like, your real name?' Jay asked.

Sadie sounded vaguely offended. 'Yes, it's my real name. What's wrong with it?'

'Nothing,' Jay said anxiously. 'Just, I've never met a Sadie before.'

'It's Jewish,' Sadie said. 'I'm not Jewish, but like, my family were back in ancient days of history or something.'

Theo crouched over Noah and spoke in a whisper that was deliberately loud enough for everyone to hear. 'As you can see, my brother Jayden has a real way with the ladies and I'm starting to suspect that he'll die a virgin.'

Jay tutted as Noah smirked.

Twenty metres up the gravel path Angie and one of the production assistants started waving arms and telling everyone to stop. After being stuck at the gate for ages, this didn't go down too well.

Angie spoke to someone on a walkie-talkie, then started organising the three camera operators so that they were facing a flat strip of grass at the side of the house.

'Chopper in two,' Angie's assistant shouted.

Jay looked up as a black silhouette grew to a full-sized helicopter. The tail fin bore an image of a sinister-looking panda and *Pandas of Doom* was stencilled along the side.

One of the camera operators crouched low, as the chopper

landed, sending violent air pulses across the coiffured lawns. Once the co-pilot had opened the passenger door, four young band members emerged – a chubby boy, a pale goth girl and two others. They wore red tees with their band logo, and had to hold their Rage Cola caps in place as they stepped out beneath the rotor.

'Well, that's equality for you,' Sadie moaned. 'I have to struggle with Noah's wheelchair on Ryanair, and these dick wads get their own chopper.'

'I have no idea who the Pandas of Doom are,' Theo said. 'But I think I hate them already.'

4. Banging Cribs

It didn't quite make sense. On the one hand, *Rock War*'s producers were changing number plates to save a few quid on limo hire. On the other, Rock War Manor was spectacular.

The house's huge main door led into a marbled hallway rammed with equipment cases, AV leads taped to floors, and great looms of electrical cables heading out of an open window to a truck parked far enough away for none of the microphones to pick up the sound of the diesel generator running inside.

But for TV, the shots would be edited to show twelve bands passing through the front door, straight into the manor's main ballroom. Shorty had a gyro-stabilised Steadicam strapped to his waist, taking a smooth panning shot that caught Summer's gaping mouth as she moved into a huge, triple-height space.

The vaulted ceiling was made of vast oak beams, and the two upper floors had wraparound balconies, with some of the manor's many bedrooms branching off the sides. This classically beautiful space had been given a high-tech makeover for TV, with two walls painted with black and yellow stripes and a pair of curved metal slides.

At ground level the space had been fitted out like a youth club. But not a normal youth club, with sticky floors and busted pool cues. In the ballroom's centre there was a mound of Rage Cola branded beanbag chairs stacked four high. The two curling metal slides intertwined like DNA and gave a rapid trip down from the first and second floors.

Branching off, one direction led to ping-pong, pool, air hockey and electric massage chairs. The other revealed a mini indoor basketball court, with a proper rubber floor and electronic scoreboard, a pair of caged trampolines and an enormous ball pit of the type usually reserved for little kids. Finally, along the back wall were rows of huge flatscreens, linked up to PlayStations and Sky boxes, but currently set up to show a variety of Rage Cola commercials.

Angie had her four camera operators and some runners and assistants armed with camcorders and ready to film the kids' reactions to this amazing space. But after being left waiting for so long, Summer and all the other girls formed a line for the toilets, while the boys – who'd been willing to pee against tree-trunks – gathered around a pair of neon-decked vending machines and helped themselves to free bottles of Rage Cola.

When Theo saw he was being filmed, he played up for the camera. After a big smile, he raised his plastic bottle.

'Rage Cola,' Theo said dramatically, before taking a sip. 'Looks delicious. Smells refreshing. Tastes like something scraped out of a monkey's arse crack.'

The purple-haired camera operator started to laugh, along with half a dozen boys. Some began their own variations on Theo's monkey's arse line, while others acted like the cola was choking them. Jay clutched his stomach and fell down dead. A kid tripped backwards over Jay's legs and apologised in a Scottish accent.

'I'm Dylan,' the kid said, as he gave Jay a hand up. 'Pandas of Doom.'

Dylan was fourteen, good-looking, slightly chubby, with bleached hair turning black at the roots.

'Jay, Jet. What was with the helicopter?'

Dylan shrugged. 'My dad knows a guy with a chopper. The TV people loved the idea of a band arriving by air and they turned up this morning to stick the logos and stuff on it.'

'Never been in a helicopter,' Jay said. 'What's it like?'

'Cramped and noisy,' Dylan answered. 'But ninety minutes in the air beats eight hours on a train, even if you're a bit squished.'

Angie was heading over, and started by telling off the purple-haired camera operator for filming the boys dissing Rage Cola. Then she spoke firmly to the boys, and a couple of girls who'd finished their toilet break. 'I need you all to spread out. Explore the room. Don't just stand here like bowling pins.'

Theo tutted. '*You* kept us waiting in the sun for half the day. People need a drink and a piss.'

Angie put her hands on her hips. 'Same as I said earlier, Theo. The quicker I get the shots I need for the show, the sooner you guys will be free to do what you want.'

After treating Theo and the camera operator to a grimace, Angie turned around as a few kids reluctantly set off to explore the ballroom. But Theo still bore a grudge from Angie's schoolboy comment earlier. Remembering that he'd pocketed one of the clingfilm-wrapped sandwiches that had been served down by the gate, Theo mashed it into a ball and threw it hard.

The clingfilm ruptured, breaking into shards of cheese and pickle as it hit the back of Angie's head. She spun around furiously.

'Who did that?' she roared.

None of the laughing boys wanted to grass Theo up, and the camera operator she'd just had a go at wasn't about to tell tales either.

'I know it was you,' Angie said, as she stopped in front of Theo and made a dramatic throat-cutting gesture. 'I can have you and your band kicked off this show like *that*.'

Jay didn't like the sound of this, but Theo wasn't fazed. 'It wasn't me, miss,' he said innocently, as some of the kids behind him stifled laughter. 'I think maybe it was an old sandwich. Stuck up in the roof for hundreds of years, and it just fell down.'

A lot of contestants found this funny, but Theo's band

mates, Adam, Jay and Babatunde, glowered at him as Angie stormed off again.

'If you get us kicked out . . .' Adam said, tailing off because he didn't want to push it with his big brother.

'Don't sweat it,' Theo said casually. 'They need twelve bands to make the show work. They're not gonna kick anyone out.'

Jay shook his head. 'Only ten bands get through boot camp and make it to the Battle Zone stage in September.'

'Whatever,' Theo said dismissively. 'I never did what I was told at school and I've no intention of doing what I'm told here, either.'

By this time the band members were finally spread across the ballroom and Angie was getting some of the shots she needed: girls on the trampolines, Brontobyte diving en masse into the ball pit, a basketball going through a hoop and Adam and Summer grinning like mad as they kicked off their shoes and tried to work out which button you pressed to make the massage chairs work.

5. Summer's Summer

'So is it recording now?' Summer asked.

Dylan stood up and pointed at the light above the tiny camcorder's viewfinder. 'It's recording when the dot goes green.'

'Right,' Summer said, as she rested the camcorder on a window ledge and sat at the edge of her bed.

'So here we are in my room. Well, the room I'm sharing with my band mate Michelle. Michelle's not here right now, but this is Dylan from Pandas of Doom. Say hi, Dylan.'

Dylan stuck his face into the camera and waved.

'Anyway, it's just after six thirty. We got into Rock War Manor about three hours ago. My room's not massive, but it's pretty awesome. I've got, like, amazing thick towels, and a robe, and all these bars of soap in bright colours, and nice smellies and stuff. I took a shower, but it's got like these nozzles . . .' Summer paused and looked at Dylan. 'Do they have a name?'

Dylan shrugged.

'So yeah,' Summer continued. 'Erm . . . There's like one nozzle at the top like a normal shower, and two extra ones that squirt water out from the side. And there's like four levers and I couldn't work out how to make it so that it wasn't either freezing or scalding.

'Oh, and the other cool thing is that we've all been given one of these little camcorders. The actual *Rock War* TV show doesn't start airing for a week. But there's, like, a whole *massive* website and we've all been asked to make video diaries. Though I'm not really sure who's gonna be interested in me wittering on. We have to give our diaries a name, so I'm calling mine "Summer's Summer".'

Summer looked anxiously at Dylan. 'What should I say next?'

Dylan shrugged. 'Tell 'em how you feel. Or what you've been doing since you arrived.'

'OK,' Summer said, taking a big breath and thinking for a couple of seconds before speaking again. 'They made us wait outside for *ages*, not letting us into this manor until a *certain* band turned up in a helicopter.'

Summer paused, and Dylan sat down beside her, cutting in. 'We spent two hours on the ground, while someone from Venus TV faffed around putting Pandas of Doom and *Rock War* stickers all over my dad's helicopter.'

Summer shot a glance at Dylan. 'Your dad's got a helicopter?'

'That came out wrong,' Dylan said, a touch anxiously. 'Of

course he hasn't. My dad just knows a guy that runs choppers out to the North Sea oil rigs and he got a cheap rate. So then, all the other bands had to wait outside for two hours because we were late taking off, and now I'm pretty sure everyone thinks we're a bunch of boarding school toffs and hates us.'

'I don't hate you,' Summer said. 'You came and rescued me!'

Dylan smirked. 'You ran out in your robe and I showed you how to work the shower.'

'Anyway,' Summer continued. 'When we finally arrived, they let us into the ballroom and there's a whole bunch of cool stuff down there. Then we had to go for this really long meeting. There's always a welfare officer on duty, who we can talk to if we're upset, or getting bullied and stuff. And they told us where to assemble if the fire alarm went off and a bunch of other health and safety stuff and rules about trying really hard not to swear on camera.'

'Pretty boring,' Dylan added. 'But I suppose they had to do it.'

Summer nodded. 'After the meeting, they said we had a couple of hours to do our own thing. So a lot of kids went crazy down in the ballroom, but I just wanted to chill out. I called my nan, who's staying in a respite home while I'm away. She'd been playing Scrabble all afternoon and sounded like she was having an OK time. And then . . .' Summer looked at Dylan as her voice tailed off.

'You've probably told 'em enough already,' Dylan said.

Summer's eyes lit up. 'Oh, yeah! So we've all got to assemble up on the roof terrace at seven forty-five. They're not saying what it is, but we've been told to dress up. Which is actually kind of stressful, cos I'm pretty much a scruff to be honest and I'd rather just bum around in a T-shirt and some baggy jeans. Speaking of which, I suppose I'd better stop recording Summer's Summer and dig something out of my luggage.

'Do you think that was all right?' Summer asked, looking at Dylan. 'Not too long-winded?'

'They'll probably edit it, anyway,' Dylan said.

As Summer grabbed the camcorder to stop recording, her room-mate Michelle burst in.

'Rock and roll!' the fourteen-year-old shouted, waving arms madly as she leaped on to her bed and did a forward somersault that reminded Summer of primary school gym class. 'I see you've got a boy in here already, you dirty cow!' Then, as Summer went to press 'stop' on the camcorder, 'No, keep recording. I'm about to do something *amazing*.'

Michelle was always hyper, and Summer had hoped that she'd get one of her other band mates as room-mate. But Coco and Lucy had been BFFs since year two, so she'd been lumbered.

'Are you OK?' Summer asked. 'Your eyes look kind of . . . glazed.'

'I drank four bottles of Rage Blue,' Michelle explained. 'That stuff is ahhhhh-mazing!'

'What's Rage Blue?'

Dylan explained. 'It's the super-caffeinated energy drink version. It's what people drink when they want to stay up all night cramming for exams, or clubbing.'

'Michelle, you need caffeine like I need a bullet in my skull,' Summer said. 'Go take a cold shower or something.'

'Bug off, I feel fantastico!' Michelle sang, as she charged towards the window and threw it open.

Summer thought Michelle was going to spew out of the window, but instead she shouted down.

'You watch *this*, Theo. You say I'm not hardcore?'

Summer had heard Theo mouthing off at the gate and she'd been coming out of the loo when he threw the sandwich at Angie's head. He was clearly trouble and the idea of Theo and Michelle egging each other on filled her with dread.

Summer was bigger than Michelle and tried to grab her by the shoulders. 'You need to calm down,' Summer said firmly. 'That shit's made you hyper.'

But Michelle was slippery and Summer stumbled. Summer glanced out the window, where she could see Theo, Adam, plus kids from Half Term Haircut, along with a pair of camera operators.

Theo began a group chant, 'Do it, do it, do it . . .'

'Do what?' Dylan asked, as he stood up to get a look.

'What's the most rock-and-roll thing you can do when you check into a hotel?' Michelle shouted, as she grabbed the little LCD TV from a table near the wardrobe and ripped it violently out of its AV and electrical leads.

Summer had no idea what was going on, but Dylan knew exactly – his dad had fronted a legendary rock group called Terraplane, and according to some sources he still held the world record for throwing TVs out of hotel windows.

'Stand clear,' Michelle shouted. 'Nobody calls me chicken!'

The little Sony flatscreen lacked the drama that would have been caused by heaving a hefty old-skool vacuum tube TV out of a window. The LED panel was light enough for Michelle to lob it overhead, two-handed like a football throw-in.

'Keep filming,' Michelle ordered.

The TV hit a stone path with a huge smash. Down below, the crowd instinctively jumped back as plastic splinters flew in all directions. More contestants came outside to see what was going on as Michelle stood by the window, punching the air to adoring shouts of her name and calls to *throw something else*.

Summer and Dylan didn't quite know what to do. Fortunately the responsibility was taken away as two of the welfare officers charged in, ordering Michelle to step back from her window, sit on her bed and take deep breaths.

The welfare officers were closely followed by Zig Allen, the too-old-for-his-tight-jeans-and-spiky-hair producer who'd created the *Rock War* concept for his production company, Venus TV.

'What are you playing at?' Zig shouted. 'Why are TVs being thrown out of windows? Aren't you ladies supposed to be keeping an eye on these kids?'

'Aww, Zig,' Michelle said dismissively. 'We had three cameras on that. You've got some great footage for the opening episode!'

Dylan was in a mild state of shock, but even though he'd never met Michelle before, he instinctively defended her.

'Unifoods made ten billion last year,' Dylan said. 'I think they can buy a new telly out of the Rage Cola marketing budget.'

Zig looked furious. 'Rage Cola built this place no expense spared, smartass. But *my* company, Venus TV, signed a contract to produce the series. That TV will come out of my *fixed* production budget. Do I look like a billionaire to you, kiddo? Do I?'

Dylan shrank back towards Summer's bed as Zig turned cherry red. He wiped a foaming mouth on his shirt cuff before tearing into the welfare officers.

'I'm not paying you to sit in the office. Your job is to stop these brats from running riot!'

One of the officers seemed more concerned by Michelle's eyeballs. 'Honey, have you taken drugs?' she asked, with a soft New Zealand accent. 'I want you to be honest with me. You're not in any kind of trouble.'

'Drugs!' Zig shouted. 'Are you kidding me? If we get a drug scandal, Rage Cola will pull this project faster than a cheetah with a firework up its arse.'

'Mr Allen,' the other welfare officer said firmly. 'We need you to leave the room. Your hostility isn't appropriate in this situation.'

'Get these kids in line,' Zig yelled, as he stormed out. 'Or I'll find someone who will.'

Michelle put on a shamed face, but Summer knew her well enough to realise she was faking.

'I . . .' Michelle said weakly.

The Kiwi officer moved in closer and spoke soothingly. 'You're not in trouble, honey. I just want you to tell me what you've taken.'

Michelle opened her mouth, winked at Summer, then puked violently in the officer's lap.

6. Caribbean Jerk

While production assistants and runners scoured Rock War Manor, enforcing Zig's order to remove every bottle of Rage Blue from vending machines, in-room fridges and kitchen cupboards, the *Rock War* contestants gathered at the bottom of the slides in the ballroom.

Angie had retired for the day, leaving Joseph to direct three camera operators, light and sound technicians, four knackered-looking runners and forty-seven irritable teenage contestants. Michelle had wanted to join in, but Zig insisted she spend the evening recovering in her room, with one of the welfare officers outside her door to prevent escape.

'How much longer?' Adam shouted. 'I've been up since five and all I've eaten is sandwiches.'

Summer was one of the last to arrive. Adam thought she looked great in her simple striped top and black miniskirt, but Summer felt underdressed when she saw a couple of the other girls, with fancy hair and inch-thick make-up.

Fortunately, her sixteen-year-old band mates Coco and Lucy had also kept things plain.

'That girl from The Messengers,' Coco said, pointing with her little finger and speaking quietly. 'How high are those heels? And the stockings! They're supposed to be a Christian band, but she doesn't look it.'

Summer giggled. She always felt awkward in social situations, and had always been a giggler.

'And what's that on her head?' Michelle's big sister Lucy added. 'It's like someone stuffed a dead rat and sewed on a bunch of sequins.'

Summer was still smiling when presenter Meg Hornby aimed a microphone in her face. The camera operator gently nudged some lads standing nearby, so that he could get Summer and Meg in the same shot.

'Summer, how's your first day been?' Meg asked.

'It's almost too much,' Summer said. 'I can't take it all in.'

'And what do you think we've got waiting for you up on the roof?'

Summer couldn't think of an answer, so Coco butted in. 'It better involve food. If they don't feed me soon, I might have to resort to cannibalism.'

Meg saw Joseph waving at her from the bottom of the stairs, as one of the runners cleared a path so that Noah could back his chair on to a stairlift.

'Here we go, people,' Meg shouted, flicking one eyebrow up for the camera. 'Let's see what the contestants have got waiting for them.'

There was a contrast between some of the elaborately coiffured girls, and the lads who were mostly in shirts and shorts with trainers. The walk upstairs was dictated by the pace of the whirring stairlift.

Noah was first to see what lay in wait, rolling out on to a candlelit terrace on the roof of the manor's modern extension. The candles encircled a large oval swimming-pool with steaming hot tub at the far end. His best friend and band mate Sadie didn't do dressing up, and walked alongside in cutoff jeans and tatty All Stars.

'It's Joe Cobb,' Sadie said, almost squealing and feeling embarrassed because a camera on her left caught the moment.

Noah's head was half a metre lower than Sadie's so he had to wheel a bit further before he could see up to the highest part of the terrace. He wasn't into cooking shows, but his mum bought all the books and he recognised the handsome young TV chef, who was the curly-haired and recently famous son of an even better known TV chef.

Noah also recognised the kitchen cabinets and appliances from the show, though it was only now that he realised the whole lot was built on wheels so that it could be set up anywhere, even by a rooftop pool, with gas cylinders and a tangled mass of power cables, just out of shot.

Noah had two cameras on him as his eyes scanned a wooden counter top covered with barbecue goodies. In the background, two of Cobb's assistants were loading beef ribs and spatchcock chickens on to a huge barbecue.

'Welcome to my kitchen,' Cobb said exuberantly. 'Is there anything that catches your eye?'

Noah felt pressured, with an on-camera light beaming on to his chest. 'What are the different types of chicken?'

'I have beautiful chicken pieces marinated in lime and yogurt, with almonds on top. This one is just herbs and garlic butter, and the shiny black one at the end is Caribbean jerk. Sweet, but fiery.'

'Spicier the better for me,' Sadie said, as Noah dithered. He liked his food simple, so he went for a salmon fillet and a cheeseburger. After loading her styrofoam plate with rice, wedges and the inevitable serving of Rage Cola, Sadie settled on one of the terrace walls with Noah parked alongside. The pair looked out at hundreds of candles flickering in the gently lapping pool.

'How's the food?' Meg asked.

'Great,' Noah said. 'Best barbecue I've ever tasted.'

Sadie nodded, as she licked hot sauce off her thumb. 'I was starving, and this is so perfect!'

'My mum is an amazing cook,' Noah told the camera. 'But I'm sorry, Mum, Joe Cobb might just be better.'

Sadie laughed. 'Your mum might stop feeding you if you're not careful, Noah. But she can still invite me round for dinner any time she likes.'

'That was splendiferous,' director Joseph told the pair. 'Funny, short and snappy. Exactly the kind of footage we're after.'

As Joseph followed Meg towards some other kids sitting

down by the pool, the pretty runner named Lorrie came by, picking used paper plates off the terraced walls.

'How much do you reckon it cost to get Joe Cobb to cook our dinner?' Sadie asked.

As a runner, Lorrie was one of the most junior people on set. She seemed pleased that someone had asked for her opinion.

'Nothing,' Lorrie explained. 'It's tit-for-tat. *Cobb's Kitchen* and *Rock War* are both Venus TV productions. So Cobb comes here and cooks for you, and later on, a couple of you contestants, or more likely the *Rock War* judges, will get a guest spot on his show.'

'So Cobb gets publicity on a show watched by young people, and *Rock War* gets publicity on *Cobb's Kitchen*,' Noah said. 'Neat.'

'Yep,' Lorrie said, as she reached down beside Noah's chair and wiped a blob of dip that had dropped off the edge of his plate. 'I've actually worked on *Cobb's Kitchen*. These chefs will do *anything* for publicity. They practically *give* their shows to the big TV channels, and make all their money selling cookbooks and putting their name on restaurants.'

After a second serve of barbecue and summer-fruit trifle for dessert, Noah felt fat as he rolled down a ramp to join a dozen kids who'd gathered close to the pool. Quite a few sat on the pool's edge with their feet cooling in the water. Everyone was stuffed and it seemed nobody had an appetite to move, let alone start swimming.

Sadie threw off her Converse and joined in, so Noah slid

out of his chair, rolled up his chinos and did the same.

'This is kind of pointless,' Noah said. 'This water could be boiling and I wouldn't know until I saw my skin blister.'

'That's dark,' a girl lying behind said gravely.

Noah looked back and studied her. She was a textbook emo/goth, ignoring the hot weather and wearing thick black leggings, DM boots and knitted black top with long sleeves.

'I'm Dylan,' the boy who had the goth's head nestled in his lap said. 'This is my girlfriend Eve.'

'Pandas of Doom,' Noah acknowledged.

'We saw your helicopter arrive,' Sadie added, a touch acidly.

Dylan laughed. 'We're not gonna live that down, are we?'

There was a yelp amidst a smaller group of kids a few metres along the poolside. Noah's head snapped around in time to see Tristan from Brontobyte getting a three-pronged soaking from band mates armed with super-soakers.

'Where did they get those from?' Dylan asked, as Tristan grabbed his little brother Alfie.

Alfie had just turned twelve, making him the youngest kid in *Rock War*, but he fearlessly tussled with his much bulkier brother, who was trying to grab the empty soaker.

'Give it here or I'll batter you,' Tristan shouted.

But Erin had other plans, stepping behind her boyfriend and yanking down his shorts.

'The cameraman got it,' Jay, who was sitting with his feet in the water, shouted. 'Nice pants, Tristan. Did your mommy buy them?'

'Aaargh!' Tristan yelled, laughter erupting around the pool as Alfie broke free, dived into the pool and began refilling his soaker. 'I'll get you, Erin. I know you set this up.'

Erin didn't try too hard to run away, grappling briefly with Tristan before letting him push her into the pool.

Erin's dress was soaked, but she didn't seem to mind as she grabbed Tristan around the chest and tried to pull him under. The availability of water guns had caused a chain reaction, and at the far end of the pool, contestants were lining up to grab them out of a wheeled wicker hamper.

Dylan was enjoying staying still, with Eve's head in his lap, but he found it hilarious that after Tristan, some kind of universal decision seemed to have been taken to target the most elaborately dressed girls.

The one with the stuffed rat on her head squealed under a barrage of water jets. She ended up on her knees, somewhere between tears and laughter. After lobbing a red stiletto at her closest opponent, the girl scrambled barefoot towards the staircase.

'I'm coming back in my swimmers,' the girl shouted. 'You *will* live to regret that.'

'Get a squirter for me,' Noah shouted, as Sadie rushed off.

Dylan got a soaking from his room-mate Leo and sprang reluctantly into action. Noah was pissed off that nobody wanted to be seen squirting the wheelchair kid, so he slid off the edge into the deepest part of the pool.

Noah's legs didn't work, but he had massive arms and

swam upwards, surfacing in front of Summer and scaring the life out of her.

'Where did you come from?' Summer gasped.

Summer had a soaker, but Noah decided that he didn't know her well enough to try stealing it. Fortunately Sadie threw one to him, and yelled, 'Start without me, why don't you?' as she dived into the pool.

As Noah filled his water gun, he caught sight of a large man in Union Jack shorts and a chef's hat charging towards the water.

'Cannonball!' Joe Cobb shouted.

Noah scrambled out of the way, but still caught a huge bow wave. The water forced his eyes shut, and for some reason he remembered someone telling him that you weren't supposed to swim with a full stomach. He rubbed his eyes and looked up to find himself being filmed by two cameras while receiving a bear hug from a TV chef who'd apparently been drinking something a lot stronger than Rage Cola.

'Stuff like this doesn't happen to me,' Noah told the camera, grinning deliriously as Sadie swam into shot. 'This is like the greatest thing ever!'

7. Let's Just Be Friends

Sadie and Noah had been up at three in the morning to catch their flight from Belfast, and it was past midnight when they got to bed. The day had been even longer for the crew, who'd had to travel out to film kids leaving home and then stay up into the early hours, snuffing out all the candles on the roof, and packing away Joe Cobb's set.

So it was no surprise that Saturday got off to a slow start. Noah and Sadie had the only bedroom on the ground floor, and it was almost noon when the pair found the dining-room, where a couple of chefs sat at a table reading the Saturday newspapers.

The chefs offered to cook omelettes or fill baguettes, but the two teenagers were still stuffed with barbecue. Sadie went for cereal and Noah put a couple of slices in the toaster and scraped them with Marmite. They took plates and mugs through to the ballroom, which was deserted, apart from seven kids on beanbags watching one of the big LCDs.

'What's this?' Noah asked, as he recognised himself on screen, wheeling towards a departure gate at George Best International.

'Dailies,' a hot sixteen-year-old from Delayed Gratification said. 'Apparently the editing team work through the night, reviewing footage all the different crews took during the day and picking out clips to go online, and in the TV show when it eventually goes out. One of the runners brought this DVD down about an hour ago.'

Of the seven kids on beanbags, the only names Noah and Sadie knew were Dylan from the Pandas and Summer from Industrial Scale Slaughter, but an hour-long water fight around the pool before bed had brought down barriers, even amongst contestants who were yet to catch each other's names.

Everyone was used to finished TV shows, so it seemed odd watching random clips, with no narration or music, varying sound levels and visuals that hadn't been colour graded. Everyone laughed at a clip of Sadie pushing Noah's chair at full speed, almost hitting the deck as she picked up her feet and freewheeled dangerously close to shopfront displays of sunglasses and travel adaptors.

The next batch of clips showed Jet, and there was an outbreak of gasps and thigh slapping when they heard Jay telling Erin that, *'Brontobyte is like the old granny contestant. The one who keeps falling on her arse on that ballroom dancing show, or the four-eyed kid who can't juggle on* Starmaker.'

'Major burn!' Dylan said, as he glanced around furtively,

making sure there was nobody from Jet or Brontobyte in their midst.

'I noticed the guys from Jet and Brontobyte were *really* getting into each other around the pool last night,' Sadie added. 'I wouldn't be surprised if we saw fisticuffs before this is all over.'

'But Jet are all bigger,' Summer said. 'Theo's massive.'

'Theo's sexy!' Delayed Gratification girl chirped. 'He gave me a piggyback last night, and he is ripped.'

Dylan was only half listening, because his eyes were fixed on Summer's legs. He thought she had cute toes, breasts out of heaven and a tired smirk that he'd love to kiss.

Dylan didn't fancy his girlfriend and band mate Eve half as much as Summer, or most of the other girls he'd seen running around the pool the night before. He'd only started going out with Eve because his boarding school was all boys, and apart from her, the only girls he got to see during term time were at joint school dances, or in town on a Saturday morning.

And it wasn't just about physical stuff. Eve was always gloomy and Dylan was half convinced she'd only started snogging him so that he didn't grass her up when he'd caught her cutting herself. But Eve had seemed happy when the Pandas spent the previous week rehearsing at Dylan's house, so now seemed like as good a time as any to break up with her.

On the downside, Dylan wanted to win *Rock War* and breaking up with Eve might cause friction in the band. But he was sick of going over the Eve situation in his head and he was desperate to take some action.

'Where you going?' Dylan's room-mate, Leo, asked.

'None of yours,' Dylan said, but not nastily.

'If you're doing another one of your epic shits, use the toilet brush afterwards,' Leo yelled, making all the girls go 'eww'.

'Nothing's worse than that crap you spray under your arms,' Dylan snapped back. 'It was so strong that pigeon keeled over on the window ledge.'

'Reminds me of a joke,' Leo said, moving to give himself more room now that Dylan wasn't sprawled out beside him. 'What do you do if a bird craps on your head?'

'Who knows?' Summer said.

'Who cares,' someone added, making Leo half wish he hadn't started the joke.

'You don't go on another date with her,' Leo said.

There were a few groans, but enough laughs to make Leo feel OK. Summer flung a little cushion at him.

'I'm not a *bird*,' she said firmly.

Three flights up, Dylan reached Eve's room and knocked.

'Hey,' Eve said brightly.

She was on the corner of her bed in the L-shaped room she was sharing with her twin brother, cross-legged and an acoustic guitar around her neck.

'Where's the Mighty Max?' Dylan asked.

'Bathroom,' Eve said, pointing towards a closed door. 'One of the make-up people told him to lose his stupid teenage moustache.'

'Good call,' Dylan said, running a hand through his tangled locks. 'So I was kind of thinking . . .'

'You want to break up with me,' Eve said purposefully.

Dylan was shocked that she'd guessed. 'What makes you say that?'

'Is it true?' Eve said, narrowing her eyes.

'I guess,' Dylan said. 'What made you realise?'

Eve shrugged, and rested the guitar against the headboard. 'All last week you barely touched me, except when you drank half a bottle of your dad's whisky and came into my room saying you needed a shag.'

'I did say I was sorry about that.'

'It was actually sweet in a weird kind of way,' Eve said. 'When you started crying and saying you were sorry.'

'I'd had a *lot* to drink,' Dylan said. 'Me, Max and Leo were completely shit-faced.'

'And then last night by the pool. I had my head in your lap, but I could see you looking at the other girls. Especially the scruffy blonde. Sarah, or whatever her name is.'

'Summer,' Dylan said.

'So you're not denying it?'

'You rumbled me,' Dylan said. 'You're always tuned in to stuff like that. What's the point lying?'

Eve half smiled. 'You're honest,' she said. 'That's one of the things I really do like about you.'

'I mainly tell the truth because I'm a bad liar,' Dylan said. 'So are we OK? You don't seem too upset. This isn't going to cause tension in rehearsals and stuff?'

'It's all good,' Eve said, twisting her long dark hair around two fingers, and sounding a little sad. 'Boarding school is a complete bubble. You don't exactly get much chance to spend time with the opposite sex. I learned a bunch of stuff about myself while I was with you.'

'You must have felt shitty seeing me eyeing up other girls by the pool – I'm really sorry about that,' Dylan said. 'And it's great that you're cool about everything, but I know you bottle things up . . . If you want to scream and shout, go for it, just please, don't start cutting yourself again . . .'

Eve put one hand on the neck of her guitar. 'I need to learn this song Max wrote. It's like a duet, no drums.'

Dylan tried to kid himself that everything was OK as he backed out into the hallway. But he knew that he'd hurt Eve, and he felt completely crap about it.

8. Inbetween Days

There was a decent roast at dinner-time. Contestants unpacked in their rooms, and carried musical equipment to a converted stable block, where each of the twelve groups had been given a rehearsal space with their band logo on the door.

A few bands rehearsed, but as Saturday wore on most kids spent their time in the ballroom, or around the rooftop pool. With everyone knackered from the day before, it felt like a day that had ended before it properly began.

Sunday was the start of boot camp proper. After breakfast the twelve bands were split into three groups. Group one comprised Jet, Industrial Scale Slaughter and the Pandas of Doom. They gathered in a little classroom with one long table and a flip-chart at the end, with Michelle and Theo at the back, ready to make mischief.

'I'm bored already,' Theo said, as he snapped a pencil in half, then leaped up on a desktop and pushed the pointy end into a polystyrene ceiling tile.

He was still up on the desk when Helen Wing came in. Most of the contestants knew her face from BBC weather forecasts, but she began by explaining that she'd retired from the Meteorological Office and now specialised in media training.

Helen mostly taught business executives how to handle media attention and interviews and wasn't used to fidgety teens. Some, like Jay and Summer, made notes and paid attention, but others just looked really bored and started playing with their smartphones, or turning sheets of notepaper into paper aeroplanes and origami cranes.

'I didn't sign up for school in the holidays,' Theo moaned, when they were allowed out for a mid-session break. Then, looking at Michelle, 'You wanna bounce?'

Michelle nodded, but the pair's band mates all waded in, saying that it was the first day and reminding them that throwing TVs and sandwiches had already brought them close to getting kicked out.

'You'll screw this up for all of us,' Michelle's sister Lucy summed up. 'And if you do, I'll kick both of your asses.'

So Theo and Michelle got herded in for the second half of the media session and fortunately, things got more interesting. Rather than go back to class, Helen led them to a room that had been converted into a small training studio. There were two professionally lit sets and a plastic stacking chair for everyone.

The first set comprised a pair of sofas and a big glass table, set out like a mini version of a TV chat show. The second was a long desk surrounded by chairs, with headsets and microphones to mimic radio interviews, or alternatively the chairs could all be moved behind the desk, so that it was more like a news studio.

The three bands had to enter silently, because presenter Meg Hornby was recording a piece to camera.

'*Rock War* boot camp isn't just about music,' Meg beamed. 'Every contestant is going to be put through a range of training programmes, which will equip them with the skills they need to deal with the pressures of a celebrity lifestyle. In our modern, twenty-four/seven, uber-connected world, knowing how to be comfortable in front of a camera and handle a pushy journalist or television interviewer is every bit as important as being able to hit a high note, or play a killer riff.'

Meg's voice dropped an octave as she looked at the cameraman. 'Was that OK?'

The cameraman made a *carry-on* gesture and whispered a voice cue. 'All twelve bands . . .'

'Shit, sorry,' Meg said, then switched back to her more dramatic on-air voice. 'All twelve bands will complete a media training course today. At the end, former BBC weather presenter Helen Wing will pick six outstanding band members for a very special prize.

'They'll get to travel to London, where they'll each get a two-hundred-and-fifty-pound voucher to spend at top department store Eldridges, and an invitation to Channel

Six's network launch party at the Natural History Museum.'

As Meg said this, one camera panned around to film the band members' reaction. Unfortunately, this was all just being thrown at them and they mostly looked confused.

'OK, Meg,' the camera operator/unit director said. 'Once more from the top. And kids, try and look more excited when Meg announces the competition.'

While Meg repeated her lines, Helen took Jay aside and gave him a sheet of questions. 'I want you to be the interviewer in our first role-play exercise,' she explained. 'You can use these questions as a guide, but if you feel your interviewee is on the ropes, you're welcome to use your own follow-up questions. OK?'

Jay looked studious as he started reading through the questions. Helen spoke to the whole group, as Meg headed off, leaving the two camera operators behind.

'Now we've done the boring theory part, and I hope you were all paying attention,' Helen announced. 'We're going to be doing mock interviews. You'll each get to role-play at least two scenarios, ranging from a serious radio interview, to a newspaper reporter who collars you on the doorstep when your mum sends you out to Londis to buy a loaf of bread.

'For the first scenario, we'll be imitating a serious TV news show, similar to *Newsnight* or *Channel Four News*. Jay will be playing the presenter, and since he was paying *so* much attention, his big brother Theo can play the role of studio guest.'

There were a few laughs as Jay and Theo sat behind the news desk. 'Ready when you are,' Helen said.

Jay smirked self-consciously as he banged his question sheets against the news desk, sat up straight and spoke in a deep voice.

'Our first guest tonight is Theo Richardson, one of the contestants in a brand-new reality TV show which launches this autumn. Good evening.'

'Yo, bitches!' Theo said, earning himself a few smirks and a disapproving look from Helen.

'Theo, tell us something about *Rock War*.'

'Well . . .' Theo said. 'It's like . . . It's a talent show. But instead of pop, it's more. Well, rock.'

Helen raised a hand, then looked at the other kids. 'Stop it there, Theo. What did Theo do wrong?'

'He's so ugly he should have a bag over his head,' Theo and Jay's brother Adam said.

There were a few laughs, before Summer gave a serious answer. 'He should have prepared some answers.'

'Exactly,' Helen said. 'Before any media appearance you need to plan. Earlier on, I asked you to write down the four questions that you were most likely to be asked in an interview, and formulate some answers. I think pretty much all of you agreed that the most likely thing you'd be asked right now, is to explain what *Rock War* is all about. Theo wasn't listening, so now he's being watched by a million people going, *err, well, err* . . . Right, Jay, skip on to the next question.'

Jay resumed in his newsreader voice. 'But it's been more than fifteen years since talent shows took the Saturday night schedules by storm. And with most of these shows well past their peak, surely *Rock War* is just one TV talent show too far?'

Theo grunted. 'You can say what you like, but that's just your opinion.'

Jay didn't often get a chance to make his big brother uncomfortable.

'Thank you for that *highly* intelligent response,' Jay said, as he decided to go off script with his next question. 'Theodore, shouldn't a show such as *Rock War* aim to set an example to young people? We understand that you've been expelled from three schools, and convicted of numerous petty crimes.'

Theo shot up out of his seat, making Jay frantically wheel into the backdrop with his chair. 'If you don't shut your gob, you'll be conducting your next sodding interview with half your jaw wired.'

The backdrop wobbled and Helen looked alarmed, but Theo didn't actually lay hands on his brother.

'OK,' Helen gasped, as Theo sat back down. 'I think that was a good example of how someone who doesn't pay attention in media training can end up having a hard time in front of a camera. So how could Theo have answered that tricky second question?'

Summer's band mate Coco looked at her notes as she answered. 'You said that thing about turning a disadvantage into an advantage, like, if the interviewer asks you a loaded question.'

'That's right,' Helen said. 'So what could Theo have actually said?'

Coco shrugged. 'Something like, *I think the popularity of those shows in the past has shown how much people enjoy them. But talent shows have become a little stale, and* Rock War *is here to give the genre a kick up the backside.*'

'Perfect,' Helen gushed. 'That was a *fab* answer. And your tone was perfect, not overly aggressive, but also not allowing the presenter to intimidate you. The world is full of snipers and you're going to encounter negative questions about *Rock War* every time you speak to the media. It would be sensible for all of you to think up a few answers similar to the one Coco just gave.'

Most kids made notes as Helen sent Theo and Jay back to their seats.

'Next up, I want to role-play a slightly more comfortable scenario,' Helen said. 'The type of group interview you'd see on breakfast TV or *The One Show*. I want Industrial Scale Slaughter on the couch. Max and Eve, wheel the news desk around to face the couch and you can play the two presenters.'

9. Tide Charts For Tenby

Monday

Jay sat on the edge of his bed, filming his video diary in the mirrored front of his wardrobe.

'Media training turned out to be OK. The role-plays were a giggle. Helen taught us a lot of stuff I'd never considered, and I reckon I'll be a lot more confident if someone does interview me. After lunch we did a dance class.

'A lot of us were like, *Rock bands don't dance.* But the teacher showed us these videos of Freddie Mercury and Guns N' Roses on stage. They don't prance about doing Gangnam Style moves, but when you watch carefully there's quite a bit of choreography, whether it's Axl doing high kicks, or the way two guitar players stand facing one another during a certain song.

'Also, the guy doing it was proper fun. At the end he had us trying to do the splits. I hate exercise and sport, so I was *terrible*. But my brothers do boxing and were dead flexible.

Theo mugged it for the cameras, and poor Summer ripped the arse out of her jeans in front of *everybody*!

'So I never would have thought I'd enjoy a dance class, but I think our next one is on Thursday, and I'm *almost* looking forward to it. This afternoon we're dividing up by instrument, and there's all kind of stories going around that our tutor is going to be someone mega famous. There was even a rumour it was going to be Keith Richards from the Rolling Stones. But like, seriously, how likely is it that a guy who's practically a billionaire is gonna drive down to Dorset to give us lot a guitar lesson?

'And it's kind of weird, because in a way all the classes we're doing mean it's like being in school. But it never *feels* like school, because I've got loads in common with all the other kids and it's not like, silicon dioxide and tide charts for Tenby. I'm learning stuff that I actually give a shit about. Plus there's no homework apart from rehearsing and it's only till one so there's heaps of time for jamming or mucking about.'

Jay spent a couple of seconds trying to think if he wanted to say anything else, and realised that someone would probably moan at him for saying 'shit' on camera. His room-mate, Babatunde, had gone down to breakfast extra early so that he could get an hour's drumming practice in before first lesson. Jay felt moderately guilty that he'd lounged in bed instead of practising himself.

After sliding into tatty Crocs and checking his hair in the mirror, Jay opened his door on to the second-floor balcony.

He was immediately startled by two camera lights in his face, and fellow contestants crowding his doorway.

Before Jay could process anything, girls lunged from either side, throwing buckets of clear, sticky fluid over his clothes. He recognised Summer and Michelle in a second wave of kids that chucked baking flour and tiny polystyrene balls, extracted from one of the beanbags in the ballroom.

Jay attempted a gasp, but inhaled flour instead. After a couple of seconds stumbling blindly in the white cloud, listening to screams and howls of laughter, Jay felt hands under his armpits. As they dragged him backwards, more hands grabbed his ankles and he managed to open his eyes enough to see that it was his brothers, Theo and Adam.

'One,' Theo shouted, as they swung Jay one way, then the other, sending him out over the balcony edge.

'Two!'

Jay tried to break free, but all he managed to do was pull a muscle in his stomach.

'Let me go, dirtbags!'

Jay was more annoyed than scared, because while Theo was pretty crazy, he'd seen the camera lights and knew everyone was in on the plan, so there was no way they were actually going to throw him over the balcony.

'Three,' everyone shouted.

Theo and Adam let go. Jay felt the most unbelievable terror as he sailed over the balcony. Time froze, and he managed an entire conversation with himself during the three-second fall.

How can they do this? Will I break my back? Will I die? This has got to be a dream . . .

Jay didn't land on the ballroom's chequerboard tiles, but to a violent bounce and the sound of stretching springs. They'd moved the big trampoline, and he'd landed dead centre.

Jay cursed as he opened his eyes, staring up at wooden joists and a pair of chandeliers. A dozen contestants leaned over the balcony, snapping footage on smartphones and camcorders.

'You,' Jay gasped, as he sat up, rubbing flour in his eyes. 'I'll murder you dicks!'

As Jay sat up, the first thing he saw was the purple-haired camera operator. Zig Allen and director Joseph were smiling and clapping.

Jay was still in shock as Babatunde stepped into the cage around the trampoline and offered a hand up.

'That's your punishment for missing first lesson,' Babatunde said.

Jay shook his head as he studied his body, which was like an alien skin made of gloop, flour and polystyrene beanbag balls.

'I didn't miss first lesson,' Jay said. 'It's nine fifteen.'

Babatunde shook his head. 'Ten thirty.'

'I just checked the clock in our room.'

'Maybe someone altered the clock in the room,' Babatunde said, cracking a smile. 'And the one on your phone.'

Jay gasped. 'So when you said you were going out early to

practise, that was just normal lesson time . . .? Damn! No wonder it seemed like such a great lie-in.'

Other kids were rushing down from outside Jay's room, as, legs still shaking, he climbed off the trampoline. The fall had been among the scariest seconds of Jay's life. Part of him wanted to yell and call everyone scheming bastards, but the cameras were on, and with so many new friends on the scene, Jay knew he had to act like he was cool with the whole stunt.

Adam and Theo had raced down. They weren't a touchy-feely kind of family, but director Joseph urged them on, and got a nice shot of the three brothers hugging.

'I hate you both *so* much,' Jay said, which earned a massive laugh.

As a couple of runners moved in to clean up all the mess, Jay was led on to a patio through one of the ballroom's glass doors. After putting on swimming goggles, Shorty filmed as Damien the runner tipped a bucket of mercifully-warm water over his head.

Jay realised the gooey substance was some kind of special entertainment industry product, because as soon as the soapy water touched it the solution dissolved and the flour and polystyrene ran off his clothes in a kind of rubbery sheet.

After a second bucket of water, Jay had to sit in a chair while a make-up lady combed a few static-charged balls out of his hair, and checked his ears with a flashlight and tweezers.

It was a warm July morning, but Jay shivered as Meg hit the scene.

'Jay, I know you're cold,' Meg said. 'I know you want to get out of those wet clothes, but can you just tell us how that felt?'

'Err . . .' Jay said, and immediately imagined his media trainer glaring at him for stuttering. 'I guess it was a very interesting way to start the day.'

'It certainly was,' Meg said. 'What did you think when you were falling?'

'Terror,' Jay told the microphone. 'With hindsight it was pretty obvious that they weren't going to throw me over a balcony without a safety net. But it wasn't like I had time to think about it. And Theo has done some nutty stuff in his time.'

Meg laughed, and for once her emotion didn't seem to be pasted on for the camera. 'You've been a great sport, Jay. And as a thank you, you'll be pleased to hear that you're one of the six band members picked to attend this evening's network launch party in London. What do you think about that?'

'Cool,' Jay said, sounding, but not feeling, happy, because he always felt awkward at parties and would miss an afternoon guitar skills tutorial that he'd been looking forward to. 'I guess I'd better go find something smart to wear.'

10. Retail Therapy

Summer had never been to Central London. She excitedly rolled down the limo's blacked-out side window to gawp, commenting on everything from how much she wanted to go on the London Eye, to how all the Starbucks were way bigger than the one at the Merry Hill Centre in Dudley.

Jay was a Londoner and acted like it was all cool, though in truth the narrow streets and uber-posh shops of Mayfair weren't his natural turf either. Even the parked cars were fancy, and Theo got a few laughs as he pointed out some of the models he'd stolen.

'If you ever steal an older Mercedes, you've gotta remember that they have this weird foot-operated handbrake,' Theo said. 'Took me so long to figure out I almost got nabbed by the owner.'

Noah laughed. After Theo had given him a push up the driveway on the first day, Noah had taken a shine to Jay's big brother. Although Noah loved his life, a wheelchair made it tough to be fully independent and Theo's exaggerated tales of stealing, shagging and fighting were a window into something Noah craved.

'Hey, brain of Britain,' Jay said, looking at his brother, who faced him across the limo. 'You realise you've just admitted about twenty crimes?'

'So?' Theo said. 'There's no camera here.'

Jay smirked as he reached up and tapped a little black dome mounted in the limo's roof lining. 'You sure?'

Theo leaned forwards, glowering suspiciously at the dome. 'That's spying,' he spat. 'What about my civil liberties?'

'They *told* us we'd be filmed in the limo,' Jay said. 'But you were too busy chatting up the fit girl from Delayed Gratification instead of listening to Angie's briefing.'

'Angie's so stuck up,' Theo moaned, before looking up at the camera dome and sounding uncharacteristically unsure of himself. 'I made all that stuff about stealing cars up. And if you editors use any of this footage in the show, I'll hunt you down and slice your balls off.'

There was some uneasy laughter as Theo settled back into his seat. Traffic meant they'd have been faster walking the last mile to Eldridges department store, but they'd finally arrived. Two camera operators and two of the store's elaborately-uniformed doormen swept across the pavement, opening the limo doors.

Despite claims that the sextet who'd attend the network party would be picked based upon how well they'd done in media training, Jay reckoned there was a diversity agenda as they stepped out on to the pavement.

He'd been picked as a reward for being cool about the balcony prank. Theo – who absolutely *hadn't* done well in media training – was the good-looking rebel. Alfie from Brontobyte was the youngest in the competition. Just turned twelve, he was puppy-dog cute and could easily have passed for ten. Summer was the poor girl getting a shot of glamour, Eve the posh emo Scottish girl, and to round things off, a kid in a wheelchair?

After three days at Rock War Manor, everyone had started getting used to being filmed, but Eldridges introduced the added dimension of being filmed in public. After the store's manager was filmed shaking hands and giving each contestant five fifty-pound shopping vouchers, the kids were paired off, and sent to explore with a two-person camera crew in pursuit.

Noah was pleased to partner Theo. Summer and Eve made a beeline for womenswear, leaving Jay with Alfie. This was tricky, because the pair had known each other their whole lives, but hadn't spoken since Jay got voted out of Brontobyte.

'It's OK . . .' Jay said. The situation with Alfie, the cameraman two steps behind and all the shoppers looking around to see who was being filmed, made these two of the most awkward words he'd ever uttered. 'I know you only voted me out of Brontobyte because you were worried Tristan would batter you.'

'He's my brother, as well,' Alfie said. 'Family loyalty and

stuff. My mum bangs it into us that families should stick together.'

'So how's Brontobyte doing?' Jay asked. 'Rehearsals and stuff?'

'Good,' Alfie said. 'They're letting me do a lot more in the band. Our tutor, Mr Currie, and now the tutor at the manor are keen for me to play lead guitar, and even drums on a couple of tracks when Tristan sings back-up vocals with Erin.'

'Makes sense,' Jay said. 'We always gave you the crap parts because you're youngest. But you're a better musician than Salman and Tristan.'

'Tristan heard your comment about Brontobyte being no-hopers. He said he'd beat your arse if it wasn't for your big brothers.'

Jay felt uncomfortable. He hated being skinny and not able to stick up for himself. By now they'd reached the trainer wall. Alfie sized up some Nikes, but was told his size was only stocked downstairs in the kids' department. Jay got some Converse, and some new pool shoes to replace his battered Crocs. Alfie got his Nikes in kids, then they played with gadgets in toys. Jay bought presents for his little siblings, and Alfie got a Fisher Price baby toy.

'Isn't that a little young for Tristan?' Jay asked snidely.

'Haven't you heard? My mum's expecting,' Alfie said. 'November.'

'Bloody hell,' Jay said. 'I didn't even realise you could have babies at her age.'

They only had ninety minutes to spend all their vouchers, and after a mad scramble using up the last of their money in the stationery department, Alfie and Jay met up with the others by the main entrance.

To end the shopping sequence, they were filmed going through the store's revolving doors, each carrying at least two of Eldridges' distinctive purple shopping bags, and then walking single file to the waiting limo.

'That was so cool,' Summer said, as they drove away. Then guiltily, 'I can't believe I spent ninety pounds on perfume. That's more than two weeks' food money back home.'

'You smell nice though,' Jay said, and got rewarded with a big smile.

'Thank you,' Summer answered, as Jay tried to imagine how she'd look naked.

It was a ten-minute cruise to their next stop in Savile Row. A precariously-steep staircase took them up to a large fitting room over a tailor's shop. Noah's disability had been overlooked, but Theo ignored Angie's health and safety concerns and gave him a piggyback upstairs.

'That's thingy from *Pebble Cottage*,' Summer said, as someone passed in the hall outside.

'Who from *what*?' Theo asked, holding his hands up to mock her excitement.

'It's a Channel Six soap opera,' Summer explained. 'My nan never misses an episode.'

After a short wait, a pair of chunky wardrobe ladies came

in, each wheeling a clothes rail. One woman, one rail and the two girls went into a side room, while the other woman looked at the four boys, then at a clipboard, as Jay glimpsed a presenter from Channel Six News hissing at a publicist in the hallway outside.

'*Rock War*,' the seamstress said. 'Can't say I've heard of that one. Is it a new show?'

Noah nodded and was about to explain, but Theo took over.

'We're geologists,' Theo explained. 'We find rare and expensive rocks, then we have a war and throw them at one another. Whoever gets knocked out first will be fed to the pandas at Edinburgh Zoo.'

Alfie and Noah laughed as the wardrobe lady glowered over the top of her glasses and addressed Theo in a deadpan voice. 'Is that so, young man? Well, let's see what we have for you.'

Jay looked wary as the lady started unzipping bags covering suit jackets on the clothes rail. In Jay's family, smart clothes were only worn for weddings and appearances before a magistrate, but he warmed to the outfit when he felt the soft woollen fabric and tartan lining. He felt properly good when he had the whole kit on and looked in the mirror: sky blue shirt, pencil-thin tie, slate grey slim-fit chinos and deep red Harris Tweed jacket.

'How's that suiting you?' the woman asked.

'Good,' Jay said, unable to stop admiring himself. 'I'd never have picked these colours, but they work really well.'

'I'm glad you approve,' the woman said, as she went down on one knee.

She wasn't satisfied, and spent the best part of ten minutes pinning Jay's outfit and making marks with dressmaker's chalk. 'I'll get the girls downstairs to make the adjustments and it'll be delivered to your hotel room by five.'

Theo was a trickier customer, moaning that his shirt collar was too tight and joking that he needed lots of extra room around the crotch.

'Oww,' Theo yelped, sounding remarkably girly as the wardrobe lady jabbed him with a pin.

'I'm so sorry,' she said, not sounding remotely sincere. 'I need you to be very still, and very quiet, or that *might* just happen again.'

Jay smirked, then gasped as the side door opened and Summer came through in a strapless white silk mini-dress, worn with snakeskin cowboy boots and a cross pendant necklace faced with twelve huge diamonds. It was like she was dressed up, but still rock-and-roll at the same time.

'Wow!' Jay blurted. 'You look *incredible*.'

'Thanks. Someone's coming to do our hair at the hotel,' Summer said modestly. 'Which is great cos it's basically a bird's nest.'

'I could totally shag you,' Theo told Summer, then gave another girlish yelp as the wardrobe lady spiked him a pin.

11. Diamonds & Champagne

It was a movie moment, coming out of the limo in front of the Natural History Museum. Summer in cowboy boots and diamonds, Eve strutting like a catwalk model in a tasselled leather skirt and punk-style jacket covered in more than a hundred zips.

Jay didn't like the way his trousers felt tight around his butt, but they looked good, and the hairdresser had thinned, trimmed and gelled his hair into nifty black spikes.

Two dozen cameras flashed, but the three interviewers on the carpet looked clueless. Then one suddenly brightened, stopped Jay and put a microphone to his face.

'Welcome to the Channel Six preview evening. You look great, are you fully recovered from filming?'

'Yeah,' Jay said, as he remembered his media training: *smile, stay upbeat, don't urm and aarrgh.* 'It's just been a cool day. Riding around London in a limo, checking out our hotel – which is uber-posh – and seeing all the Channel Six stars.'

'And I understand you hurt your back while filming *Gulliver's Travels*. Are you fully recovered?'

'I'm fine,' Jay said. Then, tailing off, 'Did you say *Gulliver's Travels*?'

'You're Hugo Portman, the actor, right?'

Jay shook his head. 'I'm Jay Thomas, from *Rock War*.'

'Oh . . . Yeah, that's the new talent show. Right?'

'Right,' Jay said, as his interviewer looked disappointed.

Another limo had pulled up and the interviewer didn't give an excuse before darting off. There were a few fans at the bottom of the carpet, who'd started squealing and holding out photos and autograph pads. Jay knew the guy's handsome face from a couple of movies, but couldn't think of his name.

The others had carried on inside and Jay caught up in the museum's lobby. A publicist called Jen was giving them all the low-down, explaining that she was going to try and speak to some journalists who might want to interview them about *Rock War*.

The museum was closed for the party, and the main hall was lit up in ghoulish green, with a finger buffet, tables set up for interviews and a huge diplodocus skeleton bisecting the room. As soon as the publicist was out of sight, Theo went straight for a table covered in bubbling champagne glasses, downing two and nabbing a third. The others were more cautious, glancing around to see if anyone was paying attention before picking up glasses of their own.

'I wonder how big that dinosaur's turds were,' Theo

said, as he stared at the skeleton. 'At least the size of a Mini, I'd bet.'

Jay tutted. 'How would something the size of a Mini get out of a dinosaur's arsehole?'

'How big was a dinosaur's arsehole?' Theo asked, as he grabbed a fourth champagne and passed a second to Eve. 'Are you some kind of arsehole expert, Jay?'

You didn't win debates like this with Theo, so Jay just ignored him. As they moved deeper into the chattering crowd of journalists, advertising execs and minor celebs, Noah and Summer were taken aside by Jen to do an interview with a teen mag, while Eve dealt with being hit on by a creepy dude who seemed to be wearing his lunch on his tie and claimed to be the head writer on *Pebble Cottage*.

Everyone was on their second champagne, except Theo, who looked wobbly as he headed off to chat up a teenage presenter who was most often seen bouncing around in pink dungarees on a preschool show called *Sunshine City*.

Much to Jay's irritation, the presenter didn't fob Theo off, and was standing close, inspecting the tattoo on Theo's neck by the time Jay turned away in disgust. After taking a run at the finger buffet, Jay found himself standing alone at a table covered in brightly coloured folders.

He flipped one open and realised they were press packs for all of Channel Six's different programmes, containing show details, photos and bios of the cast, and details of who you had to contact if you wanted to set up an interview or receive a preview DVD.

The packs varied considerably, from black and silver metallic wallets for the really important shows, down to stapled A4 sheets for a German detective series that went out at two in the morning.

The *Rock War* press pack was somewhere inbetween, placed in a generic orange folder with a sticker on the front. As Jay flipped through looking for a picture of himself, a leggy female and a tall speccy bloke reached around and grabbed a folder.

'Have you heard about this one?' the man said, as he waved the *Rock War* brochure. 'It was supposed to be huge. Rage Cola put up a ridiculous amount of sponsorship, but as soon as KT signed on the dotted line, it got repositioned as a tween-to-teen show in the five-thirty slot.'

Jay didn't get time to think about this, because Summer had arrived beside him.

'I've never tasted champagne before,' she said furtively. 'It's nice, but it's going straight to my head.'

'How was the interview?' Jay asked.

'Cool, I guess,' Summer said, as she grabbed one of the *Rock War* press packs. 'It was for some kids' magazine. *Mad House*, or *Mad Hat*, or something.'

'Never heard of it,' Jay said.

'I see our brochure's on the table with all the kids' shows,' Summer said.

Jay had been so focused on finding his picture that he hadn't noticed that the *Rock War* pack was surrounded by press packs for shows ranging from *Panda Time!* to

Fairy Belle Island.

'Yeah,' Jay said warily. 'There was a guy here a second ago. He said that *Rock War* will be airing at half five on a Saturday. So I guess they want a lot of kids watching us.'

'Five thirty's not prime time,' Summer said, disappointedly. 'And if they're pitching the show at little kids, so much for all the guff Zig Allen gave us, about the show being properly hardcore and about the music.'

The spotlights on the room-spanning diplodocus skeleton dimmed and the chatter dwindled. A man in a suit mounted a small stage behind the interview tables and the Channel Six logo flashed up on a pair of projector screens.

'They said we'd never make it,' the executive said, pretending to be slightly out of breath. 'There was no room for a sixth entertainment channel in the United Kingdom. But here we are, eight years later. Profitable, innovative, and with some of the most competitive advertising rates in the television industry.'

A few laughs and a couple of cheers echoed around the stone hall.

'But one show defined our early years,' the executive continued. 'It was the first show to take Channel Six into the top ten viewing chart. It was the platform that gave my creative team and our advertising partners the confidence to invest in other shows and it was the show that made us a force to be reckoned with. When it ended two years ago we all felt like a piece of Channel Six history had gone forever.

'But tonight, I can exclusively reveal to this revered

audience of talent, press and advertising execs, that *Hit Machine* is coming back to Channel Six this autumn.'

There were a few gasps, but it was only now that Jay understood what the speccy guy had been talking about: *Rock War* had been bumped from prime time slot to late afternoon, because Channel Six's biggest ever reality show was making a comeback.

12. Just Talk

'But nobody wants to hear me waffling on,' the Channel Six executive said. 'Ladies and gentlemen, I give you, the one and only . . . Karen Trim.'

The woman who emerged on to the stage was short, with big shoulders and a boyish face. Her nickname was The Tank because she crushed everything in her path. She'd made tens of millions developing reality TV formats that aired all over the world and *Hit Machine* was the biggest of them all.

Karen had been a judge during *Hit Machine*'s first four seasons. Her vicious critiques reduced contestants to tears, and a montage of Karen's barbs had over fifty million hits on YouTube.

'I'm back, baby!' Karen shouted, as she raised her hands above her head and gave her slightly awkward grin for the cameras. 'Speeches bore me, so just ask away!'

There was a scrum in front of the stage as journalists and

photographers barged one another out of the way.

'Will you go back to being a judge?' someone asked.

'You betcha!' Karen said. 'And we'll be announcing the other two judges for the new series of *Hit Machine* very soon.'

'What about your US ventures?'

'We've signed a deal with the network for three more seasons of *Hit Machine* and *Talented*. And an all-new country music-themed version of *Hit Machine* will begin airing on CMTV in spring 2015.'

Jay and Summer recognised the next voice, rising up from a wheelchair whose owner had pushed himself right up to the stage.

'Why are you reviving *Hit Machine*?' Noah asked, sounding very serious. 'Didn't Channel Six axe the series two years ago, because viewing figures were falling and the format had gone stale?'

The Tank's reputation wasn't just for show and there was a collective gasp among the journalists as the little woman locked eyes on Noah.

'What rock did you crawl out from?' Karen asked, acidly. Then, rather than answer Noah's question, she did the weird smile and hands above head thing again, before yelling, 'I'm back baby. See you all later!'

'Answer my question,' Noah demanded. But Karen threw her wireless mic at a stage hand, before storming away looking cheesed off.

As journalists and photographers moved off, Theo came up behind Noah and gave him a high five.

'Way to go, annoying that old battle-axe. Here, you need to drink more champagne.'

'What happened to your girlfriend?' Noah asked, as he took the champagne glass.

The lights went back up as a preview reel of Channel Six's autumn shows started running on the two big screens.

'She had to go off and do a bunch of interviews,' Theo said, as he waggled his Samsung. 'But she texted me her number.'

'Nice,' Noah said, again wishing that he lived Theo's life.

Summer and Jay had spotted Noah as the crowd of journalists backed up.

'Way to go, Noah,' Jay said. 'The look on her face was *priceless*.'

Jen the publicist was less pleased as she leaned over Noah's wheelchair and hissed, 'What the hell was that? She was supposed to do a ten-minute Q and A and you made her storm off. The channel directors are livid. And . . . Are you kids drinking champagne?'

'It's sparkling apple juice,' Noah said, failing to mask a smirk.

'I can smell it on your breath,' Jen hissed, as she snatched Noah's glass. 'Give me those glasses, all of you. You've got no idea the kind of bollocking I'm going to get off my boss tomorrow.'

'So,' Jay said firmly. 'Is it true that *Rock War* has been turned into a kiddies' show, now that the witch lady has signed up for a new season of *Hit Machine*?'

Jen put on her best false grin. 'The five-thirty-p.m. slot isn't as prestigious as the one originally planned for *Rock War*,' she admitted. 'But your show will be exactly the same.'

'That sucks,' Theo said, slurring his words and leering at Jen's boobs.

'You're drunk,' Jen snapped. 'Jesus Christ, show some maturity. What kind of publicity will you get if I fix up an interview and you rock up drunk?'

'Are we doing any more interviews?' Summer asked.

Noah snorted, and pointed back towards the exit. 'The journos are grabbing their coats. *Hit Machine* coming back is the only thing they'll write about.'

'This party is not just for journalists,' Jen said. '*Rock War* is a high-budget show that's been moved to a difficult slot. We have to sell advertisements, so I'm going to try and introduce you to some very important people and you'd better behave.'

'Or what?' Theo sneered. 'I didn't sign up for this. This is about as rock and roll as a corporate box at the opera.'

'I give up!' Jen hissed, giving a little stamp with her high heel, then walking off pretending that she had something to read on her iPhone.

'More champagne?' Noah suggested.

'Wise words,' Theo said.

'I need a pee,' Summer said. 'I'll be back.'

She swayed as she headed off.

Theo gave Jay a gentle shove. 'Get after her.'

'She's not that drunk,' Jay said. 'She'll be OK.'

'No, you dick, she's into you,' Theo said.

'Summer?'

Theo tutted. 'No, the pope. Summer's flirting with you.'

'She is?' Jay said.

'You're *supposed* to be the clever one in the family,' Theo said. 'She's making eye contact. She keeps smiling at you and putting her hand on your back.'

'She says she's not used to high heels.'

Theo shook his head. 'She's not wearing high heels.'

'Oh,' Jay said dopily.

'Babatunde, Adam and half the guys at the manor are sniffing around Summer,' Theo said. 'You've got first mover advantage, but after tonight . . .'

'What do I do?' Jay asked.

'Give her a kiss,' Theo said. 'You've snogged a girl before, haven't you?'

'Sure,' Jay said, trying to sound chilled, even though he'd only kissed a girl on the mouth once and for barely ten seconds.

Jay was full of butterflies as he scurried off after Summer. By the time he'd caught up, she was on the mezzanine level with one foot in the door of the ladies.

'Too much champagne,' Summer grinned. 'I'm busting.'

'Me too,' Jay said, as he shoved his way into the gents.

He took a pee, washed hands, then tried sniffing his breath and wished he'd used mouthwash before leaving the hotel. Back on the mezzanine, he waited so long that he thought Summer must have gone back to the main hall without him.

'Thank god you're still here,' Summer gasped, glancing around anxiously as she finally came out.

'Is that blood on your dress?' Jay asked, alarmed.

'Eve's blood, not mine,' Summer said, as she yanked Jay's arm and started pulling him into the ladies.

Jay was squeamish around blood and felt even more anxious as he stepped into a deserted women's bathroom. Summer opened the door of the middle stall in a row of five. Eve was slumped on the seat lid, holding a wodge of toilet tissue over a belly wound, with tear tracks down her face.

'What happened?' Jay asked.

As he squeezed into the cubicle, Jay saw that the coat hook had been unscrewed from the door. It now lay on the floor tiles, stained red and surrounded by dots of Eve's blood.

'They must have a first-aider here,' Jay said.

'I drank three champagnes, and I felt sick,' Eve said. 'All the noise and people were too much for me. Plus Dylan dumped me. This isn't as big a deal as it looks. It's just something I do to myself when I feel bad.'

Jay looked baffled. 'Self-harm,' Summer told him. 'Google it. It's a thing.'

Jay started pulling his phone out.

'Not now, bonehead,' Summer said. 'We need to get her back to the hotel without being seen.'

'That's a lot of blood,' Jay said. 'What if it needs stitches or gets infected?'

It'll be fine,' Eve said firmly. 'If you grass me up, they'll kick the Pandas out of *Rock War*.'

'Maybe you need medical help,' Jay said. 'This isn't right.'

'We need *your* help, Jay,' Eve added. 'You're cool, aren't you?'

Summer and Jay exchanged an awkward glance. 'Eve's got thirty quid for a cab,' Summer said. 'But I've got blood all over my dress and Eve can't walk very well.'

'It's dark in the main hall,' Eve said, as someone came into the bathroom. She dropped her voice to a whisper. 'We'll go out of the hall and down the red carpet. There was a taxi rank right out front. The bleeding always stops after an hour or so.'

Jay still couldn't understand why Eve wanted to hurt herself, but he was slightly drunk, and going along with her plan seemed easier than having to think for himself.

'OK, let's do this,' Jay said, as a bolt slid across a door two cubicles along. 'Eve, put your arm around my neck. Summer, take Eve's bag, and walk behind so nobody sees your dress.'

*

Jay woke in his London hotel. The clock said ten, but after the previous day's prank he turned on Sky News to be sure. Theo's bed was a mound of white linen, but no sign of the man himself.

After a piss, Jay saw himself in the mirror. The spikes had looked great the night before, but now his hair was all flat and shiny with gel. Back in the bedroom, Jay took his phone off charge, connected to the hotel Wi-Fi and quickly checked his WhatsApp messages before looking up the Self-harm page on Wikipedia:

Self-harm *(SH) or* **deliberate self-harm** *(DSH) includes* **self-injury** *(SI) and self-poisoning and is defined as the intentional, direct injuring of body tissue most often done without suicidal intentions.*

The page was pretty dry, so after a few more lines, Jay went to Google and got some more insightful information by reading a page of personal accounts written by self-harmers. It was weird that anyone – mostly girls, it seemed – could want to hurt themselves, or that pain could somehow give them relief when they felt low.

After the accounts, Jay did a *self-harm* Google image search. But it was a bit much, so he closed his browser and promised himself he would keep a friendly eye out for Eve.

They were heading back to the manor at eleven, so Jay figured he'd take a shower, and then wander downstairs. Hotel breakfast had probably finished, but he'd seen a McDonald's down the street and he quite fancied a McMuffin. He was stripping off when the electronic door lock clicked.

'Morning, stud!' Theo said brightly, rushing over and giving Jay a thump on the back. 'I never knew you had it in you.'

Theo wore Jack Wills shorts, with a running vest balled up in his hand. His upper body shone with sweat.

'You stink,' Jay moaned, backing up as he noted a whiff of booze in his brother's BO.

'Did some weights in the gym, then five K on the treadmill,' Theo said. 'A blast of exercise is the best hangover cure I know.'

'You certainly knocked enough back,' Jay said.

'Well, who's gonna turn down free champers?' Theo asked. 'So come on, tell us. Something major must have happened, you sly dog?'

'What are you on about?' Jay asked.

Jay had no intention of saying anything about Eve because Theo was about as discreet as the chimes of Big Ben.

'Come on,' Theo said. 'I send you off after Summer and then you both vanish for the rest of the night.'

Jay had been so caught up in the drama and his curiosity about Eve's condition that he hadn't given much thought to explaining his disappearance from the party.

'Was it your first shag?' Theo asked eagerly. 'Don't worry if you shot your load. Everyone does the first time.'

'We just talked,' Jay said, thinking on the fly. 'The party was really noisy. We were both pissed off about the *Hit Machine* thing and neither of us fancied going back.'

'You *talked*,' Theo said, looking appalled. 'I send you after a hot girl, and you *talk*. Frankly, I'm ashamed to call you my brother.'

Jay smirked. 'Well, having you in the family ain't exactly a source of pride.'

Theo half raised a fist, but Jay didn't flinch. He'd known Theo long enough to sense when he really was going to swing at you.

'I need the shower,' Theo said.

'I was just about to use it,' Jay said, but Theo was already in the doorway.

He lobbed his sweaty vest, but Jay managed to duck.

'*Talk*,' Theo said indignantly, as he started running the tap to brush his teeth. 'We're gonna have to sharpen up your skills with the ladies, my young padawan.'

13. Summer Holiday

TV Week Magazine

PICK OF THE DAY – Rock War: Boot Camp
Thursday, August 6th, 7 p.m. 6point2

Once hailed as the saviour of Channel Six's Saturday night schedule, now swept aside by the surprise return of Hit Machine, Rock War *makes its debut on a satellite-only channel in the depths of television's summer graveyard.*

Boot Camp *is designed to whet our appetite for the show's knockout rounds, which debut on Channel Six proper in September.*

Despite the branding of show sponsor Rage Cola in almost every shot and a highly questionable scene in which a terrified contestant is thrown over a balcony as a 'joke', this teen talent show shouldn't be written off just yet.

The decision to film documentary-style means Rock War *lacks the whizz-bang glitz of a Karen Trim production. But the trials and tribulations of the twelve teen bands feel all the more real for it.*

Ten days later

Theo was no gift to the world of singing, but that hardly mattered when he was in front of a microphone, naked apart from cargo shorts and glowering into the camera like he wanted to nut it. Babatunde was good enough to drum for any band, anywhere. Nobody hit a drum as hard as he did and with muffler screens surrounding his kit the noise still dominated the stable-turned-rehearsal-room. Adam's bass was decent and he looked the part, but Jay wouldn't take his shirt off in front of his more muscular brothers, and the result was a sweat-drenched T-shirt and flowery swim shorts still damp from a lunch-time dip.

As Jet's version of Aerosmith's classic 'Sweet Emotion' wound down, Theo kicked his microphone stand and lunged. Shorty the camera operator stumbled backwards as the stand hit his leg. The other two camera operators looked to their director, but Joseph made a rolling gesture, indicating that they should keep filming.

'Hell, yeah!' Jay said, cracking a massive grin as silence broke out.

Adam nodded and instinctively returned the expression. 'We're getting good. Who'd have thought that hard work and daily rehearsals would actually pay off?'

Everyone was hot, but Babatunde had the additional problem of being trapped behind plastic screens. With his ever-present hoodie unzipped to show a sweaty chest, he grabbed a big bottle of water off the floor, straddled light cables and as soon as he was out of the converted stable, poured it over his head.

After checking his shoulder-mount camera for damage, Shorty looked down and saw a cut where the microphone stand had hit his leg.

'What was that?' Shorty shouted, eyeballing Theo. 'You could have knocked me out with that stunt, and these cameras cost six grand a piece.'

Theo shrugged to show that he didn't give a shit as the cameraman stepped right up to him.

'You shrug,' Shorty shouted, as Joseph rushed towards them, 'but this is my livelihood, you spoiled brat.'

'Do something else then,' Theo spat. 'McDonald's are hiring, if you're tall enough.'

Joseph was responsible for health and safety. But he was also responsible for getting great footage. He'd watched Theo's lunge and the flying mic stand on his monitor. It was the kind of anger every director hopes to capture in a rock band, and Joseph was reluctant to do anything that would blunt Theo's edge.

'Sebastian, my good man,' Joseph said, using Shorty's real name as he rested an arm on the camera operator's shoulder. 'I'll help us pack up. Why don't you go back to the manor, put a dot of Savlon on that cut and get yourself a cup of tea.'

'Savlon and tea?' Shorty yelled. 'That yobbo almost knocked me out.'

As Joseph kept up his efforts to calm Shorty down, Theo followed his three band mates into the sun. The area outside the converted stables was a former paddock, covered in wild grass and the odd dandelion. Jay was flat out on his back, with a hand over his eyes to shield the sun. Rock music was escaping from the other practice rooms, most of which had their doors open because of the heat.

'All the other bands are sounding pretty good too,' Adam said, before squishing his water bottle and spraying the last few drips in his face. 'Anyone want a refill?'

'Cheers,' Jay said, tossing his water bottle towards Adam, before doing a big stretch and yawn.

'It's actually a shame we've got to compete,' Babatunde said. 'I've been here two weeks now. Tutors are good, most of the kids in the other bands are cool. Even the weather's been great.'

Jay didn't answer, he just enjoyed the hot sun on his body and felt really relaxed. He felt another yawn coming on, but was distracted by the sound of running water and sat up sharply. Theo had pulled down the front of his shorts and stood less than a metre away, pissing on the grass.

'For god's sake,' Jay yelled, rolling away, then glowering at his big brother. 'The toilet's just up there.'

'Watering the plants,' Theo said. 'And stop looking at my knob.'

Jay laughed. 'Theo, I've seen *way* too much of your knob. You pee on Tube trains. You pee up against cars in the street. You even got suspended for jumping naked off the five-metre board at our primary school swimming gala.'

Babatunde laughed. 'Is that true?'

'When did you ever hear a wild story about Theo that *wasn't* true?' Jay asked.

By this time Theo was shaking off and Adam was coming back with a trio of refilled water bottles.

'Can I smell piss?' Adam asked.

They were about to move further along the lawn, away from the smell, but a couple of the other bands had started heading out of their rehearsal rooms, and the music seemed to have stopped in most of the others.

Theo caught Michelle from Industrial Scale Slaughter's eye. 'What's happening?' he asked.

'First the earth cooled,' Michelle said. 'Then the dinosaurs came. Now global warming means we're heading for imminent global catastrophe.'

'That girl is properly weird,' Jay whispered to Babatunde, as Summer gave a saner answer.

'Haven't you got a text?' Summer asked. 'Everyone's getting them.'

Jay had heard a little ping from his phone about a minute earlier, but he'd ignored it because the only person who'd texted him since he got here was his mum, and she just kept asking if she needed to send more underwear and if Theo was behaving himself.

Jay looked at his phone and read aloud. 'All *Rock War* contestants please report to the ballroom immediately for an important announcement.'

'Maybe they've tracked down the chef who cooked that dodgy shepherd's pie on Tuesday night,' Adam suggested.

'You're such a fussy eater,' Jay said. 'It tasted like top quality horsemeat to me.'

Seven of the twelve bands had been in their practice rooms. Soon there was a noisy train of bodies heading down the stone path towards the manor, with a camerawoman walking backwards at its head. Everyone was eager to know what the surprise was, but nobody wanted to look uncool by admitting that they cared.

There were already quite a few kids in the ballroom, who'd either already been there when they got their texts or were just upstairs chilling in their rooms. As Jay walked in, he was slightly irritated by Meg sticking a microphone in his face.

'So Jay,' she said, trowelling on the fake excitement. 'What's the big surprise going to be?'

'Err . . . I dunno,' Jay said. 'Maybe some celebrity coming here for a couple of days, or something?'

Michelle and Theo barged into shot.

'I predict a big sex orgy!' Michelle shouted.

'Drinking Rage Cola made me grow women's breasts,' Theo added.

Adam chimed in with a loud mooing sound, at which point Meg looked thoroughly pissed off and told her cameraman to stop filming.

Angie was in charge of shooting in the ballroom. She spent ages moving lights and making all the kids sit close together on the multicoloured beanbags. There'd not been an announcement like this in the two weeks they'd been at boot camp, so everyone was pretty curious by the time Angie was finally satisfied with the shot and had her three camera operators positioned so that they could film the announcement and capture the contestants' reaction.

Jay was annoyed to find himself inhaling the smell of four lads who'd been playing on the mini basketball court. On the upside, Summer was next to him and their bare knees touched.

'OK, let's do this,' Angie shouted. 'Bring him in.'

Everyone looked behind as a man ambled into the hall, dressed in studded leather jacket and straggly grey hair. He seemed very drunk as he stood in front of the beanbags, pointed accusingly at a camera and yelled, 'New album in May. "Tiger Bright" on Clarkson Records. You make sure that gets in the show. That's the only reason . . .'

Angie gave a despairing look as the slurred voice tailed off.

'Who is he?' Jay whispered, but only got blank stares.

'"Tiger Bright",' the man repeated, as Meg rushed up alongside to do a rescue act.

'Hi, everyone,' Meg said brightly. 'Thanks for being so patient. Now why don't we give a rousing *Rock War* welcome to legendary guitarist – Sammy Barelli!'

Meg looked towards Angie, who was giving a *carry on* signal. Jay was one of the few kids who knew Sammy Barelli as a legendary guitarist in several rock bands. But it took quite an effort to reconcile the handsome man on half a dozen album covers with the straggly-haired pisshead in front of them.

'Sammy who?' someone shouted, as the anticipated cheers failed to materialise.

'Isn't that the guy who cleans our bathrooms?' Noah added.

Sammy looked outraged, as Meg spoke like she was talking to a small child. 'Sammy, I think you've got an announcement to make.'

'Screw this shit!' Sammy shouted, making it about five paces before tripping on a potted plant. 'Why am I even here? "Tiger Bright", on Clarkson Records! Buy it or I'll kill your pets!'

The kids were getting properly impatient by the time Sammy had been removed from the room, and a gold envelope stripped from his inside pocket.

'OK,' Meg said, as she stood in front of the angry contestants and gave the gold envelope a little flutter. 'Let's see what we've got in store for you.'

Meg pulled out a white card and began reading from it. 'Congratulations, *Rock War* contestants. Your hard work over the past two weeks has paid off, and all twelve bands have shown massive improvement. But now it's time to put everything you've learned together and see what you can do in front of a live crowd.

'This weekend, all twelve *Rock War* bands will be performing live in front of up to ninety thousand fans at the Rage Rock festival in Sheffield. All band members will also get VIP passes for the entire festival, giving you a unique chance to hear some of your favourite bands and meet them in the flesh.'

Jay smiled, and quite a few other kids started jumping around, hugging and yelling stuff.

'Fecking awesome,' Adam said.

'Girls in muddy wellies are hot!' Babatunde added, earning himself a punch from Coco.

But when Jay turned to look at Summer, she seemed overwhelmed.

'You OK?' he asked.

'I threw up five times before we played in front of a hundred and fifty people at the Old Beaumont,' Summer explained. 'What am I gonna be like in front of ninety thousand?'

14. Key Demographic

The Medway Festival had been going for more than twenty years, but for 2014 it had taken major sponsorship from Rage Cola and controversially been renamed Rage Rock. Jay was squished up alongside Summer as their branded chopper swept over housing estates and partly-demolished industrial sites.

It was late afternoon, but the sun was still bright. The first sign of the festival was a bird's eye view of a packed train, unloading at a tiny station. From there, the helicopter flew over roads dotted with backpackers weaving amongst snarled traffic, before finally reaching the festival site proper, where a huge scrum filtered through the festival gates.

'It's massive,' Summer shouted.

The chopper roared as Jay lifted off one cup of his ear protectors. 'What?'

'Massive,' Summer repeated.

Jay nodded as the chopper turned, opening a vista of

fields filling with tents. Sheffield Park was originally a vast steelworks and a World War Two bomb factory with adjoining airfield. Now, two brick chimneys were all that remained of this industrial past, with the festival's iconic main stage running between them. A second, smaller, stage had been built at the opposite end of the site, at the end of a long-abandoned runway.

Jay felt important as the crowds looked up, wondering who was flying overhead. After buzzing a main stage dotted with technical staff, they landed on a pristine concrete helipad.

Ducking under the rotating blades and handing his ear protectors to a ground marshal, Jay began a swift walk towards a VIP area, shielded from the main festival site by a four-metre log fence. A few keen festival-goers stood along the path, hoping to catch an autograph from someone famous, but disappointed to see just Jay and Summer, plus Angie the director, three Rage Cola marketing executives and a couple who'd won a radio competition.

The festival didn't kick off for another three hours, so they walked into a mostly-deserted marquee with a buffet and bar. Jen the publicist was on hand, and she gave Jay and Summer their VIP lanyards and a no booze, no sex, no drugs warning before taking them across the floor to meet the executive who'd given the speech at the Channel Six launch party.

'This is Mitch Timberwolf,' Jen said, clearly nervous around her boss's, boss's, boss. 'And Rophan Hung, sales and marketing VP at Rage Cola Europe.'

Jay and Summer both felt like they were in the headmaster's office as they shook hands with the two uber-powerful executives.

'You kids are doing real great,' Mitch said, as Jen smiled and Rophan nodded in agreement. 'Viewing figures are solid for the three episodes of *Boot Camp* we've aired so far.'

'And heading upwards,' Rophan added. 'Which is a sign that word of mouth is building.'

'So how many people are actually watching us?' Jay asked.

'Around twenty thousand on 6point2,' Mitch said. 'Which is good for daytime on a satellite channel, and at least that number again online.'

'Social media looks good too,' Rophan added. 'And being here at the festival is going to raise your profile even higher.'

'How many viewers did *Hit Machine* get?' Jay asked.

Mitch cast an awkward glance at the Rage Cola executive before answering. 'The last season of *Hit Machine* averaged eight-point-six million viewers. But that's prime time on a free-to-air channel. It's early days for *Rock War* right now.'

Rophan spoke brusquely, as Jen gave Jay a *why-did-you-have-to-ask-that* look. 'So what's our target for *Rock War*, once the knockout rounds begin?'

'Two million viewers in a five-thirty slot,' Mitch said.

'That's tough going for five thirty on Channel Six,' Rophan said brusquely.

Mitch smiled, and thumped his back. 'We're putting everything behind this show, Rophan.'

Summer broke an awkward silence. 'I've just gone past a thousand followers for my video diary on YouTube. There's a little battle going on at the manor to see who gets the most followers.'

Rophan looked intrigued. 'Who's winning?'

'Theo,' Summer said. 'I'm third.'

Jay didn't like this part of the conversation, because he'd taken his video diary more seriously than almost everyone else, but still only had a hundred and sixty YouTube followers.

After an awkward silence, Mitch shot a *now-the-grown-ups-have-to-continue-their-conversation* look at Jen, who practically wrenched Jay and Summer away.

Next stop was a tent city within the VIP compound. There seemed to be plenty of mobile loos and a large shower block. Jay didn't even need to duck as he went through the flap of a large hexagonal tent.

As Summer headed for the girls' tent next door, Jay inspected a large space, with a fake wood floor, bunk beds against five walls and an area in the centre of the tent with rugs and floor cushions. The centrepiece was the inevitable giant Rage Cola can. The bottom half was a Rage-stocked fridge, while the top had USBs for charging phones and details on how to connect to Wi-Fi.

It wasn't exactly luxurious, but Jay realised his first festival experience was going to be a lot more comfortable than that of the ordinary punters he'd seen crowding around the entry gates and pitching their pop-up tents in the surrounding fields.

Jay was pleased to find that his luggage had arrived before him, but he'd been on the last chopper in, so he wondered where everyone else had disappeared to.

'Knock, knock,' Jay said, once he'd crossed to the girls' tent.

'You can't come in,' Michelle shouted. 'We're all having a naked tickle fight.'

Jay knew better than to believe anything Michelle said, but was still wary as he peeked through the flap before stepping inside. Summer had one arm in the air, squirting her pits with body spray.

'They've all gone off to explore the site,' Summer said. 'But we're meeting up to eat at the Burrito Shack at half six.'

'What about the camera crews and stuff?' Jay asked.

Michelle smiled. 'Zig's trying to save money again, so the camera crews won't be here until tomorrow.'

Jay didn't exactly hate being filmed, but it was often a pain being asked to repeat something for the cameras, or waiting for lights to be set up, or having everyone gawping because you were wearing a lapel mic and being followed around by a cameraman.

'Freedom,' Jay shouted, and Summer copied, once she'd tucked her deodorant back into her big shopping bag.

*

By seven the festival site was rammed. Jay sat at a picnic bench, eating a giant steak burrito and chilli cheese fries. All the other *Rock War* contestants were there, apart from a couple of girls who'd sought out a more veggie-friendly option. The festival had a strict ID policy, and Theo's attempts to get a beer were thwarted by the red circle on his VIP badge.

The sun was setting as the *Rock War* contestants, stuffed with burritos, headed towards the festival's main stage. Most contestants used their passes to get into a special VIP area close to the stage, but Jay, Dylan, Adam and Alfie decided that they wanted to be among real fans rather than executives drinking wine and staring at their iPhones.

It took twenty minutes shoving bodies to reach a good spot, centre stage. A rap act went off to modest cheers, and a light drizzle began as one of the night's two headline acts started to play. The rain was just enough to cool a hot crowd.

'My mum would freak so badly if she knew what I was doing right now,' Alfie said, grinning ear to ear.

Jay had seen a few bands with his stepdad, but nothing on this scale. For an hour and a bit he jumped around like a loony, catching the odd elbow and getting carried by the swaying crowd. Friday night's second headliners were a Norwegian thrash band called Brother Death. They'd hit it big in the past couple of years, but Jay didn't know any of their songs apart from the hit that they played as their encore.

It was near midnight as the stage crew set up for the next band, an esteemed singer-songwriter designed to calm the crowd down. Sweaty bodies were streaming away. Jay thought he'd lost everyone until Alfie tugged his T-shirt.

The twelve-year-old's hair dripped sweat and the retro-Nikes he'd bought at Eldridges were covered in mud.

'You good?' Jay asked. Even though the band had finished, he still had to raise his voice over everyone else.

'I think we've lost Adam and Dylan,' Alfie said, grinning. 'And I've never seen so many girls with their tops off!'

'They were on about going to see some band on the second stage,' Jay said. 'I need a piss, and a drink.'

'VIP toilets are our best bet if we don't want to wade through pee,' Alfie said.

After using the loos, the two boys left the VIP area carrying giant cups of Rage Cola, on a mission to see a band called Urban Fox on the second stage. The kilometre-and-a-half runway that led towards the second stage was lined with food stalls and tents, offering everything from hot dogs to fortune-tellers and penalty kick competitions.

They were less than halfway to the second stage when Jay caught a whiff of smoke. At first he thought it was barbecue, but the crowd on the runway ground to a halt and it was one of those smells that stung the back of your throat.

'Smoke,' Alfie said.

There was also some kind of megaphone announcement being made. It was too garbled to understand, but it didn't take a genius to work out that they were asking people to clear the area.

'Looks like a food van on fire,' Jay explained, as Alfie went up on tiptoes to try and see.

Both boys jumped at a loud bang, and a collective yelp shot through the crowd.

'What was that?' Alfie yelled.

It was a girl who answered. 'I was there when it first caught fire. Apparently there's three gas bottles inside.'

Jay looked around at a pair of girls, his age or maybe a year younger. Both wore blue football shirts with *Bamford FC* crests and *Harris Hairdressers* as their sponsor's logo.

'It's a hot donut stall,' the smaller of the two girls said, then smiled as she flicked the plastic badge around Jay's neck. 'So how come you're a VIP?'

A bunch of festival stewards pushed past as Jay answered. 'We're playing here tomorrow,' Jay said.

'No *shit?*' the girl said, massively impressed. 'What's your band called?'

'We're in different bands,' Jay said. 'We're from the Channel Six show, *Rock War.*'

Both girls looked blank.

'So you're in a football team?' Alfie said, trying to break the awkwardness.

'Our church team,' the smaller of the two girls said. 'I'm Lucy, this is Freya.'

Jay felt panicked as his brain cut out the smell of smoke, the bustling crowd, and processed the fact that two OK-looking girls had started up a conversation with them.

'Alfie,' Alfie said. 'This is Jay.'

'So your whole team's here?' Jay asked. 'Or just you two?'

'Whole team,' Freya said, stepping closer to Jay as the

breeze blew a fresh waft of smoke over them. 'The festival's our reward for winning our league and the county cup.'

'Champ-e-on-ay!' Lucy sang.

'Looks like they've found a fire crew,' Alfie said, as the light coming off the surrounding stalls caught a water jet being aimed into the smoke.

'We kind of lost our team-mates,' Lucy explained. 'We're supposed to be going back to our tents to play board games at ten thirty.'

'But that's lame, so our plan is to stay lost for as long as we can get away with it,' Freya added.

'Sounds good,' Jay said.

'So do you guys wanna hang out, or what?' Freya asked.

15. Debauchery

'Hi, it's me. Theo Richardson, boxing champion and sex icon, with my latest video diary entry. This is my first video for a few days, because one of the girls from Half Term Haircut dumped my first camcorder in the pool after I posted that vid of me filming her from behind singing "Fat Bottomed Girls" by Queen.

'So it's eleven in the morning, and everyone else still seems to be asleep. I'm gonna take you on a tour of our tent here at the Rage Rock Festival.

'Of course, everyone in *Rock War* is under age and doesn't consume alcohol, because the only thing we like to drink are the wholesome non-alcoholic Rage Cola beverages, created by the Unifood Corporation of Delaware, USA.

'At this point, I'd also like to alert you to the shocking fact that *someone* found out which marquee all the VIP booze was being stored in, ripped out a plastic side panel and made off with beer, Krug vintage champagne and a selection of disposable glassware.'

'Don't forget the napkins!' Noah shouted.

Theo turned the camera on Noah, who was transferring himself from bed to wheelchair. 'Morning,' Theo continued. 'I can further confirm that eighty packs of napkins were stolen, but a wheelchair definitely *wasn't* used to escape with all the booty.

'Now, as we move around the tent, you can see things are a little chaotic. Martin from The Reluctant Readers appears to be passed out naked on the floor with hearts drawn on his buttocks. This is my brother Jay's bed, and as you can see, Dylan has vomited all over it. No sign of Jay himself though, and I'm starting to suspect that my skinny-assed half-brother is actually something of a ladies' man on the sly.

'There are more remnants of Dylan's gastric adventures in the main doorway and on top of the giant Rage can.'

Theo zoomed the camera on a dark red stain amidst a tangle of duvets and pillows on the floor between two beds.

'But this is what I really want to show you. Because this isn't just blood. This is hundred per cent authentic Norwegian rock star blood. You see, viewer-kins, around about two this morning, we had the pleasure of hanging with all three members of Brother Death. Sadly, Asbjørn got a bit too interested in Sadie from Frosty Vader. Despite Sadie keeping her distance, and the fact that she's fourteen, Asbjørn kept hassling her and of course, I had to help the damsel in distress.

'And this,' Theo said dramatically, as he pulled a small

white object from the pocket of his jeans, 'is an authentic Norwegian rock star tooth. The only thing I haven't decided is whether I'm gonna make this into a necklace, or auction it on eBay.'

Noah wheeled through bottles towards Theo as he stopped recording.

'They'll never let you upload a video like that,' Noah said. 'It has to be edited, and then either Angie or Joseph has to approve it.'

'What about "Fat Bottomed Girls", smartass?' Theo asked.

'Right,' Noah said curiously. 'How did that one get through?'

'There's forty-eight contestants,' Theo said, cracking one of his most mischievous grins. 'How do you think they remember all of our passwords for Facebook, Twitter and our video blogs?'

Noah smiled. 'I suspect I'm about to find out.'

'There's a printout, pinned to the wall in the production suite. My password is *NutJob*. Yours is *legless*.'

'Legless,' Noah spluttered. 'The bastards! You just wait and see what I upload in *my* next video.'

*

On the edge of the festival site, beyond the last tents and with the twin stages barely visible, was a field of prickly, dry grass. Jay had ended up with Freya, Alfie with Lucy. They'd held hands, snogged and probed inside each other's clothes. It wasn't the first time Jay had kissed a girl, but it was the first time he'd been relaxed enough to actually enjoy it.

'Wakey-wakey, hands off snakey,' Alfie said, waking Jay up with a flick on the chest.

It took Jay a second to work out why he had grass in his hair and ants trekking across his arm. After flicking the ants and picking a little stick out of his ear, Jay sat up and blinked morning sunshine into focus.

'They've gone,' Alfie said. 'The girls.'

'Bummer,' Jay said, remembering the taste of his football-shirted friend. He felt sad as he looked down the hill at the festival site and a rainbow of twenty thousand tents. 'Did Lucy say anything?'

Alfie shook his head. 'I woke up about four a.m. and they'd already gone. I've got a bunch of text messages from Jen. I think some of the crew are out looking for us.'

Jay saw Freya's shape in flattened grass and ran his hand across it. 'Probably never see her again,' he said gloomily.

But while Jay felt sleepy, Alfie was completely hyper.

'I got my hands on her boobs and we French-kissed,' he blurted. 'Tristan's been banging on about me never kissing a girl. I'm gonna stick this *right* in his face. And you're my witness so he can't say it's bull.'

'Seven texts, three missed calls,' Jay said, as he stared at his phone. 'Guess we'd better head back to VIP land.'

'You think we'll be in trouble?' Alfie asked.

Jay didn't seem too worried. 'They won't be happy,' he said. 'But Theo's a great lightning conductor. I'd bet my left bollock that he's been up to something ten times worse than us.'

The field was dotted with plastic pint glasses, puke, cigarette butts and the sorriest human casualties from the night before.

'People are animals,' Alfie said, as he placed his muddy Nikes carefully.

Jay agreed. 'People have only been here a few hours. Imagine the state it'll be in by Monday morning.'

'I certainly won't wander out here in the dark again.'

Jay was out of money, but Alfie was in a great mood and paid for bacon and fried egg baps and two cups of tea. It was a quarter to one when the scruffy pair showed their plastic badges to a suspicious bouncer at the entrance to the VIP compound.

While the main festival site was mostly sleeping off the night before, the compound bustled with corporate guests who'd been flown in for the day, courtesy of Unifoods. Their conversations as they plundered a seafood buffet sounded boring. Jay and Alfie crossed the marquee, exited out of the back and headed for their tent.

'Christ,' Jay said, heaving as he opened the tent flap and caught aromas of body spray, puke and booze.

None of the contestants were around, but he recognised the three runners tasked with clearing the evidence of the previous night's debauchery.

'And I think we're in the clear,' Alfie grinned, before pulling his T-shirt up over his mouth and nose.

'My bed's covered in sick!' Jay gasped. 'They'd *better* have a spare duvet.'

Lorrie, the uni-aged runner, was down on one knee, wielding disinfectant and a giant sponge. 'There's people out looking for you,' she said harshly. 'They're filming the draw in the tent down at the end.'

'What draw?' Alfie asked, as the boys stumbled back into the bright morning.

Publicist Jen was outside the tent puffing an e-cigarette, and tore into them both with vapour wafting out of her nostrils. 'What were you playing at?' she spat. 'You were all supposed to stick together.'

'We tried,' Jay said. 'But it's not easy when it's pitch dark and there's two million people jumping up and down.'

'We've been calling the pair of you all night.'

'I think my phone got knocked on to silent while we were jumping around at the gig,' Jay said.

'Signal's terrible,' Alfie added. 'We got really lost and when I was in Scouts, they said it's always better to stay where you are and wait for it to get light, rather than go wandering off in the dark.'

'I'm responsible for you kids,' Jen said, as she pocketed her cigarette. 'I was worried sick.'

Jen didn't strike Jay as the kind of person who'd lie awake worrying about the contestants. But she had probably worried about the repercussions for her job if something bad had happened.

Jen opened a sliding door into a marquee which was like a big octagonal brother to the one Jay and Alfie were supposed to have spent the night in. It was kitted out with studio lights, grey rubber flooring and a curved *Rock War* backdrop.

Presenter Meg Hornby stood in front of a bowl of lotto balls, with all the contestants lined up behind. They'd been told to act enthusiastic, but they mostly just looked sleep-deprived.

'So, so, so!' Meg said, faking jollity as the cameras rolled. 'All twelve bands will get to play here at Rage Rock today. But where will they be playing? Six will play inside the Rage Talent Tent, an indoor showcase for new bands with room for six hundred. Four bands will play the second stage this afternoon, watched by over ten thousand festival goers. But two super-lucky bands will get to play the main stage, immediately before tonight's headline act, in front of an audience of up to one hundred thousand people—'

'Cut!' someone shouted.

'Cut,' Angie repeated, before looking to the purple-haired camerawoman, who'd made the first call.

'Sorry,' the camerawoman said, as Meg looked put out. 'The sun ruined the shot when the door opened.'

Jen had stayed outside, so Jay and Alfie took the heat as Angie and the rest of the crew stared accusingly at them standing in the doorway.

'Sorry,' Jay said meekly.

'Get a runner outside the door,' Angie's assistant ordered. 'Nobody else in or out please!'

'Nice to know you're alive,' Angie said irritably, as she waved Jay and Alfie towards the other contestants standing three rows deep behind Meg. 'Alfie, I don't want to know why you look so happy. But I so want you in front of all the other miserable buggers.'

After Meg did another take of her spiel, there was a half-minute pause while the lighting director cut the main lamps. Now, Meg's face and the clear bowl of lotto balls was lit spookily from below.

'Does this make me look like a witch?' Meg asked.

'No more than usual,' Theo quipped.

As Meg gave Theo evils, Angie blew her stack.

'Can everybody please focus,' Angie yelled. 'We've only got this studio booked for another twenty minutes, and Zig's gonna love me if they charge us overtime.'

'The first four bands will play the second stage,' Meg said, as she reached in to take a ball from the large acrylic bowl. 'And our first group is . . . Crafty Canard.'

A cameraman turned on the four members of Crafty Canard, who looked moderately happy with their slot on the second stage. They were followed out of the bowl by I Heart Death, Noah's band Frosty Vader and Half Term Haircut.

'Now just eight bands remain in the draw,' Meg said, building suspense and, just in case anyone watching was stupid enough not to remember what she'd said two minutes before, 'Two bands will be picked to play the main stage, the remaining six will play in the Rage Talent Tent.

'The first band to play on the main stage in front of a hundred thousand rock fans this evening . . . is . . .'

As Meg's hand delved into the bowl, Jay and several others wondered if they actually wanted to play in front of a hundred thousand festival-goers, impatient for the main act to come on.

'Brontobyte!' Meg shouted.

Whatever doubts they'd had, Alfie, Tristan, Erin and Salman did what Angie had asked and jumped out of the crowd, squealing and hugging each other.

Meg put a microphone in front of Erin. 'How are you gonna feel playing for Brontobyte up on that stage in front of all those people?' she gushed.

'Invincible,' Erin said defiantly. 'Piece of cake.'

'No nerves?' Meg asked.

Erin smirked. 'Maybe a few.'

As Brontobyte got waved out of shot by Angie, Meg delved into the bowl again.

'The final band, who'll play right before tonight's headliners and to a global TV audience estimated at over forty-five million are . . .'

Seeing Erin and Tristan looking all excited had made Jay feel jealous, even though he hadn't been sure he wanted it until a few moments before.

'Are . . .' Meg repeated. 'The four girls from Industrial Scale Slaughter!'

Summer looked mortified at the thought of having to play the main stage, but the camera focused on her band mates. Coco and Lucy jumped around and hugged each other. As always, Michelle went for maximum attention and jumped on Meg Hornby, hoping for a piggyback ride.

Taken by surprise, Meg collapsed under Michelle's weight, the former model's skinny frame sprawling across the floor as Michelle's flailing legs sent a microphone stand flying.

As Meg stumbled to her feet, fighting an urge to swear loudly, Michelle picked up the acrylic bowl, tipped out the remaining balls and put it over her own head.

'Look at me, I'm a goldfish,' Michelle shouted, as her breath misted inside the bowl.

After head-butting a camera, Michelle tried lifting the bowl off, but it caught on her ears. 'I can't get it off,' she yelled.

Most people thought Michelle was mucking about, but when her sister Lucy tried to help, people started realising that she really was stuck. A few were concerned, but most, including the crew, started laughing.

'Get some butter from the buffet,' someone suggested.

'Screw that, leave her in there,' Meg screamed, as she ripped off her lapel mic. 'I'm sick of working with these maniac brats. You can all take this dumb kiddie show and shove it up your arse, because I quit.'

As Meg stormed out into the sun, Lucy yanked the bowl extra hard. Michelle screamed as it popped off her head, tearing an earlobe and sending her stumbling backwards into an equipment case.

'And cut,' Angie said, as she looked up pleadingly, hoping to see salvation but only finding fibreglass marquee panels.

16. Meet the Groupies

Jay felt good as he walked across the festival site, guitar around his neck, cameraman behind and Babatunde and Adam alongside. While Jay was focused on his performance, his two band mates were rating girls.

'Two o'clock, ginger hair, muddy cutoffs,' Babatunde said. 'Eight out of ten.'

Adam shook his head. 'Six tops. What about the girl with the ice cream?'

Babatunde erupted in laughter. 'She's like, eleven!'

Adam tutted. 'She's way older than eleven.'

'Jay,' Babatunde said, poking Jay and pointing so blatantly that the girl looked right at them. 'Adjudicate, brother. How old is she?'

Jay found the banter annoying, so he was relieved when Zig Allen saved him from answering. Zig's default mode was stressed and grumpy, so Jay was surprised by a smile and a slap on the back.

'What a beautiful day,' Rock War's creator said cheerfully, giving off red wine breath as he put arms around Jay's and Babatunde's backs. 'I came here with my boyfriend back in ninety-six, and we were up to our armpits in mud the whole weekend.'

'That must have been a laugh,' Jay said.

'Festival mud is a novelty that wears off *very* quickly,' Zig explained. 'After that, it's just bloody cold and bloody wet.'

Jay had never had Zig in such close proximity before, and stumbled for something to say.

'I thought you'd be all stressed over Meg quitting,' he said finally.

Zig wagged a finger knowingly. 'We were paying that woman a *fortune*. Rage Cola wanted a big name to present *Rock War*, but I always said a younger presenter would be better suited for a youth format. Meg thought I was going to grovel for her to come back. You should have seen her face when I revoked her VIP pass and gave her directions to the bus stop.'

'And I suppose a younger presenter is also way cheaper,' Adam observed.

'I might just deliver this project on budget yet,' Zig said, taking his arms away from the boys and punching the air. 'Ker-ching!'

The Rage Talent Tent was pretty empty, so the crew on the door waved Zig and the three boys through. Inside, Dylan and Eve's band Pandas of Doom were playing The White Stripes' 'It's True That We Love One Another', with

Summer's band mate Coco doing a guest spot as second female vocalist. Eve, Jay was pleased to see, looked happier than she had in a long time.

Most people were using the Talent Tent as a place to eat lunch while sheltering from the sun, and the sound crew kept the volume low enough to accommodate conversation. As Jay led the way towards the stage, he noticed a clump of seven girls, aged from tween to mid-teens. Their eyes were fixed on the stage, until one of them eyed Jay and ran over.

She was a skinny little thing. No older than twelve, with sunburned shoulders and a Ramones logo on her vest. 'Oh my god!' the girl said, bouncing on the balls of her feet as the rest of the gaggle rushed over. 'It's Babatunde!'

'Jay, you're the best thing on the show!' an older girl blurted. Then, looking at Babatunde, 'I tried drumming when I was in year seven and it's *so* hard. But you're amazing.'

'So you're all fans of *Rock War?*' Adam asked, feeling extremely awkward.

'I started watching by accident but me and my sister love it,' a freckled redhead said.

'I wish *Rock War* was on more than twice a week,' the girl's sister added.

'Every day would be better,' the oldest girl agreed. 'I follow you on Twitter and watch the diaries on YouTube.'

'I'm actually amazed there's so few of us here,' someone said. 'I thought we'd have to fight to get into the tent. When Taylor Swift did her CD signing in London, I had to queue for five hours.'

Jay shrugged; Babatunde answered. 'I guess we're not as famous as Taylor Swift.'

'Yet,' Adam added, making all the girls laugh.

'So can you sign the back of my shirt?' a girl asked, as she waggled a marker pen under Jay's nose.

Jay flushed red, as the girl turned and leaned forwards. Within a few seconds, there was a second marker and the three lads each faced an orderly queue of girls who wanted their shirts signed. The last girl to approach Jay was the youngest. Too shy to speak, she held out a manga-style drawing of his band. It wasn't professional standard, but Jay clearly recognised his own face and admired all the little details like Theo's tattoos and the Jet logo on Babatunde's drum kit. It was an impressive effort for a ten-year-old.

'Wow, that's cool!' Jay said. 'I don't think anyone's ever drawn me that well before.'

The girl almost blew up with pride, but remained too shy to speak. After snapping a photo of the drawing on his phone, Jay signed it, before lining up with all the girls and his band mates while Jen the publicist and an assortment of the girls' parents snapped photos.

'Is Summer coming here?' one of the girls asked. 'I'd really love to meet her.'

A couple of the other fan girls nodded, and one spoke. 'The bit in the first episode when she hugged her nan goodbye was soooo sad.'

'So you prefer Summer to us?' Babatunde said, acting like he was affronted.

'Don't you get hot, wearing a hoodie in this weather?' someone interrupted.

'Summer will be playing the main stage tonight,' Jay said. 'She's a nervous wreck right now.'

A burly dad who'd been taking photos reached out to shake Jay's hand. 'I just want to thank you,' the man began. 'Your show made my daughter start listening to some proper music, instead of boy bands. You're a proper rock chick now, aren't you, sweetie?'

'Dad,' the girl hissed. Then, whispering as she backed away, 'Could you be *any* more embarrassing?'

Jay didn't get more time with his fans because Jen and a member of the stage crew were urging the boys to pass through a curtain to the backstage area. Pandas of Doom had finished their set, Theo had miraculously arrived on time, and three crew members were up on stage, swapping microphones and adjusting the drum kit to suit Babatunde.

'You sounded good,' Jay told the Pandas, as Dylan grabbed a folded towel from a pile and used it to wipe the sweat pouring off his face.

'We have fans,' Dylan noted. 'All seven of them.'

'They're not the fan-babes I fantasised about,' Jay said. 'But at least we have evidence that *someone's* watching our show.'

Jay hugged Dylan's clammy band mates, and got *good lucks* from Zig and Jen before taking the three metal steps up to the stage. The atmosphere was underwhelming, with the fan-girls and their parents up front, then a big open space in the middle of the marquee before you got to fifty or so disinterested folk who'd come in to shelter from the sun. They sat against the walls, eating lunch, or playing with their phones. Jay had hoped Freya might have heard that he was playing, but there was no sign of her.

The cameraman gave Jet a thumbs-up, and Theo announced the first song. 'We're Jet, and this is a song my brother Jay wrote a few weeks back.'

'We love you Jay!' one of the fan-girls shouted.

'Theeeeo!' some more shouted.

'It's called, "USB Charger, Where the Hell Are Yer?"'

17. Bronto Bites

Zig made a few calls, but even with Rage Cola helicopters on standby, he'd been unable to find an established TV presenter prepared to drop everything on a Saturday afternoon and work for peanuts.

Three weeks into filming *Rock War*, the contestants had grown used to seeing unpaid runners changing beds, lugging equipment, mopping floors and unblocking toilets. Some couldn't hack it, coming for a month's work experience and vanishing after a couple of days. But however many quit, Zig's inbox was always stuffed with emails from eager young replacements, desperate to get their foot in the door of the TV industry.

Lorrie was one of the few who'd stuck it from day one. The twenty-year-old was studying Acting and TV Production at Durham University. She'd started the day in ripped jeans and her ex's shrunken rugby shirt. Now she held a microphone and wore make-up and clothes cobbled together from the suitcases of *Rock War*'s female contestants.

'This is the moment,' Lorrie told the shoulder-mounted camera, raising her voice above the vast crowd on the other side of the stage. 'Brontobyte are about to put everything on the line, in front of an estimated one hundred and ten thousand rock fans. This backstage area is packed with some of music's biggest stars and the atmosphere is absolutely incredible! I've got Brontobyte's lead singer with me. Salman, how are you feeling right now?'

'A little bit terrified,' Salman said, smiling uneasily. 'But we've been practising hard and we've had some amazing tutors working with us at boot camp.'

Lorrie moved the microphone down in front of Alfie. 'Alfie, you're the youngest contestant in *Rock War*. Do you think you've got what it takes to capture that monster crowd?'

Alfie shrugged, and gave a boyish smile. 'I guess we'll find out in a minute.'

'OK,' Lorrie said. 'I'll leave you guys to make your final preparations. I hope you have a total blast out there.'

'Thanks,' the boys said.

'And, cut,' Angie said, before giving a thumbs-up. 'Lorrie, that was *fab*. You look like you've been doing this your whole life.'

'Magnificent,' Zig added.

Lorrie knew that becoming Meg's temporary stand-in was the biggest break of her life, but she was too exhausted to appreciate it. She'd rarely slept longer than five hours a night since *Rock War* started and she'd been up at four that morning, making sure the camera crews had enough memory cards and fully-charged batteries to last through the festival.

Angie got caught out as the stage manager called Brontobyte on. The crowd seemed indifferent as giant screens on either side of the stage played a slick trailer for *Rock War – Boot Camp*.

'*And after learning from the biggest names in rock, the ten bands that survive boot camp will find themselves pitted against each other in* Rock War – Battle Zone. *Watch* Boot Camp *now on 6point2 or 6forU on demand.* Rock War – Battle Zone *premieres Saturday, September thirteenth on Channel Six. It's the only talent show with the volume turned all the way up to eleven.* Rock War *is brought to you thanks to Rage, the dangerously refreshing cola.*'

As the trailer ended, stage lights swivelled on to the four members of Brontobyte: Tristan on drums, Alfie playing lead guitar, Erin on bass and back-up vocals and Salman centre stage with a wireless mic. Salman cleared his throat, and a half second later the sound ricocheted out of a dozen speaker stacks, each one taller than his house.

The band mates swapped glances. Excited, but terrified.

'One, two, three, four,' Tristan shouted, counting with his sticks before their first song erupted.

After Alfie and Jay's disappearing act the night before, all the *Rock War* contestants had been confined to the VIP areas. Some had moved to the VIP area in front of the stage, but Jay liked glimpsing stars and seeing how things worked behind the scenes, so he'd joined a little backstage entourage, hanging out with the two bands that were actually playing.

Saturday night's headline act was legendary nineties indie band Smudger. It was their first UK gig in seven years, and a major reason why every ticket for Rage Rock had sold out within an hour of going on sale.

Jay couldn't resist peeking through the gap in a chipboard partition, as the three-piece hung out with wives, kids, backing singers and a fluffy sheepdog.

'What's going on in there?' Lucy from Industrial Scale Slaughter asked, coming up behind and making Jay jump.

'It's underwhelming,' Jay whispered. 'They've all got fat, Damien Smith has a hairpiece and they're talking about getting their kids into a good prep school. I actually think Barney the sheepdog is the most dangerous one in the room.'

'Cute dog,' Lucy said. 'Summer needs you.'

'Me?' Jay said, mystified.

'She's in a state about going on stage. Remember how before we played Rock the Lock, she spoke to you and you calmed her down? I thought you might be able to work your magic again.'

Jay was wary. 'What am I supposed to do?'

Lucy was half a head taller than Jay, with shoulders built for rock drumming and a whiff of armpits after a day in the sun.

'You can't make things any worse. Shift your arse!'

Lucy tugged the reluctant Jay by the sleeve. The dressing-rooms were functional, with plywood walls and Ikea furnishings. Jay felt like he was intruding, because there was girl stuff everywhere: balled-up tights, cans of hairspray, even a bra draped over the back of an armchair.

'Where is she?' Jay asked, as he noticed Coco reading a magazine and Michelle drawing wavy lipstick lines on a mirror. Rather than disguise the scab around her torn earlobe, Michelle had chosen to make an X with bright orange kiddy plasters.

The room had an L-shaped bit at the end, and Summer was in the nook, on a small black sofa that still wore its Ikea tags.

'How you doing?' Jay asked, warily.

'At least I've stopped throwing up,' Summer said, as she looked up, showing the tear tracks down her cheek. 'I guess after the fourth time, your stomach's pretty empty.'

Jay thought he'd try taking her mind off things. 'Did you speak to your nan today?'

Summer half smiled. 'When she's stuck in our flat, I'm the only person she ever sees. I think she actually likes being in the respite home, around lots of other people her age.'

'Did you tell her you're playing the main stage?'

'She knows how nervous I get,' Summer said, shaking her head. 'She'd only worry.'

'When I played the tent earlier, I just fixed my eyes on a spot and tried to imagine it was just me and the boys, rehearsing underneath the chip shop.'

'Everyone's got advice,' Summer said wearily. 'Take deep breaths, try to relax, think about something else. But I mean, how can you think about something else when you're standing in the middle of a stage, under two hundred spotlights and with a hundred thousand people looking at you?'

Jay thought she had a point, but kept up the encouragement. 'Michelle will probably do something mental,' he said. 'They'll all be looking at her.'

'True,' Summer said, sliding her hand across to Jay's knee.

Jay realised she wanted him to hold hands, and once he'd done this, Summer turned slightly and nestled her head in his shoulder. Part of Jay wanted to crane forward and kiss her, but it would have been physically awkward and he was pretty sure this was about comfort and nothing more.

'What are those numbers?' Summer asked, as she tapped the side of Jay's torso where his T-shirt had ridden up.

Mystified, Jay pulled his shirt up further and saw a bunch of smudged black characters. The F at the start and the Y were enough for him realise that it had originally said Freya. But a sweaty day had turned the mobile number written beneath into black smudges.

'Are you kidding me?' Jay gasped, pulling his skin tight in the hope that it might wring some miraculous improvement in legibility. 'Can you read it?'

Summer smirked. 'You made it into an inky mess, you sweaty boy!' Then, realising that Jay looked sad, 'I can see a seven and two zeros. Was it someone you met last night?'

'Me and Alfie just hung out with these girls. It was pretty cool.'

'All night?' Summer teased. 'What were you up to?'

Jay laughed. 'With Alfie? He's a baby!'

'Never mind,' Summer said, as she straightened up and pecked Jay on the cheek. 'You're a nice guy. Lots of other girls like you.'

Jay was surprised by the kiss, but intrigued by Summer's words. Did she kiss him and say *lots of girls like you* because *she* liked him? Or was it just out of pity?

As Jay tried to think what to say next, Coco came around the corner. 'We got the knock,' Coco said. 'Are you up for this, my darling?'

'I'm made of jelly, but I'm not gonna bail on you,' Summer said, holding on to the sofa's arm as she stood up and looked back at Jay. 'You coming to watch?'

Jay had been too focused on Summer to pay much attention to Brontobyte, but as he followed Industrial Scale Slaughter towards the stage, he realised that they were on their third and final song. Salman and Erin were singing a duet. Their voices harmonised well, but Tristan's drums were a shambles.

There was a half-metre gap in the plastic sheet wrapped around the stage. Jay squinted out into the sunset and saw a crowd that had stopped listening to a bunch of kids from a TV show they'd mostly never heard of.

Jay had quit Brontobyte because Tristan wouldn't admit that he was rubbish, and now the nightmare Jay had predicted was playing out in front of a hundred thousand people. He felt vindicated, but didn't enjoy the fact, because a sour crowd was going to make Summer's performance even harder.

Salman looked crushed as he led his band off stage. Erin looked angry, Alfie was a ghost.

'Good luck,' Jay told Summer. Once he was sure Summer was out of earshot, he clocked Tristan and cracked a big smile. '*Nice* drumming, mate,' he beamed.

Tristan lunged. Jay thought he had enough space to back off, but Tristan, a stocky judo black belt, got hold of him.

'Your brothers can't save your butt here,' Tristan spat, as he gave Jay a dead arm.

He grabbed the back of Jay's neck and kneed him. Luckily for Jay, there were plenty of people around.

Erin was first on the scene, yelling, 'Cut it out,' and charging in with enough force to knock both boys sideways.

Before either got their balance back, Jay and Tristan had fallen into the hands of burly stage crew. The dazzling stage lights and crowd noise meant that Summer and her band mates had no idea what was going on.

Jay found himself spinning around and stumbling face first into the thick plastic sheeting that enveloped the stage. The stage manager and his clipboard were on the scene half a second later.

'Escort Brontobyte to their dressing-room,' he ordered stiffly.

As three stage hands shepherded Brontobyte, the stage manager faced off Jay, who was being held in a moderately-painful armlock by the kind of man who had to duck and turn sideways to get through doors.

'Why are you on my stage, causing trouble?' the stage manager shouted.

'I'm with *Rock War*,' Jay said.

'Turf him out.'

The stage hand kicked the bar across a door marked *FIRE – EMERGENCY EXIT ONLY*, then shoved Jay through.

'I'll kick your arse if I see you back here,' he warned, before slamming it shut again.

Sore from armlock, punches, and particularly Tristan's knee in the guts, Jay took a few seconds to straighten up before realising that he was at the top of thirty metal steps, leading down to the VIP reception area below.

Moths head-butted the huge video screen above Jay's head, and he looked out on a crowd who'd paid their hundred and fifty quid to see Smudger, not a promo for some talent show they'd never heard of.

Summer looked like she was going to pass out as she took her final step up to the microphone. Coco's guitar began the jangling intro to Patti Smith's classic 'Because the Night' and Summer took a deep breath.

From this close, Jay could see the quarter-second delay between Summer's lips moving and its eruption from the vast speaker stacks. There was a fourteen-year-old schoolgirl at the microphone, but the voice had the guts of a hundred-kilo gospel singer.

In the gap between the song's two opening lines, Jay watched a hundred thousand people tune in to Summer's voice. He felt proud as a roar erupted from the crowd. He wanted everyone to know that he'd hugged that girl just before she went on stage.

After racing down the stairs, Jay spotted Noah's wheelchair and rushed over.

'She's incredible,' Jay gushed, yelling over the music. 'Her voice turned that crowd around in three seconds flat.'

But Noah lacked Jay's enthusiasm.

'What's up?' Jay said.

Noah smiled awkwardly. 'She's unbelievable,' he agreed. 'But what chance have our bands got, against that?'

18. The Week Four Problem

Coco shot with Summer's camcorder, as countryside swept past the windows of their luxury coach.

'Everyone keeps asking,' Summer said, 'but truth told, I was so nervous I can't even remember being on stage. Like, one minute I was in the dressing-room with Jay, the next I was coming off stage and everyone was going bananas.

'A lot of it's down to our choice of music. Mo, the *Rock War* music director, did us proud. I'd never heard "Because the Night" until I got to boot camp, but it's a beautiful song. And we had our set all worked out for Rage Rock, but at the last minute, Mo changed us to Smudger's "Dumb Luck". We only had time for one rehearsal, but that was the most *brilliant* choice. Everyone in that crowd was there to see Smudger, and they bloody loved it when we played their biggest hit.

'The weird thing is, I can actually remember singing "Dumb Luck" in the bath when I was like, five years old. And as we came off stage, Damien and Chris came out of their dressing-room and hugged me and told us to hang around. And after watching Smudger's set, the four of us were chilling out with Smudger's families and playing Jenga with their kids. I don't even care if we're one of the two bands voted out at the end of boot camp, because last night was officially the most amazing thing that has ever happened to me.'

Michelle bobbed up from the seats behind and leaned into the shot. 'Of course, Little Miss Superstar here would also like to thank her three incredible band mates for making it all possible.'

Michelle's tone was jokey, but Summer sensed jealousy in the mix, and also felt bad that she'd been gushing on without even mentioning them.

'I love these guys,' Summer said, putting an arm around Michelle, as Lucy leaned in from the row in front and waved. 'You would not believe how hard they had to twist my arm to join Industrial Scale Slaughter. And I'm only here because Michelle and Lucy's dad offered to pay for my nan to spend summer in a respite home. So if you're watching, Mr Wei, I love you too!'

Summer blew a kiss at her camcorder, and Michelle shouted, 'Don't blow our daddy a kiss. That's creepy!'

'We love you too, Daddy,' Lucy said, blowing her own kiss. 'And don't forget it's my seventeenth birthday soon. The car you're buying me has to be an estate so I can fit my drums in the back.'

'Don't buy her a car,' Michelle said, shaking her head

violently. 'Spend all your money on me, or I'll take you to the top of a hill and let the brakes off your wheelchair when you get old and decrepit.'

'Coco, cut!' Summer ordered, as she shoved Michelle out of shot. 'This is *my* video diary. If you two have got so much to say, go make your own.'

*

Three days at Rage Rock had pushed the crew to their limits. Zig gave everyone Monday off, except the runners, who had to clean and recharge all the equipment used at the festival, mow the lawns, wash forty-eight contestants' grubby festival gear, buy a week's food shopping and pack up the gear in Meg's room and ship it back to London.

The contestants caught up on sleep they'd lost during three days at the festival, and used a day's break from filming to rehearse, hang out by the pool and play video games. Plans were hatched to cook their own barbecue, but Zig didn't like the idea of his contestants getting wiped out by a batch of undercooked sausage, so an epic delivery from the local pizza joint was arranged instead.

Theo woke just before ten on Tuesday morning, not in the room he shared with Adam, but in an emperor-size bed, in a huge double-height room in the manor's west annexe. It had previously been occupied by Meg, and Theo felt terrifically proud of himself as he studied an elaborate gold-leaf ceiling and a ball of sheets, with Lorrie sleeping naked on its far side.

Kicking the sheets to the floor, Theo clambered over the

huge bed and gently tickled his way up Lorrie's back. As she stirred, the muscular seventeen-year-old slid his hand around her tummy and blew on her neck as he began sliding the hand towards her naughty bits.

Before he got there, Lorrie jolted, thumping her head on the ebony headboard as she sat up. Morning sun hurt her eyes, and her head had a dull ache that was nothing to do with the knock.

'Oh, shit,' Lorrie said, running her tongue around a dry mouth as things slowly came back to her.

After two days in front of the camera, filling Meg's shoes, Lorrie had thrown herself back into being a runner, working extra hard to prove to the others that she didn't now regard herself as superior.

But, bored and overworked, they couldn't resist teasing, and to make matters worse, Lorrie had been called up to the editing suite to overdub some dialogue while her comrades mowed the manor's huge lawns in blistering heat.

Unable to stomach an evening on the grass behind the kitchen, smoking and bitching with the other runners, she'd started talking to Theo. He'd come back from Rage Rock with a few bottles of bourbon and he reminded her of a guy she'd had a massive crush on in year thirteen.

The lock on Meg's old room was no problem for Theo, and after a few shots of Kentucky's finest, Lorrie put up just enough resistance to let Theo think he was calling the shots, before jumping into bed with him.

It had been fun, but bright sun and a hangover brought

the situation into sharp relief. There was only a three year age gap, and Theo was over the age of consent, but she still wondered if she'd done something wrong. Like, Lorrie was staff, and Theo was a contestant, so was it illegal in the same way that it was illegal for a teacher to sleep with a seventeen-year-old pupil?

On top of that, Theo wasn't the type to keep his trap shut. The other runners would have missed her last night, and since they'd probably been working for a couple of hours already they'd be mightily pissed off when she did show her face.

'I don't bite,' Theo said, as Lorrie shot up and grabbed jeans that were still grass-stained from the festival.

'Last night was good,' Lorrie said. 'We'll do this again, but you can't tell *anyone* about this. Not your brothers, not anyone.'

Lorrie had no intention of sleeping with Theo again, but he'd be more likely to keep quiet if she strung him along with a few broken promises. She felt her iPhone dig into her thigh as she pulled the jeans up. She noticed that the battery was down to eight per cent as she logged in with a fingerprint and checked her messages.

There was a missed call from an unrecognised number, a text from her mum, saying Lorrie had to go to a dress fitting for her cousin's wedding, and one from her boyfriend, who said he missed her even though he was spending his summer sailing in Miami and seemed to be surrounded by cocktails and women in every single Facebook update.

Then she saw a text from Zig Allen: *YRU AWOL? Great*

work this weekend! Come see me in my office ASAUGT.

Lorrie looked at Theo. 'What's ASAUGT?'

'As soon as you get this,' Theo said. 'Don't I get a cuddle at least?'

Lorrie calmed down slightly when she realised that Zig's message was only twenty minutes old. After putting her top on, she tied back her hair and used Meg's leftover mouthwash and deodorant. Theo looked boyish as he watched her.

'Gotta fly,' Lorrie said, giving Theo's bum a good slap as she rushed out. 'Put some bloody clothes on.'

After a furtive glance up and down the hallway, Lorrie used a narrow back staircase to head up to the fourth floor. She emerged under skylights in a portion of the house that had once served as an artist's studio.

Having walked past *Rock War*'s multiscreened editing computers, Lorrie rapped on a crude plywood partition and leaned through the doorless opening. She backed up nervously when she saw Zig in a meeting with unit directors, Angie and Joseph.

'Get in here,' Zig said.

His voice was headmasterly, and it flashed through Lorrie's mind that they knew about Theo and she was about to get the boot.

'So,' Zig said, keeping up the tone to make Lorrie feel uncomfortable. 'How did you like life in front of the camera?'

Lorrie squirmed and flicked hair off her face. 'It was a good experience,' she said. 'I mean, I know I'm a long way from perfect, but I think my acting background helped.'

'TV presenting is a lot like farting,' Zig said bluntly. 'Most of the time you don't have to think about it, but once in a while it goes horribly wrong.'

'The crew really helped,' Lorrie said, then aiming a hand at Angie and Joseph, 'and these two put me at ease.'

'So, do you want to carry on presenting, or go back to being a runner?'

'I'd love to carry on,' Lorrie said, but her paranoid side still suspected that Zig had invited her up here just to crush her dreams.

'This is a four-week release form, giving us your consent to use any footage we shoot,' Zig said, sliding a single sheet across the desk and unscrewing the lid of a fountain pen. 'You'll be the new face of *Rock War – Boot Camp*. But I need a decision right now.'

Lorrie picked up the contract. 'Will I get paid?' she asked warily.

Zig laughed, like this was the most absurd thing he'd ever heard. 'You're prepared to clean toilets and lug cameras for free, but for putting on a push-up bra and smiling at the camera, you want money?'

'I . . .' Lorrie stuttered. 'Meg was getting paid quite a bit, I heard.'

Zig thumped the desk. 'Meg is a four-letter word around here,' he spat. 'When your student butt arrived at the manor a few weeks back, you'd have been happy to leave with a presenter's credit on your CV, wouldn't you?'

Angie didn't like the way Zig was making Lorrie squirm.

'It's a big break, honey,' she said soothingly. 'You were a joy to work with after putting up with Meg. You'll get travel expenses and we'll have to take you up to London and get you some designer gear.'

Zig shot Angie a nasty glare, before wheeling his chair back. 'Outfits and reasonable expenses,' Zig said, nodding before sighing. 'But no hotel minibars, ever. If Elvis Presley came back from the dead and asked to host *Rock War*, I'd pay him a million bucks a show. But if he wanted to pay a tenner for a tin of bastard cashew nuts, he'd have to take it out of his own damned pocket. These hotel people make me so mad!'

The bemused expressions of his two directors made Zig realise that he'd gone into a rant.

'Focus,' Zig told himself, before taking a deep breath. 'You're actually pretty lucky,' he told Lorrie, as he drummed a finger on the release form. 'If I wasn't gay, you'd probably have to sleep with me to get an opportunity like this.'

Lorrie had seen Zig driving a bright orange Lamborghini with a ZIG64 number plate. She resented the way he was steamrollering her into signing, when paying a few grand off her student debt wouldn't have killed him. But on the other hand, this was a *massive* opportunity.

Zig smiled as Lorrie took the fountain pen. She was left-handed and made a big smudge out of her signature.

'Sorry about that,' Lorrie said. 'Do I get a copy of the form?'

'Sure, sure,' Zig said. 'There's a photocopier just outside, but bring my copy straight back.'

Lorrie took that as her signal to leave, but Zig called her back.

'Wait up,' he said. 'Has news of our *week four problem* reached as far down as the runners?'

'Err . . . Not that I know of, Mr Allen.'

'Well, me and my two esteemed directors have been chewing the fat over the past few days and getting precisely nowhere.'

'What is the *week four problem* exactly?'

Angie took up the story. '*Boot Camp* runs on 6point2 for the six weeks of school summer holidays,' she began. 'Two episodes per week. Week one, meet the contestants, tearful farewells. Week two, kids at the manor, lessons, rehearsals, Jay gets tossed over a balcony, celebrity chef barbecue. Week three, contestants go crazy at rock festival, Summer pukes a lot, bands play in front of a hundred thousand music fans. Week five, the three celebrity judges arrive and we build up suspense. Week six, final performances, tension builds, two bands get the axe in the final episode.'

'Did you see what's missing?' Zig asked.

'Week four,' Lorrie said.

'We've got the kids back at the manor. We can show some more rehearsals. Maybe fly a couple of celebrities down. I was hoping we could keep things cheap and simple, but the show is building viewers and we can't afford to lose momentum.'

Lorrie shrugged. 'What about a trip of some kind? Florida, or Paris?'

'It needs drama,' Zig said. 'Cheap drama.'

'I guess there's one thing,' Lorrie said, slightly reluctant after her first idea got shot down. 'I have an uncle.'

'So do I, honey,' Zig said, making hurry-up gestures. 'He went crazy and shot himself. We don't like to talk about it.'

'No,' Lorrie said. 'My uncle Norman. You know when firms do those days out? And like, build a raft out of barrels and sail down a river, or camp out in the woods?'

Joseph smiled. 'Team-building exercises.'

'Exactly,' Lorrie said.

'We could spin that,' Angie said. 'Put some guff on the voice-over about how building team spirit will bring the bands closer together and improve their musical performances.'

'Uncle Norman also trains actors and stuff,' Lorrie continued. 'Like, if they're gonna be soldiers in a movie, they train them how to use guns, put on camouflage and shit like that.'

'That could work,' Joseph said.

'There needs to be some kind of incentive, like a prize for the band that does best,' Angie added.

'Any idea how much it costs?' Zig asked.

'Not really,' Lorrie said. 'I don't think it's that expensive. I mean, he doesn't drive around in an orange Lamborghini or anything.'

Angie and Joseph both smiled at Lorrie's jab.

Zig looked pissed off and snapped his fingers. 'OK,' he said. 'What's your uncle's number?'

19. Shock and Awe

Dressed in jeans and a NATO-issue camouflage jacket, Lorrie stood in the semi-dark ballroom, facing a camera.

'It's Thursday morning, zero five thirty hours,' she said, whispering to add drama. 'The *Rock War* contestants think they've got a peaceful day of rehearsals ahead of them. But they're in for a BIG shock.'

The camera operator zoomed out, revealing a huge man standing beside Lorrie. Shaved bald, with black wraparound sunglasses. He had a massive ginger moustache and a sleepy Rottweiler on a metal-studded leash.

'This is Norman X,' Lorrie said dramatically. 'He's spent years training UK special forces, and we have to blur his face to shield his true identity. Mr X, what are the *Rock War* contestants in for today?'

Mr X cracked a mean smile. 'It'll probably be the toughest thirty hours of their lives,' he said. 'Physically and emotionally.'

'And what's the benefit of this?' Lorrie said, knowing the real reason was the need to add drama to week four.

'Tough physical challenges build mental strength and deepen personal bonds,' Mr X explained. 'That's true whether it's soldiers going into battle, executives on a team-building weekend, or rock bands. These kids aren't going to play a note in the next day and a half, but I guarantee they'll be stronger people and better musicians at the end of it.'

'Great,' Lorrie said. 'Mr X, over to you.'

The video would be cut to make Norman's next move seem instantaneous. But the camera and lights had to be adjusted for a close-up.

'Crews ready?' Angie asked, then looked around, seeing her camera teams giving thumbs up from positions at the bottom of staircases. 'Action.'

With a camera right in his face, Mr X took a breath and raised a dented brass whistle to his lips. Lorrie shielded her right ear as he blew mightily.

As the ballroom lights flickered on, huge dogs led an excited charge up three separate staircases to the balconies. Their handlers were ex-soldiers dressed in military gear, with camera crews in pursuit.

Dylan was fast asleep when an army boot hit his bedroom door with such force that it ripped off its hinges and slammed the floor. It made a great visual, though Zig Allen would doubtless moan about the repair bill.

'Get up, up, up!' a scarily-butch woman in camo gear shouted.

Walking over the broken door, the woman tore the covers off Dylan's bed, while her colleague did the same to his chubby band mate, Leo. Dylan was blinded by a camera-mounted light, then terrified as a huge Alaskan malamute jumped on his bed, ripping off fierce barks.

'Jesus Christ!' Dylan yelled, close to shitting in his bed. 'Get it off me!'

He rolled out from under the dog, finding himself on his bedroom floor getting his legs tangled with Leo's.

The malamute, along with a Doberman that had jumped on Leo's bed, pounced on the boys. Dylan thought he was about to lose a chunk of his body, but he just got a long lick up his sweaty back before the dogs were called to heel by their handler.

'You boys have two minutes to get out of this room and meet on the front lawn, or it's NBB,' the woman yelled. 'T-shirts and shorts only. No footwear.'

'Do you two pale-assed punks even know what NBB is?' the dog-handler yelled.

The boys looked mystified as the excited dogs strained their leashes, keen to resume the tussle.

'NBB means *no bloody breakfast*. And that might just be the only food you get for a long time.'

The same scene played out in twenty-three other rooms. In the twenty-fourth, there was a more genteel entry, and a muscular runner to help Noah quickly into his chair.

Kids streamed down the stairs in various states of tiredness and shock.

'Pom pom slippers!' one of the soldiers shouted. 'Did we say pom pom slippers?'

The slippered drummer from The Reluctant Readers passed her footwear to one of Mr X's operatives, who lobbed them across the ballroom in disgust.

'Move!' an operative with a Scottish accent shouted, giving orders from the middle of the ballroom with hands on hips. 'You're supposed to be teenagers, prime, fit and full of beans. So why are you moving like asthmatic turtles on a very steep hill?'

Mr X was waiting for them when they got out on the lawn in front of Rock War Manor. The runners had mowed it the day before and grass trimmings stuck to Jay's leg as he sat down.

'Did I say sit down?' Mr X bellowed. 'I need four rows of twelve. Stand to attention. Backs straight, arms at side. And stop looking so miserable. Anyone would think you'd never been woken up at six in the morning by soldiers with vicious dogs before.'

As Jay found his feet and joined the end of a line, he was baffled, but also highly amused. The boys didn't look much different to normal, but with no make-up and just-out-of-bed hair, some of the girls were unrecognisable.

'Look at this filthy lot of hoodlums,' Mr X shouted. 'I reckon they need a damned good wash.'

Amidst the chaos, none of the contestants had noticed a green military-style fire engine parked on the manor's main driveway. But they did when two of the ex-soldiers switched on high-pressure fire hoses.

The water was freezing. The contestants stumbled and slid as the powerful jets knocked them off balance. Those that tried to escape got knocked back by a third hose, connected to a hydrant in front of the manor. Contestants started going down like skittles, as the powerful hoses turned dry grass into mud, and blasted chunks of turf into the air.

'Much cleaner!' Mr X said, giving a signal to shut off the hoses before grinning at the tangle of gasping, mud-spattered bodies. 'Now take your kit and make it snappy.'

It was summer, but early enough for the wet kids to shiver as they stumbled across to a long fold-out table. Contestants varied from titchy Alfie up to big lumps like Theo, so the kits were folded neatly with name tags for each person.

Everyone did their best to shake off the water and mud before starting to get dressed. There was no distinction for sexes. Everyone got the same black vest, battered khaki shirt with Polish army badges, camouflage trousers, thick woollen socks and tatty black boots.

But Theo was having none of it. He fearlessly faced off Mr X, dressed only in soggy shorts and a boxing vest.

'What if I tell you to stick this, and go back to bed?' Theo asked, bristling with defiance.

'And you must be Theo,' Mr X said, smiling and sounding completely relaxed. 'I was told you might give us some bother.'

'So, ginger? What if I go back to bed?'

'Boxing champion, so I've heard,' Mr X said. 'How about a little wager?'

Two camera operators filmed Theo's suspicious expression. He was also disappointed that his rebellious streak was apparently so predictable.

'There's myself and eight operatives on my team,' Mr X said. 'Seeing as you're a fighter, I'll let you pick any one of them. If you can knock them to the ground, I'll pay you one hundred pounds *and* you and your three band mates can go back to bed with no consequences. *But*, if you go to ground first, you'll suck it up like everyone else.'

Theo looked around at Mr X's team. Most of them were huge and he didn't fancy his chances. The woman who'd kicked in Dylan's door was scarier than most of the men, but there was another woman nestling at the back. Mid-twenties, average size, blonde hair tied in a bun.

'Her,' Theo said.

Mr X looked hesitant. 'Are you sure?'

'We had a deal,' Theo said, smiling. 'You said anyone, so I picked her.'

'Some people are averse to fighting women,' Mr X explained, sighing reluctantly. 'But a deal's a deal. Amy, come over here.'

The army gear didn't do any favours, but up close you could see that Amy was pretty amazing-looking.

Theo looked at the camera, then back at Mr X. He worried that punching a girl on camera would make him look like a dick, but Amy was already down on one knee, taking off her boots. The other band members turned to watch while they zipped trousers, hooked on belts and finished buttoning their ragged Polish army shirts.

Stripped down to vest and combat trousers, Amy dropped into a proper fighting stance. Theo was slightly perturbed, but he figured that anyone ex-military would do that, and while her arms were muscular, they were half the thickness of his.

'Get going,' Mr X said, as the pair faced off, bare feet squelching on ground made soggy by the fire hose. 'Haven't got all day.'

'Smack her one,' Adam urged. 'I wanna go back to bed!'

There were a few awkward laughs amongst contestants and crew. Theo threw the first punch, but Amy dodged, so that it only glanced her shoulder.

'Not bad,' Amy teased, tapping her chin. 'Why don't you go for my face this time?'

Theo wasn't stupid enough to follow his opponent's instructions, so he went for the stomach. This time Amy parried and charged. Before Theo got his balance back, Amy had ploughed into his body and driven his legs half a metre off the ground. She then used Theo's own momentum to roll him over her back and flip him.

Everyone – apart from the other three members of Jet – cheered as Theo landed on his back with a muddy splash. Amy took a backwards step, crossed her arms and made a neat, Japanese-style bow. Angie the director knew this was TV gold, and looked at her assistant with a grin that was almost too big for her face.

Mr X dismissed the fight by wiping his hands together, then started yelling again. 'There are forty-eight contestants and forty breakfast bags on a table two kilometres east. The route has been marked with blue arrows and the last eight contestants to arrive will go hungry. After breakfast, there will be a full briefing on the day's team-building programme.'

Propelled by a sturdily-built runner, Noah's wheelchair led the way uphill towards the first arrow. With all but one contestant starting to run, Mr X looked at Theo as he stood in the mud, mildly winded by his encounter with the ground.

'Congratulations,' Mr X beamed. 'You just got beat up by a girl.'

20. Rules is Simple

Dylan, Leo and Jay didn't do sport and failed at running after a few hundred metres. Even Theo beat them to the breakfast table, despite having to finish getting dressed after the others set off. Fortunately, the breakfast bags were pretty large, so the three boys surfed other contestants' leftovers. Jay had plenty of pals and scored a pain-au-chocolat, grapes, muesli bars and little tubs of yogurt.

'This is outrageous,' Dylan moaned. 'Nobody said anything about physical activity when we signed up for *Rock War*.'

'Damned right,' Leo agreed. 'It's summer holidays. I could be on a beach somewhere, getting it on with some sweet little thing in a swimming costume.'

Eve scoffed. 'More likely sitting in your ma's house in Paisley, playing Halo 5 and stuffing your face with Pringles.'

This got a few laughs, as Alfie came over and asked if anyone wanted to swap his croissant for a yogurt.

'I reckon it might actually be fun,' Alfie said. 'Sleeping under the stars, cooking beans and that. I love doing all that stuff at scout camp.'

Alfie felt awkward as the older kids stared at him like he was from outer space.

'Boy scouts,' Dylan tutted, giving a patronising look down his nose.

Tristan had been standing ten metres away, but homed in on his little brother's embarrassment.

'Alfie still goes to scouts,' Tristan told everyone, restating the obvious. 'You should see how cute he looks with his shorts and his little woggle.'

'I don't even wear shorts,' Alfie spat, as some of the others laughed. 'Dick.'

'I was in scouts,' Jay said, as he eyed Mr X and a couple of his goons steaming towards them. 'Camp was OK, but I don't ever remember them setting dogs on us and blasting us with fire hoses.'

'You lot, stop stuffing your fat chops and listen up,' Mr X shouted, as the camera crews closed in. 'Here's how this goes down. We're going to start with a nice twenty-kilometre hike to warm you up. This evening you'll make a bivouac and—'

'What's a bivouac?' Coco asked.

'I think it's a bit like Lucozade,' Babatunde said, getting a few laughs.

'Shut your mouths,' Mr X said. 'If you have a question, you wait until I ask for questions. The next person who speaks out of turn will regret it . . .

'Once you've made your bivouac – or campsite if you prefer – you'll be given materials to make a raft. At sunrise tomorrow, a race will begin. Your rafts will have to make it two kilometres downstream. When you disembark, you'll be given several large items and your team will have to devise a method of carrying them a distance of one and a half kilometres up a cliff-side pathway.

'As a reward, the first band to finish will get to spend the weekend in London with your families, staying in a posh hotel and eating at Joe Cobb's new steakhouse, before getting to see a West End show. The next six bands to finish will get to spend the weekend at home with their families.

'Tragically, the five bands who finish at the back won't be going anywhere. You'll be given Marigolds, cloths and mops and you'll be spending the weekend making sure that every square millimetre of Rock War Manor shines like it has never shone before.'

After a pause while this news sank in, Mr X said, 'Questions?'

'If you'd actually met my family, you'd know that wasn't such a great prize,' Jay noted.

Mr X snapped his fingers and two of his men charged into the laughing kids. They dragged Jay out by his armpits, plunged him into darkness by sticking a metal bucket over his head and marched him up to Mr X.

Mr X took an expandable metal baton off his belt and used it to whack the bucket over Jay's head.

The clang was deafening from inside and Jay's ears

hummed as the bucket was lifted away. He'd only been in the dark for a few seconds, but the sunlight still dazzled him. There was another racket as Mr X threw the bucket. After crashing into a table covered with plastic water beakers, the bucket bounced and clattered into a bush.

'You heard *that*, did you?' Mr X yelled, so close that Jay got sprayed with spit. 'So you're not hard of hearing?'

Jay looked shocked, while the other contestants couldn't decide whether it was funny or horrifying.

'Right, you 'orrible lot,' the Scottish operative yelled, as he stood in front of a mound of small backpacks. 'Each of you take a pack. Use the sunscreen, drink plenty of the water. Once you have your packs, head off. The route is clearly marked, so you'd have to be a bunch of total idiots to get lost.'

*

'I think we're lost,' Jay said, looking around. 'Are you sure we didn't miss a sign somewhere?'

'There's never a camera crew when you need one,' Summer added. 'I bet those lazy buggers are sitting in some greasy spoon scoffing a full English right now.'

Jay's thighs chafed as he crunched up a steep limestone path. His foot was blistering, which was made more painful by having his feet sliding around in boots that were way too big.

'We're *not* lost,' Lucy said assuredly. Nobody had appointed her as navigator, but nobody else had wanted the job, either. 'There'll be another sign where the path splits, just after the top of this hill.'

Twenty kilometres seemed intimidating, but they did have the whole day to walk it. The route was all on public footpaths, and being high summer there were plenty of people out hiking.

A few bands had set off at a brisk pace, but since this part of the exercise wasn't a competition, Lucy had set a more relaxed pace and ended up walking in a big clump with her three band mates from Industrial Scale Slaughter, plus the members of Jet, Pandas of Doom and I Heart Death.

Jay and Summer were city kids, and despite tired legs and a minor freak-out when they realised they had to walk near some scarily large cows, the countryside trek was a novelty. The pair had stayed close all morning and had enjoyed wading through fields of heather and staring out to sea from a cliff-side path.

Adam looked around at sheep-dotted hills basking in sunshine and a cloudless blue sky. 'Why is the countryside so crap?' he moaned. 'People rave on about it, but it's just epically boring.'

He'd tied his shirt around his head, giving himself a slightly Arab look, slathered his chest in way too much sunscreen and carved a smiley face in the white cream with his thumbnail.

'There,' Lucy said, pointing at a blue sign as she crested the hill. 'Further proof that the world would be a much better place if everyone just shut up and did exactly what I told them.'

Michelle and Theo were bringing up the rear, but had got further behind as the morning had worn on. The pair had dropped completely out of sight when the main group heard a racket. Theo and Michelle were charging up the hill yelling, 'Wait up!'

As they approached, the main group stopped walking and turned to look. Michelle was carrying a stack of gold cake boxes, while Theo had polystyrene cups slotted into a cardboard carrying rack.

'Nice little cake shop back there, duck,' Michelle said, sounding like some demented Yorkshire tea lady. 'Tea un scones, wiv clotted cream. Ger 'em down yer gobs!'

Jay looked wary as Theo set down the lidded cups of tea.

'Might have spilled a drop,' Theo said, as hands dived in.

Michelle undid a bow on one of the cake boxes. Lucy and Coco were first to grab cream-smeared scones.

'These are ace,' Lucy said, catching crumbs with her spare hand, as the others dug in. Jay stayed back, looking downhill, half expecting to see an angry baker giving chase with a rolling-pin.

'Did you nick them?' Jay asked, as contestants started squatting alongside the path and taking plastic lids off their teas.

Theo tutted. 'You calling me a thief?' he said, faking indignation.

Jay laughed. 'I'm not calling you a thief, I *know* you're a thief. You spend more days in juvenile court than you do in school.'

'The cops have it in for me,' Theo said, getting a few laughs as some of the contestants sipped from steaming cups. 'Besides, I steal cars, not scones.'

Adam was also curious. 'All Jay's saying is, they made us come downstairs in shorts and tees, and there sure wasn't any money in *my* uniform, or *my* backpack.'

'Since you ask,' Theo said, producing and waggling a tatty nylon wallet.

Adam was sharing Theo's room and knew it didn't belong to him. 'Where'd that come from?'

'You remember our pert-bottomed soldier girl, Amy?'

Adam smiled. 'The one who took you down in two easy moves?'

'I could hardly punch a chick in the mouth with a camera on me, could I?' Theo said defensively.

'Oh, right,' Adam said mockingly. 'Of course, you *let* her win.'

'So after, Amy bends over to put her boots back on. I look at her arse,' Theo continued. 'First thing I notice is that said arse is a peach. Second thing I notice is her wallet poking out of her back pocket. So I did the old Artful Dodger on her. Then I used her dosh to buy tea and scones for you ungrateful twots.'

'Great scones,' Adam admitted, as he worked on a huge bite. 'Freshly baked.'

Babatunde smiled and wagged his finger. 'But if Amy finds out you ripped off her wallet, she'll kick your arse again.'

'Got no proof,' Theo said. 'And besides, I might just enjoy a little tussle in the grass with her.'

The wind had caught one of the cardboard cake boxes and released a flurry of napkins. An old fellow walking a little collie stopped and turned back.

'I hope you lot are planning to pick that mess up before you leave.'

The sniffy way he said *you lot* pissed quite a few of the contestants off. Theo gave him the finger and scowled. 'Keep walking and mind your business, you old fart.'

The man didn't like this one bit. Summer gave the collie a piece of her scone as its owner furiously waved his tweed hat in the air.

'What kind of attitude is that?' he yelled. 'What would a beautiful area like this be like if everyone let their litter blow around?'

'Slightly less boring than it is already?' Adam speculated.

'It's about time young people in this country learned some blasted—'

The man stopped as the bottom half of Michelle's scone smacked his glasses. Landing cream-side-first. The man gasped as the scone slowly peeled itself away and hit the ground.

'The ignorance,' the man roared. Then as he stormed away, 'I don't know what youth group brought you down here, but I'll jolly well find out.'

As usual, Michelle had gone over the top and she got angry when she saw the looks everyone was giving her.

'I just got you scones,' Michelle said. 'Miserable gits.'

'He was just a moany old geezer,' Lucy said, as Summer and a girl from I Heart Death chased down the billowing napkins. 'You could have just ignored him.'

Michelle hated anyone telling her how to behave. Getting lectured by her older sister in front of the other bands made her completely flip.

'Take the rod out of your stuck-up arse, Lucy,' Michelle said, as she started walking. She sounded tearful as she looked back. 'I just wanted to do something nice for all of you.'

'Michelle's a whole bag of nuts,' Theo told everyone, licking cream from a dirty fingertip as he got ready to follow. 'I think I want to marry her.'

21. The Measure

Camp was by a slow-moving river. Trouser-legs got rolled up and sore feet were bathed in the water. Mr X and his operatives had been on site when the contestants arrived and barked instructions as they struggled to put up tents. After that the operatives headed out to set up for the next day's exercise, leaving the bands sprawled in the grass.

While Lucy and her crowd had enjoyed their illicit scones, the others had eaten nothing apart from the flapjack bars supplied in their day packs. It was good to chill out after the long hike, but growling bellies made it hard to relax and the mood was surly.

Everyone looked up hopefully when a truck pulled into camp. The rear platform was stacked with plastic drums, planks, nylon rope and other stuff that was clearly intended to be used for raft building. Lorrie and a cameraman jumped down from the cab.

Two more vans loaded with runners and other crew

pulled up behind as Lorrie moved amidst the kids, holding a microphone and with a camerawoman in tow.

'How was your day?' Lorrie asked Summer.

'I'm wiped out,' Summer said, trying to sound positive. 'But some of the views and stuff were amazing.'

'Are you up for tomorrow's challenges?' Lorrie asked.

Before Summer could answer, Sadie from Frosty Vader barged into the shot. 'We're tired and pissed off,' Sadie said. 'We're not idiots. We know this looks good on TV, but we signed up for *Rock War*, not this pseudo-military horse shite.'

Several other band members yelled with approval, and some clapped as well. Lorrie looked warily back at her camerawoman, before moving deeper amidst the resting kids. She chose Alfie, because he looked the least threatening.

'Got a couple of blisters there,' Lorrie said, looking at Alfie's bare feet. 'Have you ever walked that far before?'

Alfie was conscious of how he'd lost credibility by showing enthusiasm in front of the older kids during breakfast. Now he sensed an opportunity to regain it.

He narrowed his eyes, and moved his face right up to the camera. 'I'm starving,' his unbroken voice growled. 'And whoever thought up this stupid idea of sending us out into the wild can suck my balls!'

Kids shot up out of the grass when they heard what Alfie said, clapping and laughing. Even Tristan gave him a big thump on the back, as Lorrie and her camerawoman backed away.

'You tell her, Alfie,' Jay whooped.

As Joseph and Zig arrived in a Range Rover, they were surprised to see angry-looking contestants by the river and Lorrie striding anxiously back towards the parked vans.

The kids' mood improved as runners started wheeling three stainless steel catering trolleys from the back of a truck. By the time they'd unfolded a long serving table and set out paper plates, there was a line of contestants waiting to be fed. Two camera crews fiddled about with lights, and one of the runners came around to the front of the table and planted a chalkboard that read:

Jungle Chow Menu

Starter – Sheep's eyeballs served in brain jelly
Main – Cow's udder, slow cooked and
topped with duck gizzards
Dessert – Pig's testicles, dipped in chocolate,
served with lime coulis

Vegetarian option – Seaweed stew

Most of the contestants assumed this was a joke until a runner pulled the lid from a steaming serving trolley, enabling a cameraman to take a close up of a pinkish soup, with eyeballs bobbing on the top.

There was a round of *ewws*, and one girl backed off, retching just at the sight of it. The guy behind the counter was tiny, dressed in a straw hat and green and yellow striped polo shirt with *Jungle Chow* written across the front.

'No way we're eating this,' Lucy said.

The Scottish operative laughed. 'Well, there's nothing else, so tuck in or go hungry.'

'Where's Zig?' someone demanded.

At the same time, a huge lad named Grant from I Heart Death shoved the camerawoman filming their shocked expressions, before batting the camera off of her shoulder. A second operator backed up and aimed her camera down at the grass before anyone got the chance to do the same.

'No more filming,' Adam shouted. 'No more bullshit.'

'Get back in line and shut your mouths,' the Scottish operative yelled.

But the hungry teens were having none of it. Zig was looking on warily from behind the camera teams as Lucy led a charge of contestants towards him.

'Where's the welfare officer?' Lucy asked.

Zig looked slightly baffled.

'The first day we were here,' Lucy said, 'we had a briefing. There is supposed to be a welfare officer on set at all times, to deal with any concerns we have. And we were told we could speak to our families any time we liked. But now we're out here in the middle of nowhere. We've got no phones and you're trying to feed us cow's udders.'

Angie butted in. 'All of your parents have been informed that you're on an outward bound-style exercise and will be back by lunch-time tomorrow.'

'But did you tell them about the fire hoses, and sheep's eyeballs?' Jay shouted.

'My godfather's a lawyer,' Dylan shouted. 'He'll sue all your asses.'

'Now,' Zig began weakly, as the Scottish operative sidled up to him. 'Everyone calm down.'

'My colleagues will be back any minute,' the Scotsman whispered. 'We'll soon crush this little rebellion.'

Zig glowered at the operative. 'It's not the army, it's a TV show,' he hissed. 'And in case you haven't noticed, these aren't soldiers, they're teenagers.'

Angie sensed that Zig was flapping and took the initiative. 'Kids, calm down,' she said. 'Lucy, you are absolutely right, there should be a welfare officer on site, and that's an oversight on our part. But what we're trying to do here is make a tense, exciting show. That means more viewers and more publicity, which ultimately benefits everyone.'

'Easy to say when you're not one of the ones eating eyeballs and getting yelled at,' Lucy said.

'And being hosed down, and having buckets stuck on our heads,' Adam added.

Angie took a deep breath and tried to stay calm. 'So what would you like?'

'Decent food for a start,' Lucy said. 'It doesn't have to be spectacular. Burgers, Coke, ice cream.'

'Booze,' Michelle added, getting dirty looks from everyone because the negotiations were serious and this wasn't the time to be acting like an arse.

'Second, you fake all kinds of stuff,' Lucy continued. 'You faked there being judges at our original auditions. You make us reshoot stuff when the light is wrong or the batteries run out. You set up stunts like tossing Jay off the balcony. So why can't you fake this?'

Angie looked back at Zig, checking that her boss was OK with what she was saying.

'We'll send some runners out to get you food,' Angie said. 'It might have to be McDonald's up by the highway or something, because we're not exactly in a gourmet hot spot.'

'Beats gizzards and testicles,' Lucy said, looking behind and getting nods of approval from the others.

'I'd really like some of you to try the Jungle Chow as well though,' Angie said. 'People book Jungle Chow for dinner parties and corporate events. The food is safe and tasty, and showing you guys eating it will make really great TV.'

'I'll eat a plate of that shit for fifty quid,' Theo said.

Zig stepped up beside Angie once he heard money mentioned. 'No way will I pay you,' he said. 'I'd sooner shut this production down than get into a situation where my contestants shake me down for money every time we ask them to do something they don't like.'

There were boos and jostling, and a couple of kids at the back of the crowd rocked the long serving table.

'Let me finish before you start a riot,' Zig said anxiously. 'I won't pay you off. But here's what I will offer. We'll send out to get you some food. I'll tell Mr X and his operatives to treat you nice from now on, and we can fake a few scenes of them shouting at you. I want film of *all* of you trying the Jungle Chow, even if it's just a few bites. Whoever eats most wins a prize of one hundred pounds.'

Lucy looked back at her comrades, sensing a warm response to Zig's offer. 'I also want one more thing,' she said determinedly.

Zig folded his arms and tried to look stern. 'What?' he asked sourly.

'No punishment for the last five bands,' Lucy said, getting whoops of approval. 'You can pretend for TV and take some shots of us scrubbing floors. But we've all been away from home for more than three weeks. I reckon everyone deserves to go home this weekend.'

The contestants really liked this idea and cheered with approval. Zig calculated in his head: he could make the runners clean the house for free, he'd have to pay all the contestants' train fares, but he'd save more than that in wages and food if there was nobody at the manor and he laid off all the crew members on day-to-day contracts.

'We have a deal,' Zig said, reaching forwards and shaking Lucy's hand. 'I have a feeling I'm gonna end up working for you some day, sweetheart.'

But Zig whispered a more sinister message in Lucy's ear as he pulled her in for a hug. 'I don't take kindly to people who shit on me,' he whispered. 'You and your little band mates now have more chance of landing on Mars than you do of winning *Rock War*.'

Lucy felt like she'd been slugged in the gut as Zig backed

up, all smiles as he peeled twenties out of a money clip and ordered the runners to drive to McDonald's. The hissed threat was so brief that Lucy almost thought she'd imagined it.

Over by the serving table, the little man in the straw hat was plating up cow's udder for Summer. While Theo bit into an eyeball and earned a big *oooh* of disgust from the others, Michelle had to go one better.

She crammed four eyeballs into her mouth, then bit down hard. The camera filmed and screams erupted as grey liquid dribbled from both corners of her mouth. Then she coughed and spat the whole lot out, making contestants scramble out of her way.

'They're actually not bad,' Theo told a camera, as he gobbled another eyeball. 'Now let's give the testicles a go.'

22. Four By Four

After washing the taste of Jungle Chow away with Coke, the *Rock War* contestants ate McNuggets, Big Macs, Fillets of Fish and summer fruit pies with ice cream.

As the sun began to dip, the blistered teens started hobbling around building their rafts. Tension lingered between kids and crew, while Mr X and his operatives were furious that Zig had reduced their role to little more than actors.

While the runners scoured the site, removing fast-food packaging and any sign that non-Rage Cola products had been consumed, a package of plastic oars, wooden planks, ropes, polythene sheets and barrels stencilled with Rage Cola logos was delivered to each band's tent.

The raft designs varied, from Jet's simple structure with barrels lined up and strapped beneath planks, to more daring designs that used barrels to make two sides of a boat, with the thick plastic sheeting stretched over a wooden floor.

The result bore a passing resemblance to a dinghy.

Brontobyte used Alfie's scouting skills to produce the first of these dinghy-type boats, and several other bands lashed together copies when they saw how nifty it looked. By eleven, the sky was dark and kids retired to their tents. They only had sleeping bags and thin foam pads, but the contestants were so knackered that the campsite was silent by quarter past.

The runners woke the camp up at seven the next morning. After pottering around for half an hour, eating bacon and eggs with thickly buttered white bread, the kids went back inside their tents.

This time the cameras were running, and the contestants acted out a scene where the operatives charged in with barking dogs, ringing bells and knocking down tents. Erin 'refused' to get up and acted out a scene where the instructors doused her with leftover brain jelly.

Once this charade was over, the twelve bands slid shoes over painfully blistered feet and carried their rafts down to the river's edge. Everyone was handed fluorescent yellow life vests and walkie-talkies to use in an emergency.

Although nobody now faced punishment and everyone was going home for the weekend, most of the contestants had enough competitive spirit to want to beat the other bands and nab the main prize.

Nearly all of the slow-moving river was banked with bushes and trees, so all twelve bands had to carry their rafts overhead, down a single-file path. The muddy embankment at its end was just wide enough to launch two boats at a time.

Frosty Vader were first to set off; their simple barrels-under-planks design seemed sturdy but progress was precarious because Noah's wheelchair gave it a high centre of gravity. There was a growing consensus that the stretched plastic floor design was superior as the next band, Brontobyte, set off. Their raft seemed stable, and was wide enough that all four band members could sit in the bottom and row.

They easily moved past Frosty Vader, and only the craft's tendency to pitch forwards and take on water when it picked up speed stopped them from rowing flat out.

The superiority of the stretched plastic design gave the bands waiting to launch planks-over-barrels boats a sense of doom. Two rafts of the simpler design set off on wobbly paths into the centre of the stream, before Half Term Haircut launched their stretch version.

Half Term Haircut's raft was a close copy of Brontobyte's, but was slightly narrower and had some very neat ropework.

But the four band mates began bailing water as soon as the polythene floor hit the water, and by the time it hit midstream the two girls at the back were fighting a losing battle. Moments later, the front went under and Half Term Haircut got a dunking, before wading back to shore to figure out what went wrong.

This failure made the four members of Jet more comfortable with their more primitive design. With the entire raft above water, one of the most precarious feats for the planks-over-barrels boats was getting the crew on board without tipping the whole craft over.

Jay was lighter than his band mates and found that his corner of the raft stuck out of the water and made it difficult to steer. By the time they'd drifted fifty metres, they'd been overtaken by Industrial Scale Slaughter and I Heart Death.

'Tally-ho, losers!' Michelle shouted, adding insult to injury as she tried to further destabilise Jet's raft by jabbing it with her oar.

It kept getting harder to steer and Jay's corner was rising higher out of the water. Just to rub their problems in, a more stable planks-over-barrels design manned by The Messengers passed effortlessly by.

'I think one of our barrels is leaking,' Babatunde said.

The pebbled river-bed was visible, and Theo took the initiative, jumping off the raft and starting to drag it towards the embankment. After struggling with some reeds, the four band mates got the raft on to the embankment.

It weighed three times what it had done on the way in and the boys found their feet squelching deep into mud.

'I've lost my trainer,' Jay moaned, falling down gasping as they finally reached solid ground.

After catching his breath, Jay stood up and walked unevenly to the front of the raft. Theo had the front raised and water sprayed out of several holes in one barrel, like the nozzle of a watering-can.

'Maybe we caught a rock or something,' Babatunde suggested.

Theo shook his head. 'The holes are too neat. It must have been done with a drill.'

Jay squatted down and saw what his brother meant. There was a central hole, with six more around it, forming the outline of a hexagon.

'Who'd sabotage us?' Adam asked.

'Brontobyte,' Jay said. 'That arsehole Tristan, any money you like.'

Babatunde wasn't so sure. 'They haven't got the balls,' he said. Then, looking at Theo, 'Who else have you upset recently?'

'Me?' Theo gasped. 'Is there *anything* in this world that I don't cop the blame for?'

'Loooosers!' Half Term Haircut yelled from mid-stream, as their repaired raft cruised past.

'You want me to wade out there and kick your butts?' Theo shouted back.

As Jet wondered what to do next, Amy and another of Mr X's operatives began strolling down the riverbank.

'One of you will have to walk back to the start,' Amy said. 'There's strong tape, or fast-setting epoxy to make a repair.'

'We think it's sabotage,' Adam told Amy. 'Look at the pattern.'

'Mmm,' Amy said, as she inspected the damaged barrel then clamped her hand against Theo's buttock.

Jay thought it was a weird come-on, until he saw Amy rip open the Velcro pocket on the back of Theo's camouflage shorts and swiftly extract her own wallet.

'*Thanks* for picking this up,' Amy said sarcastically, as she checked the contents. 'Looks like I'm down about twenty-five quid,' she continued, before smiling and rapping her knuckles on the leaky barrel. 'Sabotage, eh? Now *who'd* do a mean thing like that?'

23. Another Wild Ride

Jet were dead last by the time they'd drained their holed barrel and plugged the damage with fast-setting epoxy resin. A forty-minute cruise took them past an abandoned stretched skin, which had suffered major shredding after drifting into a reedbed, and an unidentified band doing a repair job on the riverbank.

'Tenth,' Mr X yelled for the benefit of the cameras as they jumped off at an endpoint marked with a Rage Cola banner stretched across the river. 'You might as well get your cleaning gear on now!'

After abandoning their raft, Jet jogged fifty metres to a riverside clearing at the foot of a gravel road, which wound itself one and a half kilometres up a steep hillside. Three huge Rage Cola and *Rock War* flags could be seen waving at the top.

'How's it been so far?' Lorrie asked, as she jogged alongside the boys and stuck a microphone in Babatunde's face.

'We sprung a leak,' he said, dripping sweat and mildly out of breath.

'You're eight minutes behind the band in sixth place. Do you think you've still got a shot at getting to see your families this weekend?'

Lucy had forced Zig to let everyone home for the weekend, but Babatunde kept up the lie for the TV audience.

'I miss my family heaps,' he said. 'I don't know if we can make it, but I'm gonna go all out to try.'

Lorrie moved the microphone towards Jay. 'We understand that your arch-rivals Brontobyte are out in the lead. How does that make you feel?'

Jay cared about winning *Rock War*, not some stupid team-building exercise. 'Good on them,' he said dismissively. 'But they still have a crap drummer!'

'Well, good luck!' Lorrie said. 'I'll leave you to get on.'

As the presenter belted off, an unmanned camera filmed as the boys were confronted by the next stage of their challenge. A wooden pallet had been laid out for each band, on which sat six objects: a double mattress, a big pirate-style treasure-chest, a large Marshall guitar amplifier, a broken wheelbarrow, and two rusted cannonballs.

The quartet had also been given a selection of poles, hammocks, wire and a plastic sled with which to carry the six bulky and/or heavy objects to the top of the hill. When Jay looked at identical pallets with the other bands' names on, he realised that Brontobyte and Frosty Vader were the only ones who didn't have to return at least once more to pick up one of their objects.

A camera operator moved in as Jet tried to work out

the most efficient way for four of them to get six objects up the hill.

'What if we roll the two cannonballs inside the mattress and carry it up between the four of us?'

'Let's see how heavy they are,' Adam said, as he squatted down to pick one up.

After much grunting, he got the ball thirty centimetres off the pallet, before dropping it.

'We'll have to roll them, I guess?' Jay said.

'I've gotta shit,' Theo said, as he headed out of the clearing. 'I don't think all the eyeballs and testicles agreed with my digestive system.'

'Well, don't take all day over it,' Jay said firmly. 'You're our strongest man.'

Babatunde shrugged. 'How about I just put the mattress on my head and run with it?'

As he said this, the four girls from Industrial Scale Slaughter scrambled on to the scene, gasping for breath and wearing layers of grit from the dusty hillside. Lucy also had a bloody gash down her leg.

'How'd you get your cannonballs up the hill?' Adam asked.

'Oh, wouldn't you like to know,' Summer teased.

'Are Brontobyte still winning?' Jay asked.

'They were,' Lucy explained. 'But Frosty Vader have been using Noah's wheelchair to carry their stuff, so they're catching up fast.'

Their last two objects were the treasure-chest and the giant loudspeaker. The girls looked like old hands as they manoeuvred the guitar amplifier on to the plastic sled and began securing it with ropes. Two pushed and two pulled as the chalkstone path crunched beneath the sled.

'So we use the sled,' Jay said, before looking left, attracted by a crunch of branches and the distinct whine of a car running in reverse.

The vehicle was a battered Land Rover Defender that Zig had hired to enable the camera crews and Mr X's operatives to get up and down the steep hillside. The horn tooted as it stopped reversing a few metres shy of Jet's pallet.

Theo threw the driver's door open. 'Can you believe this?' he said brightly. 'This is proper old-skool. No ignition lock – you just pop the hood, touch a couple of leads together and the engine starts.'

Lorrie's cameramen ran towards the scene looking anxious. 'I don't think you're supposed to be driving that,' he said, rather obviously.

He started looking around for Zig or a director, but the crew was spread thin covering all the teams in different stages of the rafting and hill climbing.

'What are you turds waiting for?' Theo asked, as he ripped open the back door. 'Load her up.'

The cameramen spoke anxiously into his walkie-talkie as Jet began lobbing their items into the back of the Defender. Jay was tying the mattress to the roof and Adam and Babatunde were struggling with the last cannonball as Mr X charged on to the scene.

'What the hell are you doing?' he shouted, as he jogged towards Jet.

'Hurry up,' Theo told Adam and Babatunde, before shouting at Mr X, 'I'm using my initiative. You ought to be proud of me.'

The cannonball made a huge crash as it got thrown in the car's boot, between the treasure-chest and the loudspeaker. The engine had been running the whole time and Jay used all his might to secure the wire holding the mattress to the roof before taking the front passenger seat.

Babatunde and Adam jumped in with the cargo and Theo hit the throttle before they'd had time to close the rear flap.

'Jesus!' Jay shouted, as the ancient four-wheel drive hit a rut and almost threw him into the windscreen.

Everything was crashing around in the back and Mr X was shouting and punching the air as Theo drove in a lazy arc. After passing behind the twelve wooden pallets, he slowed right down as he hit the gravel path leading up the hill.

'Move it, peasants,' Theo shouted, as he blasted his horn and roared up alongside the four girls from Industrial Scale Slaughter.

Assuming it was the crew, the four girls pulled their sled to the side of the road. Instead of going past, Theo slowed to a crawl.

'Michelle, my belle,' Theo teased. 'I'll give you a ride if you promise to come to my room for a bunk-up later.'

'Piss off,' Michelle said, too knackered to think of something cleverer.

Jay felt ashamed as he looked at Summer, pouring sweat, her boots and trousers white with chalkstone.

'Cheats,' Lucy added bitterly.

'Fine, if that's how you want it,' Theo said.

Theo floored the accelerator. As the Defender flew off, its big rutted tyres threw stones and dust at Industrial Scale Slaughter. Adam and Babatunde howled with laughter as they grabbed hand straps and held on for dear life.

'Lucy tried running away from the dust and fell over,' Adam reported, as he looked out the back. 'There's so much dust I can't even see the others.'

They passed three other bands, carrying various combinations of objects on sleds, in backpacks, or suspended between poles. In places the hillside path grew narrow, and there was a big grinding sound as Theo scraped one side of the Land Rover on a jutting rock.

'Oooh,' Jay joked. 'That's the sound of Zig's money going up in smoke.'

A sharp corner took them up to the final stretch, a steep five-hundred-metre run. Noah was nowhere to be seen, but the other three members of Frosty Vader were pushing his wheelchair, laden with a cannonball.

At the very top of the hill, Jay saw Tristan's bulk and Erin's curvy bum silhouetted against the sunlight. They were moving slowly, each holding one handle of a wheelbarrow weighed down by a cannonball.

'Our wheelbarrow was broken,' Adam noted.

'We never looked inside the chest,' Babatunde said.

'There's probably a wheel or something in there.'

'I really hate Tristan,' Theo said, as he hit the accelerator. 'I assume nobody minds if I kill him?'

'Splendid idea,' Jay agreed.

The gradient and loose stone path were a challenge. The Land Rover was designed for this type of terrain, but it was a twenty-five-year-old vehicle and didn't have the kind of power of the modern cars Theo usually stole.

'Tristan, you *slaaaaaag!*' Theo yelled.

As the Defender approached, Tristan panicked and let his side of the wheelbarrow go. Left in the lurch, Erin got dragged down as the barrow tipped over.

'You maniac,' Adam yelled to his brother, as he almost fell out the back of the Defender.

With Tristan diving one way and Erin the other, Theo went straight down the middle. The wheelbarrow and its contents went between the front wheels, turning a somersault as they grated under the car and lifted the rear tyres off the ground.

As the wheelbarrow sparked and dragged, the cannonball began rolling down the other side of the steep hill. At the hill's crest, a terrified-looking cameraman filmed the action, while a larger crew led by director Joseph was waiting at the finish line, expecting to film Brontobyte's victory.

Theo suspected that part of his four-wheel drive set-up had broken. Even the front wheels weren't doing much, and he ended up putting the car in neutral and rolling the last hundred metres to a line of wooden pallets where the bands were supposed to drop off their six objects.

Using the last of his momentum, Theo aimed the Defender at an empty pallet and drove his front wheel on to it. The pallet collapsed under the weight of the car, as Theo jumped out and bowed proudly towards a pair of camera operators.

On the other side, the Defender's door had buckled when they'd scraped against rocks. After several kicks to try and get his door open, Jay gave up, climbed over the gear-stick and got out behind Theo, who was making victory signs with his fingers.

With the wheelbarrow still trapped under the car, they'd gouged up a huge plume of dust on the final stretch. Tristan's hair and skin were grey as he charged out of the dust cloud, fists bunched.

'What kind of moron are you?' Tristan fumed. 'You almost killed your own cousin.'

Jay thought Tristan was about to hit him, but he went straight past Jay and landed his best punch right into Theo's eye socket. Since Theo was four years older than Tristan and a boxing champion, this was a very bad idea. Luckily for Tristan, one of Mr X's operatives jumped between the two boys before Theo had time to hit back.

'You're dead meat, mummy's boy,' Theo yelled, clutching his eye as Tristan got dragged away. 'You wait and see.'

On the other side of the lens, one of the cameramen looked anxiously at his director.

'Keep 'em rolling,' Joseph ordered. 'It's all wunderbar!'

24. Their Pies are Really Nice

'Hey it's me,' Theo told his camcorder. 'Been a few days since my last video diary, cos Michelle busted my camcorder.

'I'm feeling pretty peeved. Apparently, jump starting a Land Rover counts as initiative, but crashing it into rocks and putting the wind up Erin and Tristan was too reckless. So Jet got disqualified and now we have to clean Rock War Manor all weekend instead of going home.

'But that's not what this diary entry is all about. Because most of you know me as a sex machine and a boxing champion, but we're supposed to broaden our horizons here at boot camp. I've been doing songwriting workshops and I'm starting to consider myself as something of a lyrical maestro.

'I'm gonna read you one of my songs. We're not allowed to swear on these video diaries, so whenever there's a rude word in my lyric I'll say *bleep* instead.'

'You've got a bad *bleeping* attitude. Don't show no *bleeping* gratitude.

Bought perfume for your birthday, but you sprayed it on your dog.

Remember when we snogged in that field after the prom.

Got dog *bleep* on your dress, but you'd drunk so much you didn't *bleeping* mind.

Then I see you kissing Kevin outside Costa after maths.

Kevin, I'm gonna string electric flex around your dirty *bleeping* neck.

Kevin, you *bleep*, you'll be eating through a straw.

Gonna rip off your *bleeping* nuts off, and mount them on our school's main door.'

'So yeah, that's an example of my mad skillz. It's called "Tender Love".'

*

Brontobyte got the swanky hotel and the West End show, but thanks to Lucy Wei's negotiating skills, Jet only had to pretend that they would be spending the weekend cleaning Rock War Manor. And since they weren't officially home, there was no camera crew to bug them either.

The flat above the fish and chip shop seemed more cramped than ever after three weeks at the manor. Jay had been away long enough to notice that his house smelled of chip fat and his stepdad's back ointment. But even if the aroma wasn't great, Jay was pleased to see his mum and his three youngest siblings.

While the little kids ran in and out, Jay spent Friday evening crammed in the living-room, with his mum, Theo, Adam, obnoxious brother Kai and the latest in Kai's long line of infuriatingly fit girlfriends.

They watched the first three episodes of *Rock War*. Jay squirmed every time he saw himself on screen, and his mum played down a scary-sounding story about some guys who'd robbed the cash register when she'd been working alone in the chip shop earlier that week.

Once the little kids were in bed, Adam went out to meet his girlfriend and Theo headed out to some house party. Jay's mum and stepdad went down to help in the chip shop and Kai went to walk his girlfriend home. By half eleven, Jay found himself alone, staring out the living-room window.

Friday night after the pubs closed was the chip shop's busiest time. Drunk couples and sweary blokes queued out of the door, while those who'd been served stumbled out with their ketchup-smeared chips.

Flashing blue lights caught Jay's attention, but the cops were just stopping to buy cigarettes from the little supermarket across the street.

The scene made Jay feel nostalgic. Home was a comfortable place and he loved his family – except Kai, who he'd have been happy to never see again. But Rock War had given him a taste of a bigger, more exciting world.

Jay desperately wanted this flat to be part of his past, not his future. With twelve bands and only one winner, the odds were stacked against Jet, but the idea of going back to living here and being bored off his head all day at school was unbearable.

Downstairs, Kai pushed through the chip queue, looking like a little skin-headed bull as he took a key to the side door out of his shorts. Kai was a psycho, and with nobody else around, there was a chance Jay would end up with an arm twisted up behind his back, or suffering Kai's favourite trick of rubbing his bare arse on Jay's face.

To avoid a confrontation, Jay crept to his room as Kai unlocked the side door.

'It's almost midnight,' Jay's mum yelled to Kai, as Jay quietly closed his bedroom door. 'We'll be having words about this in the morning, young man.'

Jay's life had been easier since he'd swapped rooms to share with Adam instead of Kai, but he still felt pathetic hiding from his younger brother. He also hated the fact that Kai had a girlfriend to walk home, while Adam and Theo probably had hot girls crawling all over them too.

As Jay pulled off his shirt to get in bed, he looked down at a skinny arm and wished he was beefy like his half-brothers. Jay grabbed his mobile from his pocket, and noticed that he'd missed a bunch of WhatsApp messages.

The first was from a kid in his class, who'd spent two years ignoring Jay at school before deciding to start messaging him every day now that he was in *Rock War*. All the other messages were from a group chat of *Rock War* contestants.

The latest ones were people posting numbers that Jay

didn't understand: 456,000, 442,000, 391,000!!! Jay scrolled back until he eventually saw the explanation.

Sadie: Summer trending on YouTube! 220,000 views!

Noah: 250,000. That's 30,000 in two hours.

Grant: Is Summer on here? Does she know?

Lucy: She doesn't have a smartphone, but I've sent her an SMS.

Noah: Close to 300,000! F me!!!!

Jay scrolled up further, but couldn't find a link to the YouTube video they were all talking about. He opened up YouTube on his laptop, found the *Rock War* channel and filtered the search results by *most viewed*.

The second most viewed video was the one of Theo chasing the girl around the pool singing 'Fat Bottomed Girls', with 76,041 views. But 'Summer Smith sings Patti Smith' was just shy of half a million views.

Jay hadn't seen the edited clip, so he hit the 'play' button, and cursed the slow Wi-Fi as his screen locked on a blurred image of Summer's face.

Jay had been at Rage Rock. He'd watched the crowd's reaction as Summer broke into song, but it seemed even more real having Summer's face light up his bedroom and her voice growl from his laptop's tinny speakers.

Jay watched the whole thing with goose bumps down his neck. He remembered walking across the fields of heather with Summer, chatting like they'd known each other for years. And he remembered how she'd used her little finger to wipe jam from his top lip when they ate the scones. He'd been desperate to kiss her, but he didn't dare with so many people there.

'You fancy Sum-merr,' a little voice sang.

Jay shot up off his bed in fright.

'Hank,' Jay gasped, when he realised it was his six-year-old brother. 'Why are you awake? You scared the shit out of me.'

Hank crawled up the bed and flicked on Jay's lamp. 'Sorry,' he said meekly.

'Why are you in my bed?'

'Mummy and Daddy are working and I *needed* a cuddle,' Hank explained. 'I kept waiting for you to come upstairs, but I went asleep on my own.'

Jay smiled. Hank loathed sleeping alone, and rarely spent a whole night in his own bed. Even Theo would let him climb under the covers, rather than face a two a.m. scream-up.

'Can I *please* stay in your bed?' Hank gasped. 'I took a shower, so I smell *lovely*.'

Hank could be a pain, but Jay had missed him more than anyone except his mum. Jay took a big sniff of his brother's hair. 'You smell like dead bugs and sweaty socks,' he teased.

Hank crossed his arms. 'No I don't!'

'You can sleep with me tonight,' Jay said. 'Since I've been away.'

Jay turned the bedside light back out and the brothers snuggled up.

'Kai says you're too puny to ever get a girlfriend,' Hank

announced. 'But I think Summer Smith likes you.'

'You think?' Jay said enthusiastically, before realising that the opinion of a six-year-old probably didn't count for much.

'You looove her!' Hank teased.

'You need to calm down and go to sleep,' Jay said, trying to sound parental. 'You'll be grumpy in the morning.'

Before Hank could reply, Jay's phone started to ring.

'I'll get it,' Hank yelled, throwing off the shared duvet and grabbing the phone from its dock.

The number was unrecognised. 'Yeah?' Jay said.

'It's Jen Hughes,' a woman said.

Jay was baffled.

'The publicist from Channel Six,' she explained irritably. 'Summer's video is generating a *lot* of traction on YouTube. BBC's *Sunday Breakfast* wants to do a live interview. But it'll mean getting to Birmingham by seven a.m.'

Jay sounded excited. 'I can do that.'

'No, no,' Jen said dismissively. 'We've got Noah and Summer on board. But I'm trying to call Theo. Have you *any* idea where he is?'

Now it was Jay's turn to sound irritated. 'He went to some house party. If you can't get him on his mobile, he'll either be passed out drunk, or shagging some bimbo.'

Hank cracked a huge smile when Jay said *shagging*.

'Well, if you *do* hear from Theo, tell him to call me urgently. We'll send a car to pick him up.'

'I really don't mind doing the interview,' Jay said.

'And I'm better behaved than my brother, in case you haven't noticed.'

Jen laughed awkwardly. '*Sunday Breakfast* specifically asked for Theo. The YouTube thing is their angle on the story, and they want Theo, because his video diary has been getting more views than anyone else's.'

'Right,' Jay said resentfully. 'Well, if Theo rocks up here, I'll let him know. But don't count on him surfacing until tomorrow afternoon. He never misses my mum's Sunday roast.'

25. MediaCity

Built alongside the Manchester Ship Canal, a few miles from central Manchester, MediaCity was the northern hub of the British TV industry. BBC Sport and Radio nestled with a theatre complex that hosted quiz shows and sitcoms, while the set for long-running soap *Coronation Street* lay on the other side of a swanky steel footbridge.

Theo had his arms around a female rider's waist as their motorbike shot between metal bollards and *Pedestrians Only* signs. It was seven in the morning, but a line of nerds sat on a pavement, waiting to get free tickets for whatever was being filmed that evening.

Taking a left after a fat dude in a *Doctor Who* hoodie, the bike rolled on to MediaCity's main pedestrian thoroughfare. At the far end, a huge arena was draped with giant pictures of Karen Trim and signs that read: *We're back, baby! Hit Machine returns to Channel Six, Saturday 13th September.*

By the arena's main entrance were the three stretch

Mercedes used to ferry *Hit Machine*'s contestants around, and the even more luxurious bi-coloured Rolls Royce wearing Miss Trim's KT1 number plate.

'Are we lost?' Theo shouted.

But his female driver just took them into a side alleyway and stopped sharp in front of Studio Q. The building had more in common with an Ikea store than the more glamorous studios near the water.

'Good morning,' said a receptionist seated behind a marble plinth.

Theo walked like an old man as he took off his crash-helmet. He'd been in a club when he saw the text message from Jen. He didn't much fancy Sarah, the woman he was chatting to at the time. She was a cougar: mid-thirties, and looking for a romp with a younger guy. Sarah had bought Theo cocktails, spent some time moaning about her accounting job, before grabbing his butt and moving in for a snog.

Theo's plan was to go back to Sarah's place, shag her, then steal anything valuable he could find before doing a runner. It was a great trick to pull, because a professional woman of Sarah's age would never go to the cops and admit she got ripped off after picking up a seventeen-year-old in a nightclub.

Plans changed when Theo got Jen's message. It turned out Sarah was a biker. After a stroll to her posh flat, they'd donned leathers, straddled a giant Triumph and hit a hundred and thirty mph on the M6. On paper the bike ride had seemed glamorous, but the brutal reality of riding at speed, hands locked around Sarah's waist, had put Theo off motorbikes for life.

'This is cool,' Sarah said, oddly childish as she read the names of TV shows over doors. 'TV land!'

After eighty metres of corridor, they stepped into a waiting area, with Kermit-green carpet tiles and a view over the canal. TV folk sipped coffee and smoked outside on a balcony.

Noah was parked up next to his dad in an armchair. He felt embarrassed being with his dad while Theo strolled in, like some post-apocalyptic hero, in shabby motorbike leathers with a glamorous older woman in tow.

To make matters worse, Noah's dad stood up and grasped Theo's hand.

'Pleasure to meet you,' Noah's dad said, using a broad Belfast accent that his son hadn't inherited. 'You may be a little rough around the edges, Theo, but it's great the way you've kept an eye out for Noah these past few weeks.'

Noah looked at the ground, hoping it would swallow him, while Theo was lost for words. He got praised so rarely by an adult that he didn't have the skills to deal with it.

'You must be Theo's mother,' Noah's dad said, offering his hand to Sarah. 'Your boy's got a good heart, I tell you that.'

Biologically, Sarah was old enough to be Theo's mum, but she certainly didn't enjoy the suggestion and snorted at the outstretched hand.

'We're just mates,' Theo said, as he rubbed an aching

thigh. 'Though I'm not sure two hours on a motorbike is my preferred mode of transportation.'

'Poor baby,' Sarah smiled. 'I could feel his fingers digging into my ribs every time we went over a hundred.'

'The biscuits are good,' Noah said, trying to change the subject as he pointed at a plate covered with individual packs of Walker's Shortbread. 'Or they'll make you a bacon roll if you can track down the girl behind the counter.'

'I know what I need,' Theo said, eyeing the coffee machine.

He'd drunk beer and cocktails and missed a night's sleep, so Theo went straight for the espresso button. As the creamy black liquid dribbled into a cup, Sarah sidled up and whispered in his ear.

'You look good in leather,' she murmured. 'You wanna go find the toilet and do something dirty?'

But Sarah seemed way more wrinkly without the benefit of moody club lighting, and there was no prospect of scoring her iPhone, cash and jewellery now that she knew his real name. Fortunately, Theo was saved from answering because Jen was hurrying over.

'Ahh, you're here at last,' Jen said, going up on tiptoes and giving Theo a quick kiss. Then she turned to Sarah. 'Mrs Richardson, great to see you again.'

Before Sarah could say that they'd never met and that she wasn't Theo's mum, Jen hailed Noah and led the two boys through swing doors with a sign over them saying *Staff and Guests ONLY*.

'How was your flight?' Jen asked Noah, as they walked.

'Very cool,' Noah replied. 'Private jet sure beats RyanAir.'

Jen cracked a mischievous smile. 'Four and a half thousand euros,' she said. 'I think I heard Zig swallow his tongue when I said it was the only way I could get you from Belfast in time for *Sunday Breakfast*.'

Still holding his coffee, Theo stopped and did a double-take when he passed a little make-up room. He was sure he'd seen talent show svengali Karen Trim sat in a make-up chair, while a woman worked her over with hairspray.

'Did I just see who I thought I saw?' Theo asked.

Jen nodded. 'The big KT herself.'

'Is she on with us?' Noah asked.

'No, thank god,' Jen said. 'She's on Channel Three. The production company that owns this building specialises in breakfast and daytime TV. They have the contract to make BBC *Sunday Breakfast*, and *Shelly's Morning Break* on Channel Three. The studios are right next to one another.'

They rounded a corner and found another make-up room, this one bigger than Karen Trim's. Four barber's chairs faced a wall lined with bright LED strips and mirrors. Summer was in the chair at the back, wearing foundation and a touch of lipstick, with her usually scruffy hair combed into neat layers.

'You look good, Summer,' Theo said, as he drained his coffee and placed the cup on a counter covered with bottles and brushes.

'You really do,' Jen agreed.

'How was your nan?' Noah asked.

'Great,' Summer said, smiling. 'She seems to have made a lot of friends in the respite home. I spent most of yesterday getting cooed over by old ladies, and trying to explain what YouTube is.'

A make-up artist came into the room. His appearance was halfway between a waiter and a Nazi officer, with black shirt, slicked-back hair and a pencil moustache.

'Hey, I'm Mario!' he announced. 'Sit down, boys. I'll fix you up in a jiffy.'

'I *am* sitting down,' Noah pointed out.

Mario made Theo take a chair, then curled up his nose as he inhaled nightclub sweat and bike leather. Mario applied foundation, so that Theo didn't look shiny under the studio lights, and used a hairdryer and some fast-setting gel to bring life to hair that had spent two hours under a crash-helmet.

While Mario worked on Theo, Jen looked at Noah.

'What's up?' Noah asked.

'I was just wondering what you had on under the pullover,' Jen said, awkwardly. 'I'm just not sure it's conveying the right image.'

'I look like I'm dressed for church,' Noah admitted bluntly. 'I had to leave in a rush and I put on the clothes my mum threw at me.'

'I'm sure we can work on it,' Jen soothed, as she raised Noah's pullover and was relieved to find a bright green polo shirt with a big *Disabled & Proud* slogan, done in the same font as the Abercrombie & Fitch logo.

'Lose the V-neck and you're fine,' Jen said, smiling.

Mario looked cross as Theo turned unexpectedly and pointed at the leather motorbike jacket he'd taken off before sitting down.

'Wear that, Noah,' Theo suggested. 'I'll go on in my vest and give the chicks a beefy morning thrill.'

'He's muscular,' Mario agreed. 'It's a shame there isn't time for him to take a shower though.'

Noah was afraid the leather jacket would be too big, but doing everything with his arms had given him a powerful torso. He wasn't pleased with the jacket's aroma of damp leather and Theo's pits, but there was no denying it looked more rock-and-roll than the pullover picked by his mum.

Noah got the same make-up job as Theo, before Mario wished everyone good luck and disappeared. Karen Trim walked past a few minutes before eight. Jen kept looking at her watch, getting increasingly nervous.

'What time are we supposed to be on?' Noah asked.

'Any second now,' Jen said. 'But they usually call you over to the studio a few minutes before you go on. I guess the show must be running behind schedule.'

Jen was looking at her watch again.

'What happens if they run out of time?' Summer asked, as another minute ticked past.

'They do cut a guest sometimes,' Jen said, then after another glance at her watch, 'Frankly, it's not looking too good.'

Finally a young woman came in. She wore a striped

jersey that hung off one shoulder, held a clipboard and looked harassed.

'I'm *so* sorry!' she said. 'Our interviewer had the schools minister on the ropes, so we ran his interview a little longer. Unfortunately, that means your slot is down to three minutes. There won't be time to introduce all three of you. But the editor wants to have a chat with Summer, and show a clip from her Patti Smith video.'

'Are you *shitting* me?' Theo said, standing up and kicking the counter top in front of the mirrors. 'I was on for a bunk-up and a two-carat diamond ring before you dragged my arse up here.'

But nobody paid Theo any notice.

'Summer, you're on in ninety seconds,' the young woman said. 'We need to get you into the studio and wire you for sound.'

Summer much preferred the idea of going on with the others, and felt queasy as she stood up. Jen recognised nerves and put a hand on her shoulder.

'You're going to be fine, honey,' Jen said. 'Remember your media training, and don't talk too fast.'

'Seventy seconds,' the production assistant said. 'We need to dash.'

As Jen and Summer followed the striped shirt towards the set, Noah backed into the hallway.

'Where you going?' Theo asked.

'I think I saw a TV back here,' Noah said. 'We might be able to watch Summer's interview.'

'Waste of my time!' Theo shouted, as he gave the make-up counter a much more vicious boot.

The wooden counter top splintered away from the wall and various potions and lipsticks rolled on to the floor. Still fuming, Theo headed out into the corridor. Noah had found the wall-mounted screen, but it was showing Shelly Ross on Channel Three, doing one of her cosy interviews with Karen Trim.

'And you look so much slimmer than when I last saw you,' Shelly cooed.

'Thank you, my darling,' Karen said. 'I've been doing a lot of running. And of course, I've been living in LA where everyone's so glamorous. You have to stay slim to fit in.'

'And I understand you've bought a little doggy?' Shelly said.

'I can't see a button to change the channel,' Noah told Theo. 'Can you see anything on top?'

But Theo was deep in thought: Karen Trim was on set, so presumably she'd left some of her belongings in her make-up room down the hallway.

'Back in a jiffy,' Theo said.

Karen Trim's make-up room was only a dozen steps away. The door was open and there was a designer handbag and an iPad in a jewel-encrusted case on the make-up bench.

Seeing pound signs, Theo stepped into the room. He'd just started reaching for the bag when a deep voice erupted behind him.

'Can I help you, young man?'

The voice was a rich, Welsh bass. The voice's owner was a monster, with fingers like sausages and thighs broader than Theo's waist.

'Sorry, boss . . .' Theo spluttered. 'Wrong door. I think my make-up room is down that way.'

The giant didn't answer, but his expression said *get out or I'll smash you like an egg.*

'Where'd you go?' Noah asked, when Theo got back.

'Nowhere,' Theo said.

'I just checked Summer's YouTube,' Noah said. 'It's over eight hundred thousand views. At this rate it'll be past a million by this evening.'

'Bully for Summer,' Theo said bitterly. 'She's got a million hits and *Sunday Breakfast*. I've got a hangover, a crusty girlfriend and achy balls from two and a half hours on a motorbike.'

'Can you see if there's a button on top of the TV, so we can watch Summer?' Noah asked.

Theo gave the image of Karen Trim a two-fingered salute as he checked for buttons. 'I think you need the remote. Noah, are you up for some fun?'

Theo's reputation made Noah wary, but he didn't want Theo to think he was a wuss. 'I'm up for anything, mate.'

'Right,' Theo said, 'follow me.'

Theo stormed off, with Noah behind. They went the way they'd seen Karen and Summer go. The hallway reached a T, and Theo followed the sign pointing to *Shelly's Morning Break.*

Half expecting to find a locked door, or some burly security guard, Theo was delighted to see a scrawny production assistant standing below the ON AIR – LIVE sign above the door.

'You can't go in here,' the assistant blurted.

'Out my way, wanker,' Theo said, bunching a fist, but not needing to use it because the assistant knew he was outmatched.

The floor manager on the other side of the door was bigger, but way too slow to stop Theo from running on to Shelly Ross's pastel-coloured set. As Noah anxiously wheeled himself to the edge of the set, Theo sent a vase of sunflowers flying as he vaulted a big glass coffee table and sat himself on the sofa next to Karen Trim.

'Shelly, my baby!' Theo said, as he slid an arm behind a nervous-looking Karen. 'You may be old, but you make me so horny! Now, why are you talking to this wrinkled old bag? *Everyone* knows there's only one talent show worth watching on Channel Six and it's *not* called *Hit Machine*.'

26. The Harrassment Guy

Lucy Wei padded down to the kitchen, dressed in an oversized Ramones tee and her school PE shorts. Michelle and Lucy's dad was a successful architect, and it was nothing unusual that he had drawings out on the dining table at eight on a Sunday morning.

'My daughter gets more beautiful every day,' Mr Wei said, as he gave Lucy a kiss. 'Did you enjoy last night?'

'For sure,' Lucy said softly, as she squatted on a dining chair with one foot tucked under her bum. 'The restaurant was really great.'

'Just a pity your mother created her usual scene,' Mr Wei said.

'It's no mystery where Michelle gets her temperament from,' Lucy said, as she ran a hand through her long black hair. 'What are you working on? Opera house? Skyscraper? Olympic stadium?'

Mr Wei had made his money designing warehouses and

office parks, and knew his daughter was teasing him.

'Way more glamorous than that,' Mr Wei said. 'It's a multistorey park-and-ride facility on the outskirts of Leeds.'

'Wowee,' Lucy said. 'But if you've got a minute, there's something serious I need to talk about.'

Mr Wei closed the lid of his laptop and smiled. 'I always have time for you, but *please* start by promising me that you're not pregnant.'

'Dad,' Lucy laughed. 'You don't need to worry on that score. It's pretty hard getting to know anyone properly when there's twenty-seven cameras filming you all the time. But the thing is . . .'

Lucy explained the situation with Zig Allen. How she'd led the resistance to Jungle Chow, and Zig's whispered threat that Industrial Scale Slaughter now had zero chance of winning *Rock War*.

Mr Wei considered a while before speaking. 'Have you told your band mates?'

Lucy shook her head. 'I probably could have trusted Coco, but I reckon Summer would get really upset, and who knows what craziness Michelle would pull if she found out?'

'I dread to think,' Mr Wei said, half smiling. 'Did you get any sense that it was an idle threat? A lot of successful men feel threatened if they're humiliated by a woman.'

'It wasn't like I set out to hurt Zig,' Lucy protested. 'I just stuck up for myself when they wanted to make us eat gizzards and eyeballs.'

'That's the kind of person I brought you up to be,' Mr

Wei said proudly. 'Have you spoken to Zig since it happened?'

'Not a word. But I did think about confronting him. Maybe with a hidden recorder or something.'

Mr Wei raised a hand. 'Zig sounds like a smart operator. If you confront him, he'll just deny that the incident ever took place.'

'So what can I do, Daddy?'

'My practice has to deal with occasional sexual harassment and unfair dismissal claims. A few are genuine, but most are just ex-employees who think we'll pay up rather than see our name dragged through the mud. But I have an excellent legal guy who deals with all this stuff. I'll give him a call right away.'

'What do you think he'll do?' Lucy asked.

'I expect he'll start by calling Zig Allen. *Nobody* likes having a lawyer call out of the blue. Then he'll probably follow up with some kind of letter. If we set your story out on paper, outlining the threat Zig made, it will be very difficult for him to do anything unfair to your band further down the line.'

Lucy smiled. 'So you think we'll be all right?'

'You're too old for me to kiss you and promise I can make it all better,' Mr Wei said. 'But there's one other factor in your favour. How can they *possibly* kick Industrial Scale Slaughter out of *Rock War* when Summer is by far the most popular contestant?'

*

The editor of *Shelly's Morning Break* had to make a split-second decision. Officially, the rule was to cut to an advert if someone breached on-set security. But there was the tantalising possibility that this kind of freak occurrence could create huge publicity for the show.

With Theo sitting on the sofa and Noah just off set in his wheelchair, the editor decided to let Shelly and Karen deal with the invasion. After all, Karen's TV persona was the queen of the nasty put-down. Surely she'd be able to deal with a teen yobbo?

'Excuse me,' Shelly said, puffing herself up and eyeing Theo. 'This is a live broadcast and a closed set.'

'Freedom of speech,' Theo yelled, as he punched the air. '*Hit Machine* got axed two years ago, because it was as old and saggy as Karen Trim. *Rock War* is new. It's cool, and it's proudly brought to you in association with Rage Cola and its magnificent range of diarrhoea-inducing beverages.'

Now that she was reasonably sure she wasn't about to get stabbed, Karen Trim put on her queen bitch face and glowered at Theo. '*Rock War* is a *kids*' show,' Karen spat. 'Look at you, with your acne and your Primark T-shirt. Message to your tiny brain, Theo: I've seen your band and you've got a voice like a rusty gate. *Rock War* will go down the toilet, and toilets are what *you'll* spend most of your life cleaning.'

As Shelly grinned and gasped, Theo looked unfazed. 'I heard you had a sex change op,' he told Karen. 'Rumour has it you used to be a woman.'

'I do *love* a man with spots,' Karen replied, enjoying every moment as she leaned towards Theo. 'Let me squeeze that big juicy whitehead on your neck.'

A camera operator moved in for a close-up, as Theo tilted his head and Karen's metallic purple fingernails moved in to squeeze the zit.

'Oh god, *no!*' Shelly yelled, covering her eyes as Theo's zit popped.

As the squirt of pus hit the camera lens, Noah heard the studio door open. Karen's vast bodyguard had to duck under the door frame, before lumbering across the set towards Theo.

'I think I'd better leave now,' Theo said.

He hoped his boxer's speed would enable him to vault the back of the sofa and scramble out through an emergency exit, but his trailing leg bashed the coffee table and he ended up straddling the sofa.

There was no way the live broadcast was going to be cut now. The bodyguard stamped his boot through the glass coffee table, grabbed Theo by neck and belt loops and raised him effortlessly over his head.

'I warned you,' the bodyguard boomed.

Karen Trim was smart enough to know that her cosy morning interview had just turned into something sensational.

'Watch all-new *Hit Machine!*' Karen shouted. 'Starts Channel Six, Saturday September thirteenth.'

Although Theo tried to kick and slap, Karen's bodyguard was just too powerful for him. After pulling Theo down to his chest like a bar-bell, the bodyguard threw him across the sofa. Theo crashed into the backdrop, breaking through polystyrene columns and a plywood screen.

Karen was still ranting about *Hit Machine*, as Shelly burst into tears. Keen to impress Theo, Noah saw his chance for immortality. As the giant charged behind the set to inflict further pain on Theo, Noah wheeled into shot for the first time. He moved fast, bowling into Karen Trim and knocking her sideways.

'*Hit Machine* sucks!' Noah shouted. '*Rock War – Boot Camp*. New episode. Five thirty, tomorrow! Summer pukes and I eat eyeballs!'

'Help me!' Theo shouted girlishly, as the giant booted a huge plywood panel out of the way and grabbed him again.

Shelly stormed off set, furious that her crew hadn't stopped filming. Still wearing her wireless microphone, she screamed, 'This is not TV. It's a toshing zoo!'

Meantime, Karen Trim had stood up and was trying to tip over Noah's chair. 'Don't think I won't hit you just because you're in that chair,' she growled. 'I'm an equal opportunities bitch.'

But Noah knew how to handle his chair and backed away, sending Karen stumbling forwards into a cameraman. Then, as Theo finally broke loose and scrambled towards the fire exit, there was a bang, followed by a blue flash. One of the fill lights built into the demolished backdrop had fused, killing the mains-powered cameras and leaving the studio in the dim green glow from its emergency exit signs.

'Well,' Karen Trim said, dusting her hands and smiling. 'If that doesn't go viral, I don't know what will.'

27. PC Copper

Thirty cameras flashed as a stocky, uniformed police officer walked down a set of steps at the front of Stretford police station. He stopped at the bottom, as photographers snapped and reporters jostled to get their microphones and audio recorders close to his face.

'Good afternoon,' the officer began, his voice as dry as a mouthful of cream crackers. 'I am Inspector Philip Schumacher of Greater Manchester Police and I will now read to you from a short, prepared statement.

'At approximately eight fifteen a.m., police were called to the Studio Q building at the MediaCity complex. This followed reports of a disturbance on the set of the television programme, *Shelly's Morning Break*.

'Miss Karen Trim, along with her bodyguard Kevin Ryman, were arrested on suspicion of assault. A male juvenile, who cannot be named as he is under the age of eighteen, was arrested on the set. A second juvenile, who cannot be named, was arrested as he attempted to escape the scene on a motorbike.

'Miss Trim and the two juveniles have been issued with a formal police caution and no further action will be taken. Mr Ryman faces more serious allegations of assault against one of the juveniles and remains in custody for further questioning. That is all I have to say at this time.'

'Inspector,' a journalist in the scrum yelled. 'Is Karen Trim still inside the building?'

'Was the whole thing set up as a publicity stunt by Karen Trim?' someone else asked.

'That is all I have to say at this time,' Inspector Schumacher said, as he turned to walk back up the steps.

'Did Karen Trim cause any injuries to the disabled boy?'

'That is all I have to say at this time,' the inspector repeated. 'Good afternoon.'

*

Inside the police station, Theo stepped into a brightly lit room with a bed like you'd get in a doctor's surgery and a height chart marked on the back wall for mug shots. He wore paper slippers, and a set of disposable boxers that the police had given him.

Theo had been in enough police stations not to feel scared, and although he had blurred vision and hurt in quite a few places, he pretty much felt like his usual cocky self.

'OK,' the ponytailed police photographer said gently. 'Are you comfortable being photographed? Would you prefer it if I was replaced by an officer of the same sex?'

'I'm good,' Theo said.

The officer picked a chunky Nikon SLR out of a metal cabinet and checked the battery level. 'So I'm going to start at the top and work my way down.'

Theo flicked one eyebrow cheekily. 'I bet you say that to all your boyfriends.'

The camera whirred into focus, then flashed as the officer took three close shots of his badly swollen left eye. After pausing to check that the pictures were OK, she photographed a large swelling on his shoulder.

'If you could please turn around so I can see your back. And raise your arms above your head to tighten the skin, if that's not too painful.'

The photographer snapped a mass of bruises and small cuts, caused when Karen Trim's goon threw him into the set.

'You're lucky you didn't get a concussion,' the photographer noted.

'Boxing,' Theo explained. 'Been thumped so many times, my head's like a rubber ball.'

'Now, if it's not too painful, I'd like you to take the gauze off your arm, so I can photograph the splinter wound.

'Perfect,' she said, after a few more snaps. Then very gently, as Theo stuck the dressing back to his arm, 'Now I need to photograph the splinter wounds in your buttocks. And finally, it looks like you've got some wounds on your inner thighs.'

'They're nothing to do with Karen Trim's psycho

bodyguard,' Theo said. 'It's chafing from the motorbike ride from London. My nutsack's so raw it looks like a pepper.'

Since Theo was under eighteen, he had to be released into the custody of a parent. It'd gone three a.m. by the time his mum had finished cleaning up in the chip shop, and she'd slept less than four hours when – not for the first time in her life – she got a *Theo's been arrested* call.

'I've put your clothes out,' Theo's mum grunted, pointing to an orange plastic chair as Theo shuffled out of the photographic room and into a tiny changing area in his paper slippers.

The jeans she'd brought from London were actually Adam's, so Theo had a struggle doing up the buttons. She'd also brought one of his blue school shirts.

'This makes me look like a dick,' Theo moaned. 'And no way am I putting my school tie on.'

His mum held her thumb and forefinger a few millimetres apart. 'Theo, I'm *this* close to kicking you out of the house,' she spat as she eyeballed her son. 'I thought it might be better if you looked smart in front of the police. And you're doing all your buttons in the wrong hole.'

'Balls,' Theo said.

Once Theo sorted the buttons and slid his feet into trainers, they crossed a hallway into a larger room. Jen the publicist was there, along with a black-suited solicitor, plus Noah and Noah's dad. Unlike Theo, Noah had no experience with the police. He seemed pretty spooked and looked like he'd shed a few tears.

'It's OK, pal,' Theo said, putting an arm on Noah's shoulder. 'Police caution doesn't mean squat.'

'Stay the hell away from my boy,' Noah's dad warned. 'You're a complete bloody idiot.'

Theo's mum regularly called her son worse, but she wouldn't have an outsider doing it. She gave Noah's dad evils, as Theo felt slightly saddened by the loss of his briefly held status as a good example.

'There are two taxis waiting,' Jen said. 'We're going to leave by a side exit, so we go left and walk about fifty metres. Hopefully most of the press will be at the front, and they're more interested in Karen Trim than us. Walk fast, look straight ahead, and say *nothing*.'

The solicitor pointed at the two boys. 'The press are not allowed to ask you two questions about the criminal charges. If they try, I'll sue them.'

'Can they take our photos?' Noah asked, as he wondered what Sadie and his friends back home would make of what had happened.

'They can take photos, but they have to blur your faces if they print them in an article relating to any criminal allegations,' the solicitor said.

There were three steps at the side entrance, and the police had given the game away by coming out with a wheelchair ramp a few minutes earlier. As Jen opened the door, more than a dozen cameras flashed and a mob of photographers started shouting.

'These are juveniles,' the solicitor shouted, as he walked

out first. 'You know the rules.'

Noah glanced awkwardly at his dad, half excited, half freaked out. He set off down the ramp behind the solicitor, then wheeled towards the waiting taxi faster than anyone could run. His dad broke into a sprint behind him.

Theo grabbed his crotch with one hand and gave the cameras a two-fingered salute with the other. But the press knew they couldn't speak to Theo. Instead they focused on his mum.

'Mrs Richardson,' one of the journalists shouted. 'Your eldest son and your first husband are already behind bars. Do you expect Theo to join them soon?'

Theo's mum was about to swear, but Jen held a hand in front of her mouth. 'No comment.'

'Are you proud of the way you've brought up your children?' another journalist asked sarcastically, as they started a brisk walk towards the taxi.

'You want that camera stuck up your arse?' Theo asked, as he grabbed a lens and tried to tear it away from its owner's neck.

As the photographer stumbled, the journalists kept up their pursuit of Theo's mum.

'Mrs Richardson, can you confirm that you have eight children by three different fathers?'

'Screw you,' she shouted. 'I've worked bloody hard all my life. I've never claimed one penny in benefits.'

'Mrs Richardson, earlier in the year you were arrested and cautioned yourself after an incident with another parent at a battle of the bands competition. Do you think your children are following the example you set?'

'Leave my mum alone,' Theo roared, as Jen pushed her into the waiting taxi and climbed in behind.

The solicitor stayed on the pavement, shutting the taxi door and banging on the window to tell the driver that it was safe to go.

'Do you represent Mrs Richardson's interests?' one of the journalists asked. 'Would she be interested in telling us her side of the story?'

The taxi almost hit a photographer as it pulled away, while the one with Noah and his dad in the back was long gone. Once they'd settled in and done their seat belts up, Theo looked round and saw tears down his mum's cheek.

'Don't cry,' Theo said, reaching out to put an arm around her back.

'You!' she spat, exasperated. 'You're home for *one* bloody night, and this is what happens.'

Karen Trim was a superstar, and as a publicist Jen realised that the Karen Trim incident had turned Theo and his family into big news. Her job was to get *Rock War* as much publicity as possible, but it was supposed to be good publicity and she needed to understand where the journalists had got their information from.

'Oh I know who they spoke to,' Mrs Richardson answered, as she dabbed her eye with a Kleenex. 'Janey Jopling, superbitch.'

Jen looked baffled until Theo explained. 'That's Alfie and Tristan's mum.'

'You bloody wait until I set eyes on that cow,' Mrs Richardson said. 'And believe me, I've got *plenty* of dirt to dish on her.'

28. Back on the Farm

'Hey up!' Babatunde said cheerfully. He sat on a stool in his bathroom at Rock War Manor, filming his always-hooded torso in the mirror. 'So, I'm in bed Sunday morning, having a big lie-in. And my phone starts dinging and bleeping. First off, I thought it was because Summer's video had gone past a million hits. Then it was like, there's way too many noises for it to be that so I grab my phone and . . .

'I thought it was a wind-up. But then I click on a YouTube link and there's Theo getting battered by this *massive* dude and Noah doing his wheelchair rugby tackle on Karen Trim. It's on BBC news. It's on CNN. This morning it's front page on every tabloid. Jay's upset because they've written a bunch of stuff about his family. Making out like they're the world's biggest chavs or something.

'And Karen Trim! *I'm an equal opportunities bitch!* Attacking Noah in his wheelchair. Everyone's slagging her off, but I'd lay odds that she's loving every minute of it. And it's just as chaotic here at the manor. Our three celebrity judges are supposed to be unveiled on Wednesday. But our morning tutorials have been cancelled. They haven't even unlocked the stables, so we can't rehearse, and Zig Allen has called everyone together for some big meeting at ten.

'I'll try showing you one last thing before I go,' Babatunde said. 'If this camera's got a good enough zoom.'

Babatunde got off the stool and walked with the camera. After standing on the toilet lid, he opened a little sash window behind and went for maximum zoom. The image was shaky, but you could see what was going on.

'So that's the main gate for Rock War Manor,' he explained. 'Until yesterday I'd never seen *anyone* down there. Now there's sixty cameras on tripods, TV crews and a whole line of trucks and vans with satellite dishes on top. I think *Rock War* just hit the big time.'

*

Up in the attic, Zig Allen smashed his desktop phone into its receiver. Then he pulled it out, and smashed it back even harder.

'Karolina,' he shouted. 'Get your arse in here now.'

Zig's tall German deputy came in, looking nervous. 'I've just had three runners in here,' she began. 'The press are coming in through a side gate. They say there's a public right of way going through the manor, so we can't legally stop them.'

'Later,' Zig shouted. 'I've just had Rophan Hung from Rage Cola on the line. He's spitting blood. Are the kids gathered? I need to get them in line before they do any more damage.'

Down in the ballroom, Zig found all forty-eight contestants sprawled out on the beanbags, looking hot. The Karen Trim incident was playing on one of the big screens. Zig ordered a runner to switch it off then ordered a lone camera operator out, as he stepped in amongst the kids and stopped right in front of Theo.

'What is the first thing I told you when you arrived here?' Zig shouted furiously. 'The first thing? The very first thing?'

'The fire drill?' someone suggested.

'No!' Zig shouted. 'Not the bloody fire drill. What did I tell you about the sponsors? I told you never, ever, under any circumstances, to say or do anything that might upset the people who are paying the money to make *Rock War* happen.

'And what do I get?' Zig asked, after a dramatic pause. 'I have the most famous face in reality TV attacked by two of my contestants. I have a YouTube clip from *Shelly's Morning Break* that's already been watched twenty-one million times. And what does this idiot say, right in the middle of that clip?'

Zig paused again, and glowered at Theo.

'In the middle of that clip, Theo shit-for-brains Richardson says, *Rock War is proudly brought to you in association with Rage Cola and its magnificent range of diarrhoea-inducing beverages*. So guess what, kids? *#RageColaDiarrhoea* is trending on Twitter. We have more publicity than we can handle. We might even have a hit show on our hands.

'But I've just spent an hour on the phone with Rophan Hung from Rage Cola and they want to cut off the money. I still have a lot of begging to do, but the way things look right now, Rage Cola are pulling their sponsorship money. And without that money, there is no *Rock War*. I shit you not, children. That's how serious this is.

'So I want you all to stay in your rooms. You can use the pool on the roof, or this ballroom. But there are journalists sneaking on to the premises who you must *not* talk to. Do not leave this building. Don't tweet, don't Facebook, don't message your friends. To make sure, I'm sending the runners round to collect your phones and the Wi-Fi is being switched off. Now I'm going back up to my office to see if by some miracle I can save this show.'

As Zig stormed off, the contestants looked shocked. Three runners started collecting up phones, and Theo felt like everyone was staring at him.

'Don't blame me,' Theo said. 'We've all made jokes about Rage Cola.'

'But they get edited out, dumbass,' Sadie said. 'You said it on live TV during a studio invasion.'

One of the runners asked for his phone as Theo stomped towards the stairs up to his room. He was tempted to thump the runner, but in the end he just passed the phone over and kept walking. After Theo slammed his door two floors up, director Joseph began a more encouraging take on the situation.

'Ziggo has a terrific amount on his plate,' Joseph said.

The elderly director was always keen to gossip and he squatted on a footstool before continuing. 'Rage Cola are jolly cross, but Channel Six are over the moon. Their two big autumn talent shows have had a huge publicity boost. The dramatisation of *Gulliver's Travels* has had mediocre reviews, so they want to run *Rock War – Battle Zone* as a ninety-minute show at six thirty instead of for an hour at five thirty.'

'Prime time,' Michelle said, clapping. 'So *Rock War* will be on straight before *Hit Machine*?'

Lucy tutted. 'If Rage Cola doesn't pull the plug.'

'What about other sponsors?' Jay asked. 'If the show's looking like a hit, surely someone will step in. Or can't Channel Six pay to make their own show?'

Joseph shrugged. 'The economics of these matters is complex. But these sponsorship deals are usually set up months or years in advance. This is a very high-budget show. Rage Cola spent over two million just on the refurbishment of this house.'

'Isn't there like a contract or something?' Jay asked. 'How can Rage Cola just pull the plug?'

'Contracts running into hundreds of pages,' Joseph said. 'But those contracts would have all sorts of clauses to guarantee that Rage Cola is shown in a positive light. Zig might well sue Rage Cola. But we'll be kicked out of this manor long before he gets his day in court.'

29. Albino Gorilla

'Michelle here, with another peanut-hot vlog thingummy! Today's big questions are: *Is* Rock War *over? Are we all doomed to return to our humdrum little lives?*'

Michelle swung her camera around, revealing a dozen *Rock War* contestants squashed into her shower cubicle and the area around it. The bathroom lights were off, and they were trying to look spooky by shining torches up at their faces.

'We're doomed!' they all whispered creepily. 'Doomed!'

'My brother Theo's an idiot,' Jay added, from somewhere in the crowd. 'I knew it was a bad idea the moment I let him join my band.'

'But we have made one decision,' Michelle said. 'If Rage Cola shatters our youthful dreams of stardom and kicks us out of this house, we're not gonna leave without a fight. We'll smash every stick of furniture, use the toilet seats as Frisbees, throw our TVs out of the windows and wipe our asses on the curtains. Isn't that right, boys and girls?'

Cheers and whoops erupted from the bathroom.

'You *already* threw our TV out of the window,' Summer pointed out.

'Stay tuned, beloved viewers,' Michelle said ominously. 'The *Rock War* contestants will not be going anywhere without a bang.'

Michelle stopped recording, and everyone looked cheerful as they piled out of the bathroom.

'Jesus, who farted?' Dylan's band mate Leo asked.

'It was Noah,' Sadie said. 'I know his smell.'

'Oh you're a hoot,' Noah told his best friend, as he rolled out of the shower cubicle.

'One question,' Summer said thoughtfully. 'The Wi-Fi's off and they took our phones. How are you going to upload?'

Dylan answered for her. 'I've got an iPad with 4G data,' he announced. 'Signal's not great out here, but I can usually get a connection up by the pool.'

'Onwards,' Sadie shouted, as she led a charge out of Summer and Michelle's room. 'To the pool!'

*

Rock War was unravelling, but the weather remained perfect. Summer burned easily, so after a swim she grabbed a tub of Ben and Jerry's from the kitchen and a John Green book she'd borrowed from Coco, before chilling on beanbags in the ballroom.

Summer liked to read, but homework and looking after her nan made it a rare luxury. Irritatingly, now that she had nothing but free time, she had too many thoughts in her head to focus on the story.

Summer's instinctive feeling was that *Rock War* ending was bad. But she was shy and a big chunk of her kind of liked the idea of going back to Dudley, going to school, cooking dinner for her nan and watching junk TV.

Summer also had new feelings that she didn't understand. She'd puked before taking the stage at Rage Rock, but once the crowd got hooked on her voice, she'd felt a rush she was desperate to experience again. And while Theo's invasion of Channel Three got all the attention, she'd been sat on a BBC sofa, confidently answering questions from presenters, making jokes and subtly plugging *Rock War*, exactly like she'd been shown during media training.

Summer didn't really know what she wanted, as she laid the open book alongside her and tilted back to study the ballroom's ornate ceiling. But it seemed really weird that in two weeks she might be back at school, starting her GCSEs.

She wondered if she'd developed a taste for celebrity, but then she worked it out. What Summer really liked was that for the first time in her life it felt as if she mattered enough for someone other than her nan to care about what she did.

'Chef!' a runner shouted.

Summer sat up abruptly as two runners squeaked purposefully across the indoor basketball area at the room's far end. Matt had been around for a few weeks, while the frizzy-haired girl was the latest recruit to Zig's unpaid army.

The chef came out of the kitchen's swing doors. 'That

was bloody quick,' he noted.

Matt shook his head. 'We got up to the counter with our trolley stacked, but the credit cards are dead.'

'Which one?' Chef asked.

'Both,' Matt said.

'Did you have the right PIN?'

Matt nodded. 'I've used the card a dozen times. Worked fine last night when I put petrol in the minibus.'

'You'll have to go up and see Zig,' Chef said.

Matt didn't like the sound of that. 'He's in a shitty mood. I took a delivery up there earlier. He was yelling at the editors and his PA was almost in tears.'

'Well, what do you want me to do about that?' Chef said, as he pointed back towards his kitchen. 'There's forty-eight contestants and almost as many staff to cook for. So tell Zig, we need a wodge of cash or a bank card that works. Otherwise there's no dinner tonight.'

'Zig's got a Lamborghini,' the frizzy girl said, as Matt led her up to the top floor. 'He can't be short of a few quid.'

Summer wondered if she was some kind of financial jinx. Her nan was on benefits and Summer struggled to balance the shopping budget. Now she ends up on some big TV show, and they can't pay for food either . . .

*

There was still press camped out at the gates of Rock War Manor, but numbers were depleted because a pair of albino gorilla cubs were being unveiled less than five miles away at North Dorset Zoo.

Loyal photographers and the single remaining TV crew finally got rewarded for their week-long vigil when a black and gold helicopter swept over the top of the manor. Contestants around the rooftop pool saw the words *Karen Trim Productions* as it landed on the lawn, rotors blowing plastic chairs into the pool.

The public footpath that ran through Rock War Manor led to nowhere in particular and was rarely used by walkers. But it was a godsend for the press, who jogged past a hundred metres of wall before charging en masse through an unsignposted gate.

In best TV fashion, the helicopter landed twice. The first time, a two-man film crew jumped out of the cabin. Once a camera and boom mic were set up in the grass, the pilot took off and flew around in a tight circle before the camera filmed him landing again.

With the boot camp training programme suspended and their phones and Wi-Fi removed, contestants and crew poured out of the house to see what was going on. Zig and Joseph the director had a head start, and got the best view of Karen Trim's dramatic arrival.

Wearing gold ear protectors, sunglasses the size of dinner plates and pointy-heeled boots that didn't work too well on shaggy grass, Karen strutted theatrically towards her cameraman, before turning slightly and giving Zig two kisses on each cheek.

'Zig, Ziggy, Zig!' Karen said, as the press on the footpath snapped away. 'Long time no sees!'

'Hey,' Zig said, sweating, and clearly not comfortable with the camera. 'I thought this was a private meeting. Can we have this switched off?'

'They're filming a documentary about my UK comeback,' Karen explained, as she spotted Lorrie amongst the crowd of contestants and runners.

'You're doing *such* a great job as a presenter, my darling,' Karen told Lorrie, using the same fake voice as when she was a judge on *Hit Machine*. 'So young and fresh. Whatever happens with *Rock War*, you and I must have lunch.'

As Lorrie smiled helplessly, a couple of her former co-runners looked like they wanted to kick her up the arse.

'Runners are so great,' Karen told everyone, before pointing at Zig. 'That's how this young man got going. Zig was a runner on my first ever show. By the time *Hit Machine* started he was assistant unit director, then he decided to set up Venus TV to make some serious money of his own.'

'It's all true,' Zig said, flushing red with embarrassment.

After hearing that *Rock War* had lost its main sponsor, Karen Trim had called Zig for a meeting. Since Karen was allegedly worth half a billion and Zig was about to go broke, he hoped she was planning to offer financial help.

But Karen had spat blood when Zig set up his own company, and had spent years making snide remarks in the press that a lot of Zig's shows were just cheap rip-offs of hers. Few people would fly from Salford to Dorset to publically humiliate an ex-employee, but Zig reckoned Karen Trim was one of the ones who would.

'Do we have to have this guy filming us?' Zig repeated irritably, as he started leading Karen towards the manor, her cameraman in tow.

'Darling, I film everywhere I go,' Karen said. 'Now let's crack some numbers and see if we can patch up the holes and get this old boat of yours to float.'

30. Zigzag

'Karen Trim running *Rock War* will suck *so* hard,' Dylan said gloomily.

He was in the ballroom with a whole group of contestants and runners. Karen Trim had been upstairs in Zig's office for over two hours.

'Is she any worse than Zig?' Lucy asked. 'The guy's a total creep.'

Dylan shrugged. 'Karen's shows are all the same. The big set with the glitzy lights. The fake interviews. The crying contestants. *Rock War*'s more real. Can you imagine a *Hit Machine* contestant getting their own video diary? Or playing at a real rock festival, instead of in a TV studio?'

'They use Facebook and stuff,' Sadie said.

Dylan nodded. 'But it's all so sanitised and fake.'

'Oh yeah,' Lucy said. 'We're *never* fake.'

'Karen Trim's not stupid,' Summer said. 'Why would she change the stuff that makes *Rock War* a bit different?'

Noah laughed. 'I'm screwed if she does invest, after our on screen punch-up.'

Theo disagreed. 'You must be joking. The publicity that clip got probably made her millions.'

'Andy Warhol said that you should never read your publicity,' Jay said. 'You should just weigh it to see how much you get.'

'Who's Andy Warhol?' Noah asked.

'Some dude who liked publicity,' Jay said uncertainly. 'I think he played baseball.'

Summer tried to raise the gloomy mood. 'I just hope the show keeps going. Even if they make some changes, it's better than just going back to school, isn't it?'

'Totally,' Alfie agreed. 'The show may even be more popular with her in control.'

Michelle snorted. 'You two would say that.'

Summer was wary of biting on anything Michelle said, but Alfie was less experienced and sounded peeved.

'Why would we say that?' Alfie asked.

'Because,' Michelle began, acting like it was obvious, 'if Karen Trim gets her fangs into *Rock War* and cleans up our act, she'll get all the girly girls and grandmas watching. And who will they vote for? The girl with the amazing voice and the little cherub-faced kid who hasn't got pubes yet.'

'I have pubes,' Alfie shouted furiously. To prove his point, he shoved a hand down the front of his swimming shorts, tugged hard and emerged with a few wiry black hairs. 'There, what the hell are those, eh?'

'Was that all of them?' Dylan teased.

'Up yours,' Alfie said, giving everyone the finger as he slumped back on to his beanbag.

Everyone looked around when Joseph cut through towards the hallway.

'Hey, old man,' Theo shouted. 'Where you off to?'

'Cigarillos from the shop in the village,' Joseph said. 'Would you like me to fetch something?'

'I'm good,' Theo said. 'Any idea what's going on upstairs?'

Joseph gave a quick glance around and moved closer to the kids. 'Zig called me in to go over some financial details,' Joseph said in a conspiratorial voice. 'Zig says *Rock War* is going to be a hit show, with worldwide potential. He wants Karen Trim to buy a third of his company, in return for enough money to make this first season of *Rock War*. But Karen is playing hardball, reminding Zig that he's broke. She wants to take all of Venus TV's shows from Zig, and rename us *Karen Trim's Rock War*. In return, she's offered to pay off Zig's debts and save him the humiliation of going bankrupt.'

'Any sign of compromise?' Summer asked.

Joseph shook his head. 'They call Karen Trim "The Tank" for a reason. That lady doesn't negotiate, she blasts people into submission.'

*

As afternoon became evening, Zig's deputy, Karolina, got her hands on some cash to pay for groceries, while Karen Trim's helicopter stayed on the lawn. Contestants and runners staged a FIFA 14 tournament on the ballroom PlayStations, but even Alfie's epic penalty shootout win over Tristan only got a muted response.

It was hard to focus on anything while negotiations continued between Karen and Zig on the top floor. The pair were still locked in at dinner-time, though the growing consensus in the manor's dining-room was that it was only a matter of time before Zig gave in and *Rock War* joined Karen Trim's reality TV empire.

Just after eight p.m., Sadie and Noah had gone to their room. Sadie was a closet *EastEnders* fan and Noah half watched, half teased her about it, when there was a knock.

'We're masturbating,' Sadie said. 'Come back later.'

There was a running gag, where contestants made the grossest comments possible when someone knocked at their door. But the woman outside wasn't in on the joke.

'I need to speak with Noah,' Karen Trim said, aghast.

Noah broke into a huge grin, and Sadie covered her face as she turned bright red.

'Yeah, come in,' Noah said.

His grin didn't last, because Karen Trim was properly scary, and the last time he'd seen her close up he'd sent her flying with his wheelchair. The first thought in Noah's head was that Karen had done her deal with Zig and was about to kick him off the show. But Karen was all smiles.

'We didn't exactly get off on the best foot, did we?' Karen said.

Noah looked wary. 'That's one way of putting it,' he said.

'So, are you our boss now?' Sadie asked, back to her usual blunt self.

'I've made an offer,' Karen said. 'It may take Zig Allen a while longer to accept the reality of his position. But I'm not here to talk about that.'

'You tried to tip me out of my wheelchair on live TV, and that doesn't make you look too good,' Noah said.

Karen's eyes narrowed, like she was pissed off. But then she smiled, and gave one of her fake laughs. 'You can't bullshit a bullshitter, eh?' she said, smiling. 'For sure, it's good for my image if we kiss and make up. But in case you haven't noticed, *Rock War* is a popularity contest. My publicists will make sure the picture gets wide coverage, online and in the press, and that'll help raise you and your little band's profile too.'

Sadie interrupted. 'Who'll even care if our show dies and we get our asses flown back to Belfast?'

Karen gave Sadie a kind of *how-dare-you-interrupt* look. But Noah spoke before either could say anything.

'Ten thousand quid,' Noah said firmly.

'Oooh,' Karen said, smiling. 'That's a lot of money, young man.'

'Don't patronise me,' Noah said. 'You were in the *Sunday Times* Rich List. You're worth four hundred and fifty million, so ten grand to you is like me dropping a twenty-pence piece down the side of my chair.

'And the money's not for me. There's a little charity back in Belfast called Kids in Motion. They give disabled young people mobility training, and grants so that parents can afford stuff like running blades and lightweight wheelchairs for sports.'

Sadie looked proudly at Noah as Karen Trim tapped her nose.

'That'll work,' Karen said. 'The story will get more coverage if we swing the old charity angle.'

Then she stepped out of the room, where her entourage stood waiting. Noah and Sadie didn't hear the first bit of Karen's conversation, but half of Rock War Manor heard when she lost it with her assistant.

'I don't bloody know where you find a big cardboard cheque in the middle of Dorset at ten o'clock at night,' Karen shouted. 'But you either get me one by eleven, or your arse is fired.'

As Karen led her entourage away, Sadie jumped off her bed and surprised Noah with a soggy kiss on the cheek.

'I'll take back everything I've been saying about you,' Sadie joked. 'Standing up to Karen Trim like that was *officially* awesome.'

31. The Big Cheque

Karen Trim's assistant started by calling the press office of her bank. The bank called the manager of a local branch, thirty miles from Rock War Manor. The manager knew that he didn't have any giant cheques at his branch, but he'd once got a local printer to make one when the Mayor needed one at short notice.

The bank manager called the printer, who got out of bed at twenty past ten, opened his shop, printed a giant banner-size cheque and spray-mounted it on cardboard. The printer's van was being repaired after a minor accident, but the bank manager's sister-in-law lived nearby and was willing to drive it the thirty miles to Rock War Manor. She got lost on the way, but still arrived by ten past eleven.

Noah put one of his good shirts on and Karen Trim's cameraman took his photo with Karen and the big cheque. Then they did a selfie on Noah's phone and tweeted Kids in Motion to say that there was some money on the way.

Big cheques aren't real, but Karen promised that a real one would be sent to Kids in Motion's Belfast office the next morning. Noah didn't doubt it because she'd get unbelievably bad publicity if she promised money to charity and didn't follow through.

After painting on a smile for the photos, Karen headed to her helicopter for a flight back to *Hit Machine* HQ in Salford. She didn't like the fact that it was late and she'd had to shell out ten thousand pounds to get the picture she needed with Noah, so before boarding, Karen fired her assistant and refused to let her on.

'Not a nice lady,' Sadie told Noah, watching the helicopter blast off, as Karen's sobbing ex-assistant walked towards the house. 'If she takes over, I might just quit on principle.'

*

'People, gather up!' Joseph shouted.

Dressed in a flat cap, with his usual cardigan and slip-on shoes, the grandfatherly director waited patiently while forty-eight contestants came out of bedrooms, or drifted in from breakfast in the dining-room. There were even a couple of towel-wrapped girls who'd got up early to swim laps.

Zig's stern deputy, Karolina, stood alongside as Joseph began an announcement.

'I have good news,' Joseph said, holding his arms aloft.

'Karen Trim died in a helicopter crash and left us all her money?' Sadie suggested.

Joseph couldn't help joining the laughter. 'No such luck,

my dear. But I am very proud to announce that we have a show to make.'

There were a few claps, and cheers.

'Due to our budgetary constraints and the withdrawal of Rage Cola as sponsors, we won't be engaging our high-paid celebrity judges, or continuing with the full boot camp training programme. However, there continues to be monstrous public and media interest in *Rock War*. "Summer Smith sings Patti Smith" and "Theo vs Karen Trim" have been viewed millions of times on YouTube. Since Miss Trim's visit yesterday, we have more press than ever camped out at the front gate. And reruns of *Rock War* episodes are getting record viewing figures for a show on 6point2.

'So, while there is still no permanent deal in place, Channel Six have advanced us enough money to keep the lights on here at the manor for a few more days. They have also asked us to produce an eighty-minute compilation show, to be named *Rock War – The Story So Far*.

'This will be the first outing for *Rock War* on Channel Six's main channel. It will be broadcast this coming Saturday at seven p.m. For the most part, the show will be a compilation of material from the earlier bi-weekly episodes. Since Summer and Theo are our two online superstars, the show will climax with the pair of them singing a specially recorded duet.'

Theo gave Summer a thumbs-up. 'You and me, sister!'

Summer felt like everyone was looking at her and half smiled at Theo, before going bright red. But several other contestants weren't so happy.

'What about our bands?' Michelle asked. 'Isn't that what *Rock War* is supposed to be about?'

Joseph's nod showed some sympathy. 'It's far from perfect,' he agreed. 'I would be as delighted as you if the money fairy waltzed through the door, wrote us a big fat cheque and told us to spend it however we like. That's very unlikely to happen, but the compilation show and the lifeline from Channel Six will give Zig more time to find a partner that everyone wants to work with.'

Joseph seemed a decent guy and everyone nodded in agreement, or at least didn't make any more fuss.

Karolina handled the next part of the announcement in her authoritative German accent.

'There's one other thorny issue with continuing the show,' Karolina announced. 'Rage Cola have sent us a threatening legal letter. They're insisting that all Rage Cola branding be removed from Rock War Manor before any new filming can take place. Some of the runners have already started working on this, but we're operating with minimum levels of staff and crew to keep down costs. So, if some of you contestants would be willing to help remove—'

'Let's trash this joint!' Michelle shouted, punching the air.

Karolina didn't look pleased and raised her voice. 'If some of you could *safely* and *sensibly* give the runners a hand to remove Rage Cola branded items from around the house, your help would be enormously appreciated.'

32. Five Point Three

Saturday

'So this is my arm,' Michelle told her camera. 'Well, obviously it's my arm. But as you can see it's now got a lovely gash and twenty-two stitches. We got carried away taking out all the Rage Cola stuff. Me and Theo ended up at opposite ends of the ballroom, with vending machines on four-wheeled dollies. The idea was for us to wheel the machines towards each other and have a big smash in the middle.

'Trouble is, I'm titchy, and Theo's massive. So I'm trundling along trying to wheel this machine, and I can see Theo charging towards me with his machine, practically sprinting. I realised it wasn't going to end well for me, so I chickened out and tried to back away.

'Theo's vending machine hit mine, and there was this massive bang. Somehow my arm went through the clear plastic and . . . Well, you can all see the result for yourselves.'

Michelle kept recording as she stood up. Summer took

Michelle's spot on the edge of her bed and started her own diary message.

'Dear video diary,' Summer said, smiling at the irony of the situation. 'This is a joint entry, because what Michelle didn't mention is that her camcorder was gaffer-taped to the vending machine, and it came out of the smash-up in an even worse state than her arm.'

'The memory card survived though,' Michelle said. 'Seventy thousand YouTube hits and counting!'

'The last few days have been pretty fun,' Summer continued. 'Channel Six sent these four massive bouncers to stop the press from straying off the public path. So we've been allowed back out to the rehearsal rooms. There's been no word about Karen Trim. Zig's getting stressed because he's almost bankrupt. I don't think he's showered for a few days and he's snarling at everyone.

'Zig's not letting us have our phones or Wi-Fi back because he's in *delicate negotiations* and doesn't want us causing any more controversy. I don't really care, because I have the cheapest, crappiest phone, with no internet or anything on it. And I can still call my nan from the office whenever I want.'

'You're such a pov, Summer,' Michelle sneered.

Summer was slightly irritated, but nodded in agreement. 'I'm a pov,' she confessed. 'But the main thing I've been doing is me and Theo had to rehearse and record our duet. It's this song called "Fairytale of New York". The original version is sung by this weird-looking Irish guy called

Shane McGowan. He's got a dead gruff way of singing which is a lot like Theo. And the female part suits my voice pretty well too.

'The strangest part is that it's August, but "Fairytale" is a Christmas song. Rather than try to hide the fact, Joseph hired a snow machine. We've made this video of the song which is totally hilarious. Me and Theo are singing by the pool in bright sunshine, but there's this absolutely stupid amount of snow pelting us. They've actually cut two versions of the video. There's a more serious one which will go out during the TV show, and another version which has loads of scenes of mayhem from *Rock War* edited in. I think they'll be putting that version on YouTube.'

*

The eight big screens along one side of the ballroom were all set to the same channel. *Rock War* logos had been positioned in slots where there had once been vending machines, and with all the Rage Cola branded beanbags gone, the contestants had to snuggle with pillows dragged down from their rooms.

The contestants were being filmed, while crew - from the freshest unpaid runner to Zig Allen - sat along the opposite wall in chairs taken from the dining-room. A *Hit Machine* advertisement drew some boos, before the row of screens cut to a revolving Channel Six logo. The station announcer sounded unusually excited.

'*Now on Channel Six – and in a change to some listings – it's time to bring you bang up to date with the talent show that can't seem to keep out of the headlines. This is* Rock War – The Story So Far.'

After a brief flash of the Venus TV logo, the screens cut to a shot of Summer, standing in her little bedroom, with her two half-packed bags-for-life resting on a tangled bed. A title appeared at the bottom, *First day of the summer holidays.*

'Hi! *My name's Summer Smith. I'm fourteen years old and I'm the lead singer with Industrial Scale Slaughter . . . Sorry, can I do that again?*'

No one got to see what happened next, because there was a jump-cut. First to a shot at sunrise, of Noah going up a lift into a RyanAir plane.

'*Has there ever been a rock star in a wheelchair?*' Noah asked, in voice-over. '*I can't think of one, but I wanna be the first.*'

The final shot of this intro sequence was of Mrs Richardson, standing at the bottom of a staircase.

'*Jay, Theo, Adam,*' she yelled. '*I cooked breakfast for you idle BLEEPs. The least you can do is get your skid-marked butts out of bed and come down here to eat it.*'

Then the screen made a jump-cut to the *Rock War* logo, and there was a sound of electric guitars, before THE STORY SO FAR slammed down over the logo and made it shake.

For eighty minutes, the contestants in the ballroom laughed, mocked their on-screen appearances, drank supermarket-brand cola and scoffed Pringles. Up back, Zig took a couple of complimentary phone calls, and cheered up a touch as he joined the rest of the crew, downing beers, wine and whatever else they could raid from the kitchen.

Theo and Summer's grand finale was the only thing specially filmed for the compilation show and it didn't really fit with the documentary style of everything that went before. But it was well done and got some good laughs.

As the end titles rolled, the contestants were chuffed. They'd been sold on a show that was about rock music, and different to all the other cheesy, glitzy talent shows, and that was exactly how this *Rock War* special had looked on screen.

By now, Zig was completely sloshed and stumbled half a step before speaking. He had a huge red wine stain down his shirt.

'I don't know if we're going to survive,' Zig began sadly. 'I haven't slept for a week with the stress. But through my tired eyes, that looked like a damned fine TV show.'

Everyone clapped, and there were a few whoops and cheers, especially from the young runners, who were mostly wasted.

'Karen Trim called this morning,' Zig slurred. 'She asked me if I'd seen sense and was willing to accept her offer to buy *Rock War*. Maybe it's just pride. Maybe I'm a dick, but I told that hag-faced bitch that I'd rather go broke than let her get her fat trotters on my show.'

Zig got the biggest cheer of the night for this. Even though Karen Trim seemed like the only person with the money to bail out *Rock War*, contestants and crew increasingly seemed to agree that they'd rather *Rock War* went down the toilet than have her take it over.

As Zig moved to sit back down, Karolina held the screen

of an iPad in front of his face.

'IAB, five point three,' Zig shouted, as he punched the air. 'Holy guacamole! Five point three!'

Joseph and some of the other senior crew stood up to shake Zig's hand, but none of the contestants knew what IAB was. Lorrie hadn't touched alcohol since her night with Theo and was studying TV production at university, so she explained to the contestants.

'IAB stands for Independent Audience Bureau,' Lorrie explained. 'They have an electronic system that monitors viewing habits in thousands of homes and estimates how many people watch every show. Five point three means that they estimate five point three million people just watched *The Story So Far*.'

Is that good?' Dylan asked.

'It's superb,' Lorrie said. 'The highest-viewed shows in the UK are soap operas like *Coronation Street* and *EastEnders*. They typically get around ten million viewers. Five point three is still very respectable. It's in line with popular shows like *Masterchef*, or *Top Gear*.'

Karolina had walked across to help Lorrie out. 'It's probably the highest audience Channel Six has had since *Hit Machine* was at its peak,' the German explained. 'And the more viewers a show gets, the more money you can charge for advertising.'

'So we won't need Karen Trim's money?' Jay suggested.

'*Rock War* is a very expensive show to produce,' Karolina said. 'We still need a new sponsor, but these viewing figures could make finding that sponsor a lot easier.'

Lucy Wei had been sitting down for nearly two hours. She did a big stretch and peeled her sweaty vest away from her back.

'Get me a Coke while you're up, sis,' Michelle asked.

'Get it yourself, you lazy cow,' Lucy said, as she stepped over the outstretched legs of her band mates before heading out to get some air.

She passed through the kitchen, where a couple of runners were making out, and found Dylan outside the back door, smoking a cigarette.

'Gimme a drag,' Lucy said, then, 'Mmm,' as she sucked in the smoke.

'I'm running low,' Dylan said. 'My dad's supposed to be sending me two hundred Russian cigarettes and a big bag of weed.'

Lucy laughed. 'Your *dad*?'

Dylan shrugged like it wasn't a big deal. 'Dad says I'm old enough to kill myself if I want to.'

'I don't even smoke, really. But my dad would go ape-shit if he even saw me take one puff. What does your dad do?' Lucy asked.

'Music publishing,' Dylan lied. Then he changed the subject. 'I thought the show was really good.'

'It was,' Lucy agreed.

'I need a piss,' Dylan said, holding out the cigarette. 'You wanna finish this?'

'I guess,' Lucy said.

Lucy wasn't a hardened smoker, so she took two more drags before squishing the cigarette under her All Stars. She liked the way it got properly dark in the countryside and was tempted to take a little walk and get away from the noise inside, but Zig came out before she got the chance.

'My favourite queen bee,' Zig said sourly.

Lucy got a chill down her back. It was the first time they'd spoken since Zig made his threat about Industrial Scale Slaughter having no chance of winning. He had booze breath and looked like he'd not slept or showered in days.

'I've worked my balls off to save this show,' Zig slurred. 'Can't sleep, you know? I close my eyes, but my brain keeps running. Then on top of it all I get this call, from some smartass lawyer.'

'I'm going back inside,' Lucy said.

'No you're not,' Zig said, getting in Lucy's way. He grabbed her wrist when she tried to barge past, then forced her back against the wall.

'I'll scream,' Lucy threatened.

'All the shit I'm going through,' Zig hissed. 'And you get your daddy's lawyer to make threats!'

As Zig said this, he gripped Lucy's upper arm, digging in with his thumbnail.

Lucy gritted her teeth. 'Get your hand off, before I take it off.'

Lucy wasn't strong enough to push Zig away, so she brought her knee up hard between his legs.

'Sleazebag,' Lucy yelled, as Zig stumbled back.

She'd only hurt Zig enough to make him angry and he charged forwards and tried to grab Lucy's hair. Zig was stronger, but Lucy was fast and sober. She ducked, and without really knowing how, managed to whack Zig's nose with a flying elbow.

Zig stumbled backwards, blood dripping into the hand cupped around his nose. Lucy scrambled back into the kitchen. The two runners making out looked around. Part of Lucy wanted to do the right thing and report Zig's behaviour. *What if he attacked someone smaller, like Summer or Alfie?*

But on the other hand, she knew Zig would deny everything, and it was doubly awkward because a lot of people at the manor currently viewed Zig as the plucky underdog, fighting to save *Rock War* from the evil grasp of Karen Trim.

The two runners decided to ignore Lucy and resume snogging, but before she made it to the other side of the kitchen there was a distinctive blast from a V12 engine.

One of the two guys making out looked at Lucy. 'Is that Zig's Lamborghini?'

His partner looked annoyed as the young runner headed out the back door.

'Get back here,' the older runner moaned. 'Zig's a big boy.'

'Mr Allen,' the runner shouted, as he ran towards the revving car. 'You can barely walk.'

But the bright orange car was more than fifty metres away,

and there was no way Zig would have heard over the massive engine stacked behind his head.

Lucy followed the runner outside, in time to see Zig floor the accelerator. The powerful car lit up its tyres, then a back wheel churned up turf as it caught grass on a corner. It was hard to say how fast the car was moving, but Lucy and the two runners made it around the side of the house in time to see it rip towards the main gates.

Zig had an electronic plipper, so the manor's gates were open as he arrived, but the press parked out front were scrambling to get their tripods out of the road, and at least one photographer decided to abandon his equipment.

Fortunately – for the photographer at least – Zig was very drunk and the gates were designed for the width of an Edwardian carriage, rather than the much greater width of an Italian super-car. By the time Zig realised he'd messed up, even the car's huge ceramic brakes couldn't save him.

The front of the car deformed as it hit the post, but it still had enough momentum to grate along the side. The orange carbon fibre bodywork shattered along the entire right-hand side, sending spears of plastic in all directions as photographers dived for cover. The car's engine cut out on impact, and the press pack standing nearby jolted as several air bags exploded.

The instant the car stopped moving, a huge swarm of photographers began snapping photographs, while contestants and crew ran down from the house.

'Mr Allen?' a journalist shouted, as he raised the car's

scissor door, letting out a cloud of white smoke from the air bags. 'Mr Allen, are you OK?'

'Leave me alone,' Zig shouted, as the burly journalist pulled him out of the car.

A dozen cameras flashed as Zig stood, bloody-nosed, slowly turning around to survey the shattered body of his £300,000 car.

'No pictures, you jackals,' Zig slurred. 'Get those cameras out of my face.'

'Mr Allen, how much have you had to drink?' a journalist asked.

'Is it true that Rage Cola are planning to sue Venus TV for twenty million pounds in reputational damage?'

'Mr Allen, is it true that Karen Trim is trying to buy your company at a knock-down price?'

'Don't mention that woman's name in my presence,' Zig shouted, as blood continued to stream from his nose. 'If I ever see Karen Trim again, I'll strangle the cow. And let me tell you, if that woman dies, a whole lot of cosmetic surgeons will go out of business.

'As for Rage Cola, Unifoods or whatever you call them, I'm past caring about those assholes and their family values. Now get out of my way. I'm going home, and I'm gonna drink until I pass out.'

But Zig only made it four paces before falling flat on his face. Several cameras filmed as he gave off mighty sobs and peed in his trousers.

33. Bournemouth Kiss

It was 8:28 on Monday morning. Channel Six boss, Mitch Timberwolf, celebrity chef Joe Cobb and Zig's deputy, Karolina, sat at a long desk at the end of the ballroom. The contestants had been told to stay in their rooms and keep quiet, while TV crews set up and journalists got inside Rock War Manor for the first time.

Because Channel Six was a public company, announcements had to be made in line with Stock Exchange rules. Mitch waited until exactly 8:30 before clearing his throat and starting to speak.

'I don't think I've ever seen so many journalists gathered in the middle of Dorset,' the executive joked. 'If *Rock War* starts generating money the way it has been generating publicity over this past month, you'll hopefully be writing articles about my obscene bonus payment before too much longer.'

After getting a good laugh, Mitch began reading from a

prepared statement.

'I am happy to announce that Channel Six PLC, along with a consortium which includes my good friend and well-known chef Joe Cobb, can this morning announce the joint purchase of Venus TV, from Zig Allen.

'This deal will secure the future of Venus TV as a vibrant, independent, television production company. It also secures the long-term future of hit Channel Six shows, such as *Cobb's Kitchen*, *Benefit Bludgers* and, of course, *Rock War*. Questions?'

'Where's Zig Allen?' a man from the BBC shouted.

'Zig Allen has been suffering from high stress levels. He is currently resting in a private healthcare facility. He will have no further involvement with Venus TV. On behalf of myself and everyone at Channel Six, I would like to wish Mr Allen a speedy return to health.'

'We understand that Karen Trim was negotiating to take control of *Rock War*. Is she one of your investors?'

Mitch shook his head. 'Karen Trim was unable to finalise her deal with Zig Allen. She is not part of the Channel Six consortium.'

'Will Karen Trim be angry that you've pinched Venus TV from under her nose?' a posh woman asked.

Mitch smiled unconvincingly. 'Karen Trim is a valued member of the Channel Six family. We intend to work together to make the new series of *Hit Machine* a huge success.'

'How large a stake is Channel Six taking in Venus TV?'

'As per the formal disclosure statement issued to the London Stock Exchange, Channel Six will take a fifteen per cent stake in Venus TV, and has agreed a deal to secure the long-term future of several of our biggest shows. Cobb Entertainment will take a ten per cent stake. The new owner of the other seventy-five percent of Venus TV has chosen not to disclose their holdings at this time.'

'Will *Rock War* have a new sponsor?'

Mitch shook his head. 'Our sponsors seem extremely keen to advertise during *Rock War*. Given the excellent viewing figures for Saturday's show, I'm confident that Channel Six can cover its costs from commercials, without the need for direct sponsorship.'

'Mr Timberwolf, would Karen Trim simply have become too powerful if she'd taken control of so many of Channel Six's biggest shows?' a bearded journalist asked. 'There have been rumours in the past that she might even bid to take control of Channel Six itself.'

Mitch straightened his tie and eyeballed the reporter. 'I've said *everything* I have to say about Karen Trim. She's a valuable part of the Channel Six family, and I hope that remains the case for many years to come.'

An intense journalist with a French accent spoke next. 'With all this publicity and given Saturday's excellent IAB viewing figures, do you think it's possible that *Rock War* could actually be a bigger show than *Hit Machine*?'

'It is my hope that both shows will be immensely popular,' Mitch said, diplomatically. 'Channel Six viewers will have a very exciting schedule for their Saturday evenings between now and Christmas.'

*

With Zig gone, Karolina was in charge. The tall, composed German needed to replace Zig's TV experience, and started by rehiring Julie, the assistant Karen Trim had fired three nights earlier.

With the show's future secured, Venus TV had money to spend. Among the first acts were the erection of a press tent inside the main gates and the arrival of a construction crew to tile over the giant Rage Cola label in the bottom of the swimming pool.

Shortly before lunch, Karolina switched the Wi-Fi back on, and arranged for all the contestants to get their phones back. They made a little show of it, presenting phones and tablets to eager kids on a velvet cushion with gold piping.

The crew had been slashed to a minimum when Rage Cola pulled out, but familiar faces, like Mo the music director and Shorty the cameraman, began arriving back at the manor. Joseph called Lorrie and all of the senior crew members into a meeting.

Boot Camp's six-week format had been disrupted by the loss of Rage Cola and the decision to make the *Story So Far* episode. But while the crew had to rejig the show, the contestants had been confined to the manor for almost a week and were going nuts.

The nearest decent-sized town was Bournemouth. To lose the press, the contestants sneaked out the back of the house and hiked half a mile where they were picked up by a coach. Everyone was rowdy as they set off on the thirty-minute drive.

After a stop for Eve to throw up, they arrived in Bournemouth and split into groups. Jay spent an hour wandering shops with Sadie, Noah and Babatunde. Zig's drunken Lamborghini crash had made the front page of every Sunday newspaper, but they were surprised to see their show getting plenty of coverage on Monday's front pages too.

The most popular story, *TRIM FLIES IN TO BUY ROCK WAR*, was already out of date. But a couple of the trashier newspapers were running a story about one of the girls in Half Term Haircut, whose older brother was apparently serving time after an horrific car accident in which three school kids got killed at a bus stop: *ROCK WAR BROTHER DOES LIFE*.

'I hope the press don't start digging dirt on my family,' Noah said. 'Mind you, they're all pretty boring.'

Jay smirked. 'If any journalist starts digging dirt on *my* family, they'll probably end up being killed by the avalanche.'

'Theo's all right though,' Noah said.

'You love Theo,' Sadie teased. 'He's your idol.'

'Piss off,' Noah said defensively. 'Everyone goes on about Theo, but he's always been decent to me.'

Jay nodded. 'Theo's a nutter, but he actually has a moral compass. Like, he'd steal from a supermarket, but he wouldn't rob a charity. He'd give someone a slap if they piss him off, but he wouldn't beat them senseless.

'My eldest brother Danny and my younger brother Kai are the real shits. Danny's been banged up since he was sixteen. He robbed a betting shop with his dumb mate. Brained the assistant manager with a rubber cosh and battered the woman on the counter. The idiots thought they'd get a pile of money, but all they got was eighty quid from the tills. The rest was in a timed dropbox that none of the staff had access to.'

'How long's he in for?' Babatunde asked.

'Not long enough,' Jay said. 'I'm dreading the day Danny comes home. If I do make it big, I might just drop someone ten grand to take him and Kai out.'

Noah smiled. '*ROCK STAR'S 10K TO MURDER BROTHERS*,' he said. 'That would *definitely* make the news.'

'My family's not that exciting,' Babatunde said. 'My parents want me to follow in their footsteps and become a doctor, which is ironic because all they ever do is bitch about how awful their jobs are.'

Noah's wheelchair made him one of the most recognisable people on *Rock War*. The quartet got stopped by sunburned teen sisters as they neared a rendezvous with the others at the Odeon cinema. The girls wanted an autograph, but nobody had a pen, or paper.

'It's such a cool show,' the younger of the two girls said.

'So who will you be voting for to win?' Babatunde asked. 'Jet, I hope.'

The girls both shrugged, before the older one admitted,

'Summer's voice is amazing.'

Younger sis nodded. 'But her band's not that great. What kind of music is it again?'

'Thrash metal,' older sis said. 'It's just crap!'

Babatunde looked at Jay as they headed off the opposite way to the sisters. 'Summer's gonna win *Rock War*,' he said solemnly. 'I think the rest of us are fighting over who gets to be runner-up.'

'It's not certain,' Jay said. 'Summer's voice gives Industrial Scale Slaughter a wow factor. But they're no way the best band in the competition.'

'One Direction finished runners-up on *X Factor*,' Noah pointed out. 'They seem to be doing OK.'

By this time the Odeon cinema was in sight and some of the others were already waiting outside. A few of the girl contestants – and a couple of reluctant boyfriends – were going to see some romantic comedy. But all the boys wanted to see *Guardians of the Galaxy*.

The afternoon showing only had a few people in each row, so everyone spread out. Jay looked around and smiled when Summer sat next to him.

'Gotta love a hunky superhero,' Summer said, smiling broadly.

'Popcorn?' Jay asked, tilting the big box towards her. 'It's just salted.'

Summer grabbed a handful as another advert came on.

'Put the bastard film on,' Theo shouted, as he lobbed an empty Coke bottle across the cinema.

Summer smirked. 'He'll get kicked out in a minute.'

'Hopefully,' Jay said.

Summer thumped his arm gently. 'He's your brother.'

Jay tutted. 'So, you're another in the long line of girls who's fallen for Theo's charms?'

Summer smiled. 'Well, he's got a torso like an underwear model and he was surprisingly easy to work with when we rehearsed our duet. But . . .'

Summer paused like she wasn't sure whether to say something or not.

'But what?' Jay asked.

'I'd go for brains over brawn any day,' Summer said, before leaning across and kissing Jay gently on the lips.

Jay tried to be cool, but couldn't stop himself breaking out in a helpless smile. After freezing for a couple of seconds, he nervously put his arm around Summer's back. She put her head on Jay's shoulder and grabbed more popcorn.

'I've been waiting ages for you to make a move,' Summer said softly. 'I was starting to think you didn't really like me.'

34. Judge Not

Tuesday

There was talk of hiring a big-name presenter for upcoming battle zone rounds, but for now, ex-runner Lorrie remained the face of *Rock War*. She held a big umbrella, as lightning flashed and rain pelted the gravel in front of Rock War Manor.

'Over the past six weeks, the *Rock War* contestants have had a lot of fun. They've been to glamorous parties, they've been tutored by top talent and they've all made friends. But now it's time to get—'

Lorrie stopped speaking as a gust of wind caught her umbrella, strong enough to knock her off balance.

'Cut,' Angie the director shouted.

'Can we do this inside?' Lorrie begged. 'My back is soaked.'

'It's all about atmosphere,' Angie said. 'We're trying to create drama, and this weather is perfect. Take it again from *now it's time*.'

'Quiet on set!' Angie's assistant shouted.

'Sound!'

'Camera rolling!'

'And, action!'

'But now it's time to get serious,' Lorrie said, keeping going as another gust blew up her hairdo. 'We're awaiting the arrival of our three rock legends. After each of our twelve bands performs live on Saturday night, the legends will give them marks out of ten. Then, it will be down to you, the viewer, to cast your votes by phone and save one of the three lowest-scoring bands.'

'Cut,' Angie said, giving Lorrie a double thumbs-up. 'Spot on, Lorrie, thanks for persevering.'

As Lorrie dashed inside, where a runner handed her towels and a make-up man set about fixing her hair, the crew started working on the next shot. Set-up took half an hour, arranging six cameras, lights and getting forty-eight reluctant contestants to line up in the rain.

By the time they were ready, and the camera drone was in position, fifty metres up, the rain had died off. Angie called, 'We're burning ten grand's worth of tyres here. It's a one-shot deal. Is everybody ready?'

Because there were cameras by the gate, along the path and in front of the house, the assistant director signalled *action* by firing a starting pistol.

Three red Ferraris rolled through the main gate, its pillar still scarred from its encounter with Zig's Lamborghini. With stunt drivers at the wheel and rock legends in the passenger seats, the cars sped up the path towards the front of the house.

When the first Ferrari got close to Lorrie and her microphone it slowed like it was about to stop. But then the driver floored the accelerator, lighting up the back tyres and leaving her standing in a rubbery haze. As the first Ferrari spun donuts on the courtyard in front of the house, the second and third joined in.

Half choked by rubber smoke and deafened by exhausts tuned to be extra noisy, the contestants laughed and clapped as the three cars finally stopped in front of them. The legends emerged and started walking towards Lorrie. There was a middle-aged man with straggly hair, a punkish woman in a black kaftan and a hot young guy in cowboy boots, tight jeans and mirrored sunglasses.

'How was that for you?' Lorrie asked, sticking a microphone in the middle-aged man's face.

He spoke with a working-class London accent. 'I'm 'ere,' he told Lorrie. 'But I think my guts are still somewhere back down the road.'

Once all three legends stood alongside Lorrie, she cleared her throat and tried to ignore the rubber smoke stinging her eyes.

'If you don't know already,' Lorrie began, 'this is guitarist Earl Haart. He's sold over twenty million albums and his guitar riff on "Find My Love" was voted the greatest of all time by Terror FM listeners.

'Our second legendary judge,' Lorrie said, as she put her

microphone in front of the punkish woman, 'is Beth Winder. Singer with eighties band Gristle, sometime actress, composer of scores for more than thirty movies and nominated for two Best Soundtrack Oscars. Welcome to *Rock War!*'

'Good to be here,' Beth said. 'I'm a massive fan of the show. So many talented young bands, playing proper music!'

Some of the contestants cheered as Beth punched the air.

'Last, but definitely not least,' Lorrie said, as she smiled at the handsome young cowboy, 'Jack Pepper is an indie sensation. His albums have sold millions of copies around the world, he's also written two novels and set up the Peace Camp charity, which has helped to educate hundreds of thousands of children living in refugee camps around the world. All that and he's still only twenty-four years old! Jack, it's *so* great to have you here!'

Jack pushed down his shades and gave Lorrie an intense stare. 'Can I get your number?' he asked. 'You're beautiful.'

Lorrie turned bright red and some of the girl contestants went *oooh* as Jack kissed her on the cheek. Jay saw the way Summer was looking at Jack and felt wildly jealous.

'There's a guy who gets to have a *lot* of sex,' Babatunde noted.

'So . . .' Lorrie stuttered, showing her inexperience as Jack looked very pleased with himself. 'Jack . . . Over the next three days, each legend is going to be tutoring four bands, honing their performance for this weekend's show.

Are you looking forward to the challenge?'

'Baby,' Jack said, flicking up his left eyebrow and staring Lorrie in the eyes. 'I'm always up for a challenge.'

*

Jay had been on good form since getting off with Summer the previous day. There was the *I've got a girlfriend* thrill, followed by the new-found respect from his male peers when he'd spent half the evening cuddling and snogging Summer on a poolside lounger.

But if having a girlfriend was great, having one of the world's greatest guitarists come into Jet's rehearsal room as well seemed ridiculous. Jay kept expecting to wake up at home, with his mum yelling and brother Kai about to thump him.

'You're a quiet bunch,' Earl Haart said, as he walked into the former stable, followed by a runner, filming on a little camcorder.

The floor was cobbled and the air sticky because the door provided the only ventilation. The runner squatted against the wall and screwed a wide-angle adaptor over her lens, so she could get a decent shot in the cramped space.

Earl reached out to shake hands. Jay, Theo, Adam and Babatunde introduced themselves politely, before Earl dragged a piano stool out of a corner and squatted on it.

'So you're North London boys?' Earl said. 'Whereabouts?'

'Do you know Tufnell Park?' Adam asked.

'My old student stomping ground,' Earl said warmly. 'I studied maths at North London Polytechnic. Played some of my first gigs in the student union and the pubs thereabouts. Happy days!'

Adam smiled. 'It's North London *University* now. We get loads of students from there in our ma's fish and chip shop at lunch-time.'

'Good fish and chips . . .' Earl said fondly. 'Bloody hard to get now. It's all McDonald's and five pound for a cup of poncy coffee. I used to go to the chippy just down the road. Next to the White Horse pub.'

Jay looked up from his guitar. Now he *knew* he was dreaming.

'That's our mum's,' Adam said proudly. 'Been in our family more than fifty years. And the pub next door as well.'

'Small bloody world,' Earl said. 'The old man who ran the place. Big 'tache, hard as nails. Anybody gave him trouble he'd be over the counter and BAM. Punch their lights out!'

'That was our grandad,' Adam said.

'How's he doing?' Earl asked. 'Must be in his seventies now.'

'Died before any of us were born,' Adam said. 'Cancer.'

'Pity,' Earl said. 'I remember the alley around the side. Shagged this girl down there, and I swear to god, she kept eating her chips the whole time.'

The four members of Jet all started laughing.

'They should put one of those blue plaques in the alleyway,' Theo suggested, as everyone kept laughing. '*Earl Haart – rock guitarist – shagged a bird here, 1980.*'

'It was seventy-four,' Earl corrected.

'So, you still live in London?' Babatunde asked.

'Flat in Chelsea,' Earl said. 'But I moved out to LA in the late seventies to avoid tax. Ex-wives, kids and grandkids are all in California, so I guess that's home now.'

As the conversation lapsed, Earl reached forwards and tapped Jay's knee.

'Let's hear it, then.'

'Uh?' Jay said dopily, looking up from his guitar.

'He's got a girl on his mind,' Adam explained.

'Batting some way out of his league,' Babatunde added.

'Well, he's strumming my riff,' Earl said indignantly. 'So let's hear it, young Jay.'

Jay had a brain clogged with thoughts, and wasn't even aware that he'd been plucking Earl's famous riff from 'Find My Love'.

'Sorry,' Jay said. 'You must get sick of hearing that.'

Earl laughed. 'I never get sick of hearing "Find My Love". As far as I'm concerned, that song is the sound of money pouring into my bank account. Now play it, kiddo!'

Jay felt dead uncomfortable as he reached down to turn up the volume on his guitar amp. He didn't know the riff well, and was surprised by how well it came out.

'Looks like we have a decent guitar player in the room,' Earl said, as he stood up and gestured for Jay to hand over his guitar. 'Can you play it like this?'

The runner crept around to get a better shot, as Earl hooked Jay's guitar over his neck, then swung it behind his back. Earl's hands had to twist awkwardly to reach the fret board, but he didn't even look around as he played his most famous riff behind his back.

'Is it true you can do it with your teeth as well?' Jay asked.

'I could,' Earl said. 'Back in the days when I had my own teeth.'

After another lull, Earl said, 'So, before we get to work, I'd like to hear you boys play a tune.'

As the boys debated what song they should play for Earl, they heard Michelle shouting on the lawns outside the stable.

'No way,' Michelle screamed, as Jet and members of several other bands stepped out of their rehearsal spaces and saw Michelle facing off ex-punk Beth Winder. '"We Built This City" is the cheesiest rock ballad ever. We're called Industrial Scale Slaughter, for Christ sakes. We're supposed to be a thrash metal band, not rehashing some god-awful seventies glam rock shite pile.'

'You need to play to your strengths,' Beth said, as Michelle glowered at a camera operator standing between them. 'Summer is your biggest asset.'

'Screw that,' Michelle said. 'Is that all we are now? Summer Smith's backing group? Nobody gives a shit as long as the pretty little blonde girl gets her bit of warbling in?'

'Calm down, Michelle,' big sister Lucy said, charging out of the rehearsal room. 'It was just a suggestion.'

'We'll find another song,' Summer said, as she followed Lucy and Coco on to the lawn. 'I totally agree with Michelle.

Ever since Rage Rock it's all been about me and it's not fair on you three.'

Beth backed away from Michelle, and pointed at the four girls. 'I don't need this,' Beth said. 'I've been in the music business for thirty-five years and I get paid the same whether you win or lose.'

'Thanks for sticking up for me, roomie,' Michelle said, as she pulled Summer into a hug.

Summer was smiling as the four girls walked back into their rehearsal room, but Lucy was furious.

'You could have at least listened to what Beth said,' Lucy spat, glowering at Michelle as she sat back behind her drum kit. 'In case you haven't noticed, you just pissed off one of the people who can vote to get us kicked out of the show.'

35. Bright Blessed Day

Jay sang Louis Armstrong's 'What a Wonderful World' in the shower and came out wearing a towel and a big smile.

'Shut up, you happy bastard!' Babatunde said, as he gently lobbed a drumstick, forcing Jay to duck and drop his towel.

Babatunde erupted in a deep laugh as Jay scrambled towards his bed and hurriedly tugged on boxers.

'How can any woman resist a body like that?' Babatunde teased, as Jay pulled a T-shirt over his skinny chest.

'Got it figured,' Jay said, as he rummaged in the plastic bag the runners had delivered his clean laundry in. 'I'll have a couple of hits with Jet, but my career won't really take off until I ditch you losers and go solo. Summer will have released a few best-selling albums of her own by then. Our wedding will be on the cover of *Hello!* magazine. We'll keep a flat in Mayfair, but mostly we'll live in LA. Three kids, a pony paddock for our little girl and two Rottweilers to keep the fans out. I'll give you a job as our head butler, but you'll have to lose the hoodie.'

'You're on quite a trip,' Babatunde said, as Jay pulled on socks. 'Heading for a fall if your little romance comes crashing down.'

'Sun's back,' Jay said, ignoring his band mate's warning as he looked out of the window. It was a bright morning and a bunch of journalists stood smoking outside their newly-erected marquee. 'You wanna head down for breakfast?'

'I'll come down in a bit,' Babatunde said. 'My mum's been working nights and I promised I'd call.'

There had never been much wrong with the food at the manor, but now celebrity chef Joe Cobb owned a stake in Venus TV, he'd insisted on replacing the kitchen staff with some of his own. Jay was disappointed when he looked around the dining-room and couldn't see Summer, but was consoled by the smell of freshly-baked bread and croissants.

There were a couple of girls up back who Jay barely knew, so after ordering an omelette he sat with Leo from the Pandas of Doom, and bit into an apricot Danish.

'Loving the new food,' Jay said.

Leo didn't seem like his usual chatty self. 'Jen was looking for you, did you speak to her?'

Jay shook his head. 'Jen the runner, or Jen the publicist?'

'Publicist,' Leo said, then after an uncertain pause, 'There's some stuff about you in the papers this morning.'

Jay didn't look bothered. 'With my family, it was always gonna happen. Is it my brother Danny?'

'You don't know?' Leo said. 'It's about *you.*'

'I've never done nothing,' Jay protested. 'I'm like, the most innocent member of my family. Which paper was it?'

'*UK Today.*'

There were usually a few discarded papers kicking around the dining-room. As a cook delivered Jay's omelette and a pot of tea, he scrambled around, finding a copy of every paper except the one he was looking for.

'Here,' Leo said, sliding a Samsung tablet across the table when Jay came back empty-handed.

The *UK Today* website was designed in the same red and black as its paper cousin. Even the headlines were done in the same font, and the one on Leo's screen read:

ROCK WAR JAY BORN AFTER MUM SLEPT WITH COP

Jay didn't like the headline; he liked the article even less when he saw who'd given the paper an interview:

In a sensational turn of events set to once again rock TV's most controversial new show, UK Today *secured an exclusive interview with Jane Jopling, mother of contestants Tristan and Alfie. Speaking from her £2.5-million home in North London's prosperous Hampstead, the heavily pregnant Mrs Jopling made a number of startling allegations about Heather Richardson, mother of rival contestants Jay Thomas, Adam Richardson and Theo Richardson.*

Mrs Jopling claimed that Jay Thomas is actually the child of

Police Inspector Chris Ellington (33). Mrs Jopling alleged that as a nineteen-year-old virgin and newly qualified police constable, Inspector Ellington caught mother of eight Heather Richardson driving a vehicle filled with property stolen by her husband, the notorious North London gangster Vincent 'Chainsaw' Richardson.

According to Mrs Jopling, Heather Richardson had three young sons and was 'desperate not to get banged up', so she threw herself at the young officer. Following a brief sexual encounter, Inspector Ellington's son, Jayden Ellington Thomas, was born nine months later, while his mother was never charged with handling the stolen goods.

Jane Jopling, whose story has been verified by a former employee of the fish and chip shop where Heather Richardson works, said that she was a close friend of Heather Richardson from the start of secondary school. The pair's friendship ended when Jane married wealthy businessman Gideon Jopling in 1996.

'Heather was mad jealous,' Mrs Jopling said. 'She can't handle the fact that I've made something of myself, while her family's still in the gutter.'

Earlier this year, Jane Jopling and Heather Richardson were given police cautions after fighting outside a London music venue. This followed an incident in which Mrs Jopling's £65,000 Porsche Cayenne was knocked into the Regent's Canal in mysterious circumstances.

Further allegations . . .

Jay sat with his mouth gaping as he scanned the rest of the article.

'You OK, mate?' Leo asked. 'Do you want me to see if there's a welfare officer on duty?'

'It's fine,' Jay lied, as his eyes glazed over. 'I don't want one of those welfare idiots asking about my *feelings*. I've just got to make a call.'

Jay scrambled through the dining-room and out of the door at the back of the kitchen. There was nobody out there smoking, and he checked to make sure his phone was getting a signal before looking up his dad on the speed dial.

'Hey, son,' Jay's dad, Chris, said, after a couple of rings.

'Hey,' Jay said. 'I wasn't sure if you were on duty or not.'

'I'm not working. I take it you saw the paper?'

'For sure,' Jay said. 'I'll get major stick from everyone when I get back to school. But it's you I'm worried about. Is this going to affect your job?'

'The journalist from *UK Today* called me last night, asking if I could confirm the story. I met with the Commander this morning, and handed in my resignation.'

Jay felt like he'd been punched. 'You *what*? Couldn't you have denied it?'

'I don't mean to criticise your mum, but she's long regarded the incident as a bit of a joke. She told quite a few people over the years.'

'You've been a cop my whole life,' Jay said. 'What the hell will you do?'

'The Commander said that since the incident came early in my career, and that I'd had a clear record ever since, it was highly unlikely that they would take further disciplinary action.'

'But that's not fair,' Jay blurted, as his heart raced. 'Everyone makes mistakes. It was *fourteen* years ago.'

Jay's dad tutted. 'I was young, naïve and curious about sex. But that doesn't excuse me catching a baddie and letting them off in return for a shag. For a cop, that's about as serious as it gets.'

'Shit,' Jay said, stamping his foot and realising he'd walked outside in his socks. 'I never would have entered this stupid show if I'd known this was gonna happen.'

'Don't blame yourself for something I did,' Chris said firmly. 'Maybe it happened for a reason. Sleeping with your mother was probably the dumbest thing I've done, but having a son like you is by far the best.'

A tear welled in Jay's eye, as he picked one of his feet off the ground and saw that his sock was all soggy.

'Are you on your own?' Jay asked. 'Are you going to be OK?'

'I'm staying with Johno. The one you met at my thirty-third party.'

'The fat guy,' Jay said, nodding.

'I tried to get home, but when I arrived there must have been twenty journalists on my driveway. I had to hand in my police uniform before I left the station, so right now I'm wearing some old tracksuit bottoms I had in my locker and one of Johno's T-shirts, which is like XXXL and hangs off me like a dress. Johno's wife said she'll pick a couple of bits up for me in Primark on her way home from work.'

'But what will you do with yourself?' Jay asked.

'I've got five seasons of *Battlestar Galactica* to watch on Blu-ray,' Chris joked, but he turned more serious when he heard a sob. 'Are you OK, son?'

'I'm just . . . shocked,' Jay said. 'When we started getting publicity I thought they'd dig up some dirt on Chainsaw and Danny. But I never thought this could happen to you. If I see Mrs Jopling at parents' evening or something, I'm gonna slap her *so* bloody hard.'

'Oh no you won't,' Chris said firmly. 'Maybe it's for the best, anyway. I was under a lot of stress. I won't make as much money working as a security guard in Sainsbury's, but I'll probably sleep a lot easier. Or maybe I'll study. Go to university perhaps.'

'That would be good,' Jay said encouragingly. 'You're smart. Maybe you could become a lawyer, or something.'

'And if all else fails, I'm sure my millionaire rock-star son will look after me.'

36. We've Wanted This to Happen For Ages

Jay felt agitated. Part of him wanted to run down to the press tent and throw boiling coffee over the journalist from *UK Today*, part of him wanted to go up to his room and hide from everything and part of him wanted to leave Rock War Manor and be with his dad.

Jay's dad took his job seriously. All his mates were cops, his social life was based around police squash and darts leagues. He lived alone and Jay was certain that his dad was lying when he brushed it all off and said it wasn't a problem. Chris Ellington hadn't just lost his job, he'd lost his whole identity.

'I spoke to Mum,' Adam told Jay when he met up with his band mates in their rehearsal room. 'She's furious. But *UK Today* have offered six grand to tell her side of the story, *The Post* has offered eight, but she's holding out for ten. And Len decked a reporter who stood on top of a van, trying to take photos through our upstairs window.'

Jay felt bad for his mum, but with eight kids aged between five and nineteen and a fish and chip shop on one of London's rowdiest streets to run, getting branded a slag by a national newspaper would worry her a lot less than important stuff, like getting her three youngest to eat properly, stopping casual staff robbing her till and making sure there was enough in her account to pay the electric bill.

'If I see Mrs Jopling . . .' Theo snarled, pounding his fist into his hand.

'It's a shame she's got two sons,' Adam said. 'If Mrs Jopling had a daughter, Theo could really piss her off by sleeping with her.'

'I could probably sleep with Tristan,' Theo joked. 'I bet he'd be up for it.'

Jay felt nice knowing that his brothers were on side, but he wasn't comfortable with the way they'd turned it into a joke.

'I need some air,' Jay said.

He strolled past a couple of rehearsal rooms, one empty, one with crew inside, filming Frosty Vader. The third was Industrial Scale Slaughter's room. Summer sat fanning herself with a magazine, while her three band mates worked on an arrangement.

'Awww,' Lucy said, when she saw Jay. 'You doing OK?'

Jay felt loved as Coco gave him a hug and even Michelle made a kind of sympathetic purr. He met eyes with Summer, who put her magazine down and looked around at her band mates.

'If you're talking music, can I take fifteen minutes?' Summer asked.

They kissed once they were outside. Summer's eyes took a while to adjust to sunlight as they walked twenty metres and sat in the rough grass, on what had once been a riding paddock. Jay felt a lot better with Summer beside him. She was hot from the rehearsal room and he admired her legs as she kicked off her slip-ons.

'It sucks,' Summer said. 'Printing all those lies about you.'

Jay half smiled, as he lay back in the grass and picked a daisy. 'It's not lies,' he sighed. 'I wish I was like Noah, or Babatunde. You know: Mummy, Daddy, regular jobs and a reasonable number of siblings.'

Summer nodded. 'Just so you know, before it hits the front page: my mum's a junkie. She's been in prison a couple of times and I haven't seen her since I was eight. She has no idea who my dad is, probably because she got pregnant when she was sleeping with guys just to get drugs.'

Jay smiled. 'That's why I like you,' he said. 'We have *so* much in common.'

He'd picked a few more daisies by this time and he sprinkled them over Summer's belly. She rolled over and they had the most amazing kiss.

'I had to get blood tests every year until I was nine,' Summer said, when they finally broke apart. 'Because my mum shared needles and shit. I used to lie awake when I was little, terrified that there was this invisible thing in my blood that was going to kill me.'

Jay didn't know how to reply to that, so he nuzzled Summer's neck. 'You have the best smell,' he told her.

'Sainsbury's Basics antiperspirant spray,' Summer said. 'Forty-nine pence.'

'You smell like it cost at least a pound,' Jay teased.

Summer was pushing her hand up the front of his T-shirt, which felt really sexy until she tweaked his nipple.

'Cheeky boy,' Summer said. 'You smell like you ate the spicy sausage baguette at lunch-time.'

'Is that bad?'

'Smells are funny, aren't they?' Summer observed. 'Like, food smells amazing when you're hungry, but nasty when you're full. Spicy sausage and a touch of sweat actually smells pretty great when it's coming off you.'

Jay smiled, but he didn't want to answer, because it was nice just to lie there with Summer's hand on his chest. He tried to shut out the stuff in the papers, and how he was way out of his depth with the whole girlfriend thing, and how Jet might get knocked out of *Rock War*. Both of them managed to enjoy being in the moment until Tristan's shadow loomed.

'Nice write-up in the paper, butt face,' Tristan said.

Jay sat up and eyed his former best friend. He hated the way Tristan had paired off with his cousin Erin, so having Summer alongside made him feel like he'd evened things up on that score.

'Butt face,' Jay mulled. 'You walked fifty metres from rehearsal room to here, and that's the best insult you could come up with?'

'Your dad resigned,' Tristan said. 'It's all over the *UK Today* website. So I guess he'll be on benefits now, like the rest of your family.'

'You spend way too much time listening to your Tory mamma,' Jay said. 'We're not rich, but nobody in my family is on benefits.'

Tristan scoffed. 'You must get *some* benefits, the rate your mum spurts out babies.'

Jay was used to being baited by Tristan and was more irritated than annoyed. But Tristan had inadvertently pushed Summer's buttons as well. She shot to her feet and jabbed him with her pointing finger.

'What gives you the right?' Summer yelled. 'I guess it's nice, living in your two-million-pound house, with your mum driving around in a new Porsche. But some people don't get that, through no fault of their own. Some people are on benefits because they're sick and they can't do anything about it. Some people have to scrimp just to get enough food to last the week. Some kids go to school with their feet bleeding because they can't afford bigger shoes.'

Summer's fury had caught the attention of kids in the rehearsal rooms. A break in Babatunde's drumming meant that Adam and Theo were among them.

'You flapping your trap again, Tristan?' Adam shouted, as he charged out with Theo behind him.

Seeing Jay's two hulking brothers put Tristan into such a panic that he barged Summer out of the way and started to run. Jay stuck his foot out, catching a painful whack on the shin, but leaving Tristan splayed out in the grass.

The camera crew that had been filming Frosty Vader recorded the action as Theo scooped Tristan off the ground and threw him over his shoulder.

'Right, you gobby little shit,' Theo said. 'You've been asking for this for a *long* time.'

'Theo, put him down,' a cameraman said half-heartedly.

But neither the cameraman, his assistant or their runner fancied taking on a fiercely-muscled boxing champion, so they pursued with their camera instead.

For a moment, Jay was scared that Theo would do Tristan serious harm. But he quickly worked out where Theo was headed, and realised there was humiliation rather than pain on the agenda.

At the end of the stable block there was an outdoor toilet. Built in the days when the block was used by a couple of stable hands rather than fifty-plus crew and contestants, the stall tended to get grungy, to the extent that most of the girls would take the short walk back to the manor rather than step into the lake left behind by the boys.

'Let me go,' Tristan demanded. 'I'll make you pay for this! You let me go!'

Theo booted the toilet door, much to the alarm of a lad from The Messengers who was having a pee.

'Shift,' Theo roared, as the boy looked around and was startled by Theo's bulk and Tristan's flailing legs.

As the boy scrambled away, forced to resume his pee

in the weeds around the side, Tristan gave a final desperate shout.

'I'll kill you, you bastard!'

Theo leaned forwards, lowering Tristan head first towards the bowl.

'The more you wriggle, Trissie-kins, the more chance you're gonna come out with that big skid mark stuck to your forehead.'

Ever the loyal girlfriend, Erin had sprinted all the way from Brontobyte's rehearsal room.

'You put him down, Theo,' Erin demanded. Then she looked around at the camera crew. 'Why are you filming this instead of stopping it?'

'He's bigger than us,' the runner pointed out.

'Theo,' Erin yelled, diving into the stall as Tristan's head touched down inside the toilet bowl.

'My father is very influential,' Tristan shouted, as he caught a noseful of shit and old drains. 'He'll sue your ass. He'll take every penny you've got.'

Theo laughed. 'Trissie, as you're so fond of telling us, my family are all povs. I haven't got any money.'

The toilet had an old-fashioned thunderbox cistern, with dangling chain. As Theo reached to pull it, Adam realised that the most likely outcome from Erin's brave attempt to save her beloved was that one of Theo's elbows or Tristan's flailing legs would clobber her.

'You'll get hurt,' Adam warned, as he grabbed Erin around the waist and dragged her out backwards.

Erin thought Adam was trying to protect Theo. As Theo yanked the chain to give Tristan his bogwashing, Erin broke free from Adam's grasp. Not realising how angry his cousin was, Adam made no attempt at defence as Erin launched an almighty punch his way.

'Help me!' Tristan yelled, before realising that he had to shut his mouth to stop it filling with toilet water.

'That'll teach you,' Theo said, wearing a huge smile as he staggered out of the stall. Then he walked right up to the camera, pounded his fist into a palm and yelled, 'Anyone else wanna dis my family?'

Theo looked less sure of himself when he saw Adam, clutching his face, blood gushing over his chin and down his arm.

'She broke my nose,' Adam moaned, the blood blocking his nostrils giving his voice a comic twang. 'I can feel the bone moving!'

While Adam staggered about, Tristan fell off the toilet bowl, coughing and spluttering as water dripped from his hair and nostrils.

'Stop filming,' Tristan shouted, close to tears as he flopped on to the toilet's piss-soaked floor.

About twenty kids had witnessed the whole thing; there were a few nervous laughs as Tristan crawled out and got a hand up from Erin.

Jay ripped off his T-shirt and gave it to Adam to hold over his nose, then looked anxiously back at Summer. He had a horrible churning feeling. Theo had done all kinds of crazy stuff, but he'd never assaulted another *Rock War* contestant before. There was going to be trouble, maybe even enough to get Jet kicked out of *Rock War*.

37. SD

The camera panned around a seedy concert venue. The bar was shuttered, the low ceiling yellowed by ancient cigarette smoke and every wall and pillar scrawled with graffiti. Lorrie stood centre stage, with an unlit neon *Rock War* sign set on top of a metal packing-case directly behind.

'Welcome to the Granada Room, Liverpool,' Lorrie said, as the camera stopped panning. 'The Beatles played some of their first gigs here in the sixties, and it was the hub of the Liverpool punk scene in the seventies.

'This Saturday, all twelve *Rock War* bands must take to this historic stage and impress the three *Rock War* legends. Then it'll be down to you, the viewers, to decide who makes it to the competition's knockout phase. So, make sure you tune in to *Rock War – The Boot Camp Showdown*. Live, from six thirty this Saturday. Only on Channel Six!'

'Keep rolling,' Joseph said. 'Nice one, Lorrie, but I think we picked up bleeps from a truck reversing outside. So let's do that one more time, from the top, whenever you're ready.'

*

Zig Allen was a creative type, better suited to dreaming up shows like *Rock War* than the daily grind of making them happen. Karolina Kundt was a different beast. She lived by spreadsheets, memorandums and electronic calendars, but didn't get flustered when she had to deal with a chef who'd called in sick, or a thunderstorm that trashed the whole day's shooting schedule.

Since Karolina had taken charge, the crew seemed happier and things ran more smoothly than under Zig's reign of mild chaos and moody rants about people spending his money. But now, the tall, slightly greying German faced her first big challenge.

Zig's former office wasn't big enough, so Karolina was perched on a desk in the open-plan admin area outside it. Her newly-appointed assistant, Julie, and the on-duty welfare officer stood at the side, while seven angsty contestants sat facing her on office chairs.

Brontobyte were on Karolina's left. Alfie looked mortified, Salman annoyed, Tristan with just-washed hair and Erin with strapping around her knuckles. On Karolina's right was Jay, who felt like he was about to get a bullet through the head, Babatunde, as inscrutable as ever in hoodie and sunglasses, and Theo, who looked a lot less cocky than usual. Adam couldn't attend, because he was in casualty, waiting to get his broken nose reset.

'You all signed these before filming began,' Karolina said, as she waved some stapled sheets of A4. 'I wrote these personal conduct statements myself. They outline the standards of conduct and behaviour required of all *Rock War* contestants. The punishment for violating these rules is also outlined: anyone who breaks the rules will be eliminated from *Rock War* and sent home, along with the other members of their bands.'

Karolina threw the papers down. 'Unfortunately, very little notice has been given to these agreements up to this point. But that dates back to a time when I was not in charge. So to begin, why should I not send all of you home immediately?'

Tristan spoke. 'Surely it's Jet you should be kicking out. I was assaulted, *I'm* the victim here.'

Jay sounded bitter. 'You started this whole thing by having a go at me and upsetting Summer in the process.'

Karolina pointed at Erin. 'Adam is in the hospital and has suffered the most severe injury. Members of both bands committed assaults that should lead to their dismissal from *Rock War*.'

Brontobyte's lead singer Salman raised a hand warily. 'How can Saturday's show work if you boot two bands out?'

Jay had wondered about this himself, and it was the one hope he was holding on to.

Theo crossed his arms, and suddenly sounded like his usual self. 'If you *could* kick us out you'd have done it already,' he said.

Karolina glowered at Theo. 'You think the competition won't work without you? It's actually very simple. This weekend, we eliminate one band instead of two. Then we leave it a couple of weeks, before announcing that there was a fault with the electronic voting system during week three. Because of this fault, no band will be eliminated. So, I *can* kick Jet and Brontobyte out. The consequence to *Rock War* will be minimised within three weeks.'

'My dad will sue,' Tristan spat and, pointing at Theo, continued, 'I made a joke. He overreacted massively. He should be arrested for common assault.'

'You think that was bad?' Theo spat back. 'Next time I'll make sure the toilet's clogged before I dunk your head in it.'

Jay tugged the sleeve of Theo's T-shirt and made a *calm-down* gesture.

'Enough,' Karolina ordered, as she picked an SD memory card off the desk she was perched on. 'I am going to give you two options. The first option is the one I've already outlined. When you leave this room, you all go downstairs and start packing your bags to leave. You can whine and moan. You can threaten to call in the cops, or sue Venus TV, but this card has all the footage I need to justify kicking Brontobyte and Jet out of *Rock War*.

'Or,' Karolina said dramatically. 'There's a second option. Luckily for you seven, it *would* be better for *Rock War* if all twelve bands wěre to appear on Saturday's live show. Especially as Theo is one of our most popular contestants.

'So here is what I propose. We act like this unfortunate

incident *didn't* happen. Tristan didn't upset Jay and Summer. Theo didn't overreact. Erin didn't break Adam's nose. Everyone stays in the competition and I take this SD card with the only copy of the footage from the incident and drop it into our paper shredder. The choice is yours, but I'll only play ball if your vote is unanimous.'

There was a moment's silence before Jay raised his hand. 'I'm good with that,' he said, as Babatunde's hand followed his into the air.

Salman raised his hand next, Alfie looking anxiously at his older brother before doing the same.

'I'm the one who really suffered here,' Tristan said angrily.

Alfie corrected him. 'You could shower. The runners will have to wash your clothes, and Adam's the dude with the broken nose.'

'Oh,' Karolina said. 'I should have mentioned. Joseph is with Adam at the hospital. I've discussed this proposal, and Adam is happy as long as everyone stays in the competition.'

Erin and Theo raised their hands upon hearing this, leaving Tristan as the only holdout.

Salman kicked the back of Tristan's chair. 'Do you want to be in *Rock War* or not?' he asked.

But it was the stern look from girlfriend Erin that finally persuaded Tristan to briefly flip his arm into the air.

'Whatever,' he said. 'I'll keep my mouth shut. It's all about the music, isn't it?'

There were a few nods from both bands as Karolina took three paces and switched on a big paper shredder by the door. The memory card made a satisfactory crunching sound as the metal rollers inside ripped it up.

'Meeting over,' Karolina said, as she moved towards her office door. 'Try getting a good night's rest. Tomorrow's your last chance to rehearse before the big brouhaha on Saturday night. And think of this as your final warning. I will *not* be lenient if this kind of incident happens again.'

As the kids strolled out, followed by the welfare officer, Julie stepped across to her new boss and spoke quietly.

'The last time I looked we were using GY-150s for all of our small-unit shooting,' Julie said. 'On Karen's shows, we'd always use the dual-record mode in case one of the SD cards failed.'

Karolina smiled. 'Very sensible, we do the same here.'

'So . . .' Julie said, smiling.

'The other SD copy is locked in my safe,' Karolina explained. 'Tristan's a sly one and by all accounts his mother's a complete monster. If Brontobyte get knocked out in the early rounds, I say the odds of him trying to sue Venus TV are still fairly high.'

38. The Forty-eight

Friday

Summer got up to pee first thing, and found that the runners had slid a note under her door:

MEMO

TO: All contestants

FROM: Karolina Kundt

Rock War contestants who are voted out will NOT be returning to the manor. Before leaving this afternoon, all contestants must ensure that personal belongings are collected from the pool, ballroom and other areas and placed in your rooms.

All of your musical equipment must be left in your band's rehearsal room. If you have borrowed equipment from the store room, or from other bands, please return it before departing to Liverpool.

Eliminated contestants will have their personal belongings and equipment delivered to their homes within three working days.

Summer felt emotional as she stepped out of her room, looking down two floors at a ballroom littered with magazines, mugs and pool shoes. She remembered the afternoon when she'd first walked in, and couldn't believe it had been six weeks ago.

Jay was waiting by the stairs. After a kiss, they used the metal slide to get downstairs and noticed stacked desks, plastic chairs and whiteboards in the lobby. All were brand-new, wrapped in polythene and cardboard.

'It's gonna be so weird having to go to lessons here, now school holidays are over,' Jay said.

'It'll be even weirder if we get voted out and have to go back to our real lives.'

'You won't get voted off,' Jay said. 'You're the *Rock War* superstar.'

Summer waved her hand, uncertainly. 'But we've already upset one judge and we're doing a Pantera track, so we're not gonna get the little old ladies who like my voice voting for us.'

Most of the crew were already in Liverpool, setting up for the live show. Karolina's schedule had Friday morning marked down as rehearsal time, but most of the band's equipment had already been sent north for the show, and since it was a fine morning, the contestants mostly hung out by the pool until it was time to leave.

The three rock legends got a chopper ride, while the twelve bands had to slum it in giant Mercedes limousines, with their band logos on the doors. While uniformed chauffeurs loaded overnight bags into the backs of the limos, the last camera crew at the manor set up benches on the front lawn for a photo shoot.

Lined up in three rows of sixteen, the contestants tried not to squint as their picture was taken by a tripod-mounted Nikon. The grand house with ivy crawling up the front gave the picture the air of some posh boarding school photograph, except the kids had bleached hair, studded wristbands, ripped jeans and nose rings, in place of uniform.

A couple of tame members of the press had also been invited up to join the shoot, and ask a few informal questions. Dylan, Jay and Noah ended up together as a radio journalist put a little voice recorder in front of them.

'I'm Tash, from Rok FM,' the woman said. 'Do you think I can get a couple of soundbites from you boys?'

'Sure, I guess,' Jay said, as Dylan and Noah nodded.

The journalist pulled out a voice recorder, with a big microphone bulb on the end.

'So, are you guys feeling nervous?'

'A little,' Dylan said. 'Lining up for the photo, I felt like I was in one of those old movies, where the squadron passes training before being sent off to fight in the Battle of Britain or whatever.'

Jay and Noah both laughed.

'Of course,' Noah added, 'the major difference is that those guys risked getting their heads shot off by Nazis, while the worst thing that can happen to us is that we make tits of ourselves and get voted out of a TV show.'

'And given all the controversy around the show, do you think your parents are proud of you?' the journalist asked.

'Controversy made the show,' Dylan said. 'Before everything kicked off, *Rock War* was a teen show heading for oblivion. Now we're prime time.'

'I'm not sure if my mum's proud,' Jay said. 'But she got fourteen grand off *The Post* to tell her story and she's gonna use the dosh to refurbish our fish and chip shop.'

'What about your father? That must have been difficult.'

Now Jay was less comfortable, but he remembered the thing about staying positive from his media training and faked a smile. 'My dad's a great guy. It's a shame he had to resign, but it's an opportunity for him to do something new.'

'Will he be at the Granada Room tomorrow night?'

'I don't think so,' Jay said.

'My parents are flying in,' Noah said.

'Great answers, boys,' Tash said, as she looked at her recorder's display to make sure it was still running. 'Finally, can you just say who you are and *Rok FM rocks*.'

The boys looked a little awkward, making a quick discussion about how to do it before speaking in unison.

'We're Jay, Noah and Dylan from *Rock War*. And we say Rok FM rocks!'

'Short and sweet, boys,' the journalist said cheerfully. 'Ta very much.'

Everything was going wrong down by the limos. There was a remote camera positioned at the top of Rock War Manor and Angie had planned to film a dramatic shot of all twelve band limos leaving in a line. Unfortunately, nobody had told the drivers and a couple had driven off as soon as their four band members were inside.

Jay was first into Jet's stretch Mercedes. There were two luxury recliners facing the same way as the driver at the rear, and two facing backwards at the far end more than four metres away. The area between was all bling, with a three-seat leather couch along one side, while the other had a wooden console with flatscreen, PS4 and an illuminated cocktail bar.

'Me likey!' Jay said, as he got in first and went down to the seats at the far end.

'My dad's car's way bigger than this,' Babatunde lied, earning a few laughs.

In preparation for the young band mates, the bar had been stripped of alcohol and a pair of ultra-wide-angle cameras were attached to the roof.

'Man,' Theo gasped. 'Get a girl in here and you're guaranteed a shag.'

The only one who didn't seem too enthusiastic was Adam, who was drowsy from his painkillers and had a plastic mask covering his nose.

'Holy shit!' Jay gasped, as he pressed random buttons,

until he found himself reclining, getting massaged and watching the panoramic roof open, all at the same time.

It seemed they'd finally given up on getting all the limos to leave in line. But as Jet's ride was about to pull off, Dylan rapped on the glass.

'Can I bludge a lift?' Dylan asked. 'I told the others I needed a crap. When I came out they'd left without me.'

'No room,' Theo teased, before opening the door into the car's vast interior.

'OMG,' Jay yelled, as he pressed a button that made a fan whirr above his head and sent a stream of bubbles out of a nozzle and up through the open roof. 'This car is better than sex!'

'How would you know?' Adam asked.

The car started a slow cruise out of Rock War Manor as Dylan sank back into the sofa. Jay looked behind out of the back window at two limos following and the big house shrinking from view.

'Might never see it again,' he said sadly.

'Who gives a damn?' Babatunde said, as he grabbed a Pepsi from the fridge. 'Even if we get voted off tomorrow, I've still had the best summer of my life.'

39. Theo's Dimensions

Dorset to Liverpool was a five-hour drive, with decent traffic and a single toilet stop. For the first part of the journey, the twelve identical limos ran pretty close. Cars going the other way honked when they realised who was inside, contestants in different limos texted one another, and a few stood up with their heads through the roof until the limo drivers gave them grumpy warnings not to do it again, and locked the panoramic roofs if they did.

While most of the limos went for the A34 and a direct ride to Liverpool, it had been arranged for some bands to stop off and shoot some footage with their families en route. For Jet's limo, this meant a hundred-mile detour into London and a fight with Friday rush hour.

'Check what Summer sent me,' Jay said, as he showed Babatunde a WhatsApp picture message. It showed the leopard-print carpet inside Industrial Scale Slaughter's limo and a heart shape made from the tops of Pepsi bottles.

'Sweet,' Babatunde said. 'But that says it's from Michelle.'

'Summer's got that old Nokia,' Jay explained. 'I don't think it's even got a camera on it.'

The traffic around Camden was completely snarled. Theo had his chair fully reclined and was half asleep when he was startled by a thump on the glass next to his head. They were going through the busiest part of Camden Lock and the pavements heaved with bodies, out to enjoy the canal and trendy market stalls.

Theo opened his window and five sets of painted nails shot into the vehicle.

'We love the show,' one of the girls said. 'Good luck tomorrow.'

A couple of other people thumped on the roof and the owner of a juice stand was shouting for them to get out and have a freebie.

'Best OJ in Camden! You know you want it!'

Wary of dragging some poor girl along the street, the limo driver stopped and put his hazard lights on, which immediately got him honked by the bus behind.

Theo shook the final hand, then put his window back up. A couple more people had seen the Jet logo on the car and were waving, even though all the limo windows were blacked out.

People were taking pictures on their phones as the driver pulled away. Tufnell Park was another ten minutes, and he stuck to the back streets. When they turned into the brothers' home street, the boys could see a crowd of about sixty right outside their mum's chip shop, plus another twenty across the street.

'How could they know we were coming?' Jay asked. 'They must have announced it on the website or something.'

The driver rolled back the roof, and the four members of Jet, plus Dylan, stood up so that their heads stuck out the top. Phones flashed, while *Rock War*'s camera operator filmed from a traffic island. Shorty was balanced at the top of a ladder, getting a dramatic shot over the heads of the crowd.

'This is mental,' Jay said, smiling, but at the same time he wasn't sure how much he liked the idea of getting mobbed outside his own house.

As the limo stopped, a couple of humongous dudes in grey suit jackets cleared a space for the boys to get out. Theo got a big cheer as he balanced precariously on a roof bar, before jumping down on to the pavement. Jay and the others made more conventional exits through the doors.

As well as the crowd outside, the chip shop itself was rammed, but Jay's eye was drawn away from the shop and towards large white graffiti that had appeared on the alleyway wall. It read:

THEO RICHARDSON HAS A TINY PENIS

'Looks like you've been outed by one of your ex-girlfriends,' Adam said.

Theo looked furious as Dylan and the Jet boys cracked

up. Jen the publicist was holding out Sharpies. Jay grabbed one of the pens and signed an autograph book for a girl of about ten.

'Move along the line,' Jen ordered, as the others started signing autographs. 'The cameras are all set up inside. We want to film you boys serving fish and chips behind the counter.'

'Sorry,' Jay said, stepping on someone's toes as he squeezed into the crowded chip shop. The TV lights made it way brighter than usual. After passing behind the counter, one of the runners handed Jay a striped apron, but he ignored it, gave his mum a quick hug and kept walking.

'Where are you going?' Angie the director asked, frustrated.

'I've been in a car for three hours,' Jay said. 'Where do you think?'

Jay's six-year-old brother Hank was at the bottom of the stairs. 'Hey!' Jay said fondly. 'Sorry, pal, I'm busting.'

'They showed you kissing Summer,' Hank said, as he followed Jay up to the loo. 'Why would you do *that*?'

'You'll understand when you're older,' Jay said, not bothering to close the toilet door as he unleashed a much needed pee.

Dylan was queuing behind as he shuffled out. While Angie got her shots of the three brothers serving in the chip shop, Jay's stepdad, Len, took Jay's three youngest siblings for a tour of the limo.

Once Angie had enough footage of the lads behind the

counter, they settled at a table on the other side, joined by Babatunde, Dylan and their limo driver.

Jay's mum laid chip paper across the tabletop, before bringing across pieces of cod, salmon and calamari and a huge pile of chips.

'Good grub,' the limo driver told her, as he smiled for the camera.

'Best chippy in London,' Jay told him. 'And I'm not just saying that cos she's my mum!'

A few people snapped pictures of the boys eating their dinner and Theo signed a couple of chip bags, but most of the crowd had decided that the limo was more interesting. The two heavies kept things orderly as groups lined up for photos at the kerbside. Jay was on his last ring of calamari when two kids from his class banged on the glass.

'Hey, guys,' Jay said fondly.

'Wanker!' the two lads shouted, flipping Jay off before legging it down the street.

Jay had heaps in common with all the kids at Rock War Manor, but this was an uncomfortable reminder that he wasn't exactly Mr Popularity at school. And when he did go back, being on *Rock War* and the stuff about his parents in *UK Today* would make him a target for untold stick.

*

Night was drawing in and they'd just passed a *Liverpool – 30 Miles* sign when Babatunde felt a weird jolt in the bulky armrest between his seat and Theo's. His first thought was that he'd accidentally pressed a button, but the second push seemed firmer and was accompanied by a determined grunt.

The arm-rest went up and down, but like most modern cars there was also a secondary panel, which opened a hole between the seats and enabled you to grab stuff out of the boot.

'What's happening?' Theo asked, annoyed that he'd been woken up as Babatunde pressed the catch.

The sight of a small hand made Babatunde jump. Hank grabbed the edge of the seat and yanked himself through the hole. Figuring that Jay would be gentler than Theo, the six-year-old scrambled to his feet, vaulted Dylan's outstretched legs in the middle of the cabin and jumped into Jay's lap.

'Surprise!' Hank announced, as his knee caught Jay in the stomach.

Slightly winded, Jay shot up in fright and almost knocked his little brother to the floor.

'Hank, what the hell?' Theo shouted. 'Mum'll kill you.'

'Please don't be cross,' Hank begged, putting his hands together in a praying gesture and giving Jay his most pitiful eyes.

It was an awkward one. Part of Jay thought his little brother stowing away was cute, but his parental side came out first.

'You're really silly,' Jay said stiffly. 'Mummy and Daddy are probably looking for you.'

'Nah-uh!' Hank said. 'Daddy put me to bed. So I came downstairs, and sneaked back into the car while nobody was looking.'

Jay grabbed his phone, which was charging inside the arm-rest.

'What are you doing?' Hank gasped. 'Don't tell them. I just wanted an adventure.'

'I've got to,' Jay said, as Hank wriggled off Jay's lap and perched himself grumpily on the arm-rest. '*Don't* disturb Adam. His nose is swollen and he's sleeping off a headache.'

'Richardson's takeaway,' Jay's stepdad answered.

'Hey, Len,' Jay said, jovially. 'Have you mislaid a child, by any chance?'

'Pardon me?' Len said.

'Hank hid in the boot,' Jay said. 'We just found him.'

'Oh balls,' Len said. 'I put him to bed while you were eating. Your mum'll blame me when she finds out.'

Jay laughed. 'Yeah, I'm glad I won't be in the room for that moment. But he's fine. You're coming up for the show tomorrow anyway, so he'll just have to bunk in with me tonight.'

'Tell Hank to behave himself and that he's in big trouble when I see him.'

'I'll be sure to. See you tomorrow.'

Hank was close enough to hear both ends of the conversation, and smiled as he slid down to sit on the floor between Jay's legs.

'Daddy's a softie,' Hank said. 'I'm not even scared of him.'

'Mummy will be really cross as well,' Jay warned. 'What if

the car had to stop suddenly? You could have been knocked out by flying luggage.'

Hank was definitely scared of his mum, and he looked anxious for a few seconds before starting a crawl towards the fridge.

'Can I have something?' Hank asked, but he'd already grabbed a little can of sparkling orange juice.

40. Cute Stowaway

The Thorne Hotel was a bland four-star, situated closer to John Lennon Airport than Liverpool's city centre. After their London detour, Jet's black limo was the last of the twelve to pull into a reserved corner of the hotel's car park.

Jen had sorted all the accommodation and handed over keys to a pair of third-floor rooms. Jay kept Hank out of sight, because he knew she'd make some huge fuss about him and they'd end up having to have some stupid conversation with the welfare officer.

All the other bands and most of the crew were in the same third-floor corridor. Quite a few contestants had propped their doors open. There were room service trolleys all along the hallway, and Hank was a massive hit.

'Oh he's so cute!' Eve said, before letting Hank scoff the chocolate on her pillow.

Hank didn't approve when Summer kissed Jay, but he minded a lot less when he went into the room she was sharing with Michelle, making himself comfortable on a king-size bed, flipping between kids' stations on the TV.

Summer and Michelle kept an eye on Hank while Jay showered and unpacked. Adam was still suffering with his nose, so Jay got to share with Theo. Everyone apart from Hank was dressed in one of the Thorne's plush white bathrobes as the room service got wheeled into the boys' room.

Summer had already eaten, but she took a slice of Jay's pizza as Hank tucked into nuggets and beans and Theo knelt in front of the locked minibar.

'Theo, they locked the booze away,' Jay said. 'Get over it.'

Theo scoffed, as he unfolded an attachment on his pocket knife. 'If I can break into a BMW without setting off the alarm, I'm not gonna let myself be defeated by the crummy lock on a hotel minibar.'

'Your spaghetti's getting cold,' Summer noted.

'Alcohol, here I come,' Theo said, as he probed the lock. 'Just a gentle twist, and voilà!'

Theo tugged the fridge handle. Nothing happened, so he did it a lot harder. The lock remained in place, but he managed to snap the plastic hinges on the other side and the entire fridge door assembly came off in his hands.

'Oh!' Theo gasped, as little bottles of whisky and cognac inside the door came tumbling out, and he rolled backwards, ending up with his feet up in the air.

'Nice move!' Jay said, howling with laughter.

'Was that supposed to happen?' Summer teased, as Hank

laughed so hard that the sauce off his baked beans started bubbling out of his nose.

'I'm pretty sure I know what I did wrong,' Theo said, as he picked a miniature bottle of Gordon's gin off the floor, undid the top and downed it in two gulps. Then he stood up and went for the door.

'I'm gonna try the fridge in your room,' Theo told Summer.

'I want a Coke,' Hank said, abandoning his plate and scooting down the bed towards the doorless minibar. The move stopped when Jay grabbed his ankle.

'No way José,' Jay said, before turning towards Summer to explain. 'Hank doesn't wet the bed very often, but when he does it's usually when he's overexcited and he's had a lot of fizzy drinks.'

'Ah,' Summer said, as Hank reluctantly settled back down with his plate on his lap. 'Good call.'

'Don't tell her my secrets,' Hank said irritably.

Jay got a couple of quiet mouthfuls of pizza before he heard Michelle screaming in the room across the hall.

Summer crossed the hall to see what was going on in her room and found that Theo had made a much more successful attempt at unlocking their minibar. As Jay and Hank leaned curiously out of their doorway, Michelle lobbed a little bottle of whisky at Summer.

Hank picked the whisky off the floor and looked at Jay. 'Can I have it?'

'Go for it,' Jay said, to Hank's astonishment.

'Really?' Hank gasped. 'Mummy wouldn't let me.'

As Hank nervously studied his miniature whisky, Theo and Michelle seemed to have already downed several.

'It's competition day tomorrow, guys,' Summer warned. 'Be sensible.'

Jay started to laugh. 'Telling those two to be sensible might be a *bit* futile.'

'I can't open it,' Hank said, holding up his bottle.

'He can't drink that,' Summer said, thinking Jay was irresponsible.

'You've never tasted whisky, have you? I *really* don't think you'll like it . . .' Jay said, undoing the little top.

Hank took a sip. As soon as the whisky hit the six-year-old's tongue, his eyeballs bulged like snooker balls.

'Aaaargh, disgusting,' Hank shouted, as he spat it out. 'I'm on fire!'

Hank charged back into his room and stuck his head under the bathroom tap.

'Told you so, Hank,' Jay said, as Summer turned red with suppressed laughter.

'You tricked me,' Hank shouted.

'How could I *possibly* have known you wouldn't like whisky?' Jay asked, keeping up his most deadpan voice.

Hank came back out with water dribbling down his chin and whacked Jay across the bum. 'Meanie.'

Jay was about to turn back into his room when he saw Dylan, Leo and a couple of other contestants coming out of a little room with ice machines inside. They'd nabbed a big plastic dustbin from somewhere, and it was so full of icy water that the quartet could barely lift it.

'You should come and watch this, Jay,' Dylan said. 'I think you'll enjoy it.'

'Enjoy what?' Jay said, as he followed the sploshing bin down to the last room.

Frosty Vader's four members had landed a two-bedroom suite at the end of the hallway. The living area had a long balcony with sliding glass doors. The room lights were off, and Noah was keeping lookout.

'They're still down there smoking,' Noah whispered. 'Four or five of 'em.'

The dustbin made a big *spelunk* sound as the boys put it down.

'Who's down there?' Jay whispered, as Summer and Hank followed him into the suite.

Sadie was sitting on a sofa in pyjama bottoms. 'Photographers,' she told Jay. 'There's at least one from your favourite: *UK Today*. You know the big bald guy? And the other one, who kept sneaking around the back of the kitchens at the manor?'

'Camera running,' Sadie said, opening the glass door a bit more as she stepped out. She leaned against the railing, with the camera pointing down.

'On three,' Dylan said.

'Why's it dark in here?' Hank blurted. Then he froze as eight people shushed him.

'OK,' Dylan said. 'Are we doing this? One, two . . .'

The four boys charged out on to the balcony, leaving a big wet patch behind on the carpet. Leo stubbed his toe on the door frame and lost his grip on the bin, but the other three had enough momentum to lift it up on the railing and tip it up.

A couple of photographers looked up in time to save themselves from the brunt, but the majority got the mix of water and ice cubes full force.

'Take that, you spying arse wipes,' Sadie shouted, as the journalists below scrambled off with iced water down their backs and soggy cigarettes in their mouths. 'I reckon YouTube will like that one!'

41. Freebies

Saturday

With Michelle and Theo on the rampage, Summer ended up sleeping on Theo's bed, with Jay and Hank sharing the other one.

Hank led a charge towards the lifts, and was intrigued by feathers over the hallway carpet and streaks of shaving foam along the corridor walls.

'Someone's been naughty,' Hank said, grinning. Then as Jay caught him up, 'Are we going to the TV show now?'

Jay shook his head. 'Jen the publicist has called a meeting. We're doing rehearsals this afternoon, and the live show this evening.'

One of the runners was waiting in the ground-floor lobby. Hank poked his tongue out when a photographer took their picture. As a bull-necked guard marched the photographer out towards the automatic doors, the runner pointed them towards a reception room.

The huge space was designed for conferences and wedding receptions, but right now all the chairs and folding tables were stacked up back, and there was nothing but an expanse of garish carpet and a man up a scaffold replacing chandelier bulbs.

Julie and Jen stood in the middle of the room. There were a bunch of cardboard boxes behind, and about forty contestants, half dressed, or still in nightwear. Not everyone had seen Hank, and he got lots of girls cooing and saying how much he looked like Theo and Adam.

Jay found Adam, still wearing his nose mask, but looking more cheerful than the day before. 'How you doing?'

'Way better,' Adam said. 'Swelling's down, and I haven't got much of a headache. I'll definitely be able to play tonight.'

'OK, is that everyone?' Jen asked, as a big group of contestants came through the door.

'Theo's not here,' Coco shouted.

'He never listens to a word I say anyway,' Jen joked. 'So let's start this thing.'

Jen opened up a newspaper with the headline: *ROCK WAR LOUTS URINATE ON PRESS*

'This gets on the early pages of several tabloids this morning,' she said. 'I've also received phone calls threatening legal action for damage to photographic equipment and a laptop.'

'It wasn't urine,' Noah pointed out. 'We uploaded the video. You can *see* it's water and ice cubes.'

'Is that such a surprise?' Jen asked. 'I'm sure you've all

noticed by now, a lot of what you read online and in the newspapers bears little resemblance to the truth. Now, as a publicist, I can't say I'm unhappy that my show is getting lots of coverage on the morning of our first live show. However, it's also my job to keep *Rock War* in the news. Not just today, but every week between now and the grand final in December. If you upset the media, that makes my job a lot harder. So please, please, please, no more pranks on the press.'

Julie took over from Jen to explain the day's schedule. Kids could meet their families for an early lunch if they were coming to the event. Jen had set some contestants up with pre-show interviews on national radio stations, then everyone had to be at the Granada Room at one thirty for rehearsal.

'Following the rehearsal, you'll have a half-hour break, then it'll be straight into hair and make-up. This is live TV, so you absolutely *have* to keep to today's schedule.

'The live show will kick off at six thirty and lasts for two hours. The results show airs at ten fifteen. Now, I'm sure you're all wondering what's in the boxes behind me. There's a box for each of you. Since the show started getting big, we've been sent lots of items by people who'd like to see their products in the show, and also a few gifts have been sent by fans. So in a moment, we're going to switch the cameras on, and we'll film you opening your freebies. Questions?'

Everyone was too intrigued by the gift boxes to ask anything. All the professionals were setting up for the live show at the Granada Room, so filming was down to a pair of runners with camcorders.

Even though Hank wasn't a contestant he piled in, earning himself the task of reading out names. Most of the boxes were light enough for the six-year-old to handle, but Summer's stuff had been packed into a giant Amazon box that had to be dragged.

'It's like Christmas,' Jay said, as he sat on the carpet and opened his box.

'Maybe at your house,' Summer said. 'My nan can't get out. I get one present, and I have to buy it myself.'

'That's like, the saddest thing I ever heard,' Jay said, as he gave Summer a kiss.

'What have you got?' Hank asked excitedly, as he ran, then skidded on his knees, stopping between Jay and Summer.

In the background, Eve was holding up a sexy nurse costume. 'Look what some pervert sent me!' she shouted.

'These are nice,' Summer said, as she took out a bunch of tops and some denim shorts. There was a note on the front. *Dear Summer, we hope you enjoy wearing our Autumn collection. Jess Winters, Marketing & Publicity, MW Apparel.*

'Expensive,' Coco added. 'MW shorts are about a hundred and fifty a pair.'

Jay dug down into his box, finding some cool jeans, plectrums, an effects pedal and a variety of hair gels and toiletries.

'Two watches,' Jay said, as he held up a G-Shock and a

giant black chronometer.

Adam gave Hank some chocolates from his box, as Summer smiled at a hand-knitted rabbit, wearing a mini-tee with the Industrial Scale Slaughter logo on it. Then she practically exploded as she read a message aloud: '*Hey Summer. We saw that your phone was a little out of date. Here at XTA, we think everyone deserves a top quality smartphone. The enclosed phone comes with a two-year Unlimited Everything package, and there's one for your nan too.*'

'Bloody hell,' Jay said, as Summer took the lid off a small box. 'That got five-star reviews all over the place. It's a five-hundred-quid phone.'

'Better than your phone?' Summer teased, as she hugged the box.

'Sunglasses,' Adam said, as he balanced a set of designer shades over his nose mask. 'How do I look?'

'You'll have to teach me how to work this,' Summer said, as she unboxed the phone. 'It's enormous!'

Summer was completely overwhelmed by all the free stuff that companies had sent, in the hope that it would get seen on TV. There were throat pastilles specially designed for singers, tons of make-up, strappy shoes and a stack of envelopes containing vouchers for everything from free meals in Dudley restaurants to £100 in a posh London shoe shop.

'Hank, you don't have to eat all that at once,' Jay said, as he snatched the chocolate. 'You'll be moaning that you feel sick again in a minute.'

Alfie was delighted by the clothes and video games in his box, but furious when he found that a toy company had sent him a plastic helicopter and a set of action figures.

'How old do they think I am?' he blurted, as he lobbed the toys at Hank. 'They're taking the piss.'

'Someone texted me about free shit,' Theo said, as he sauntered in dressed in boxers, looking hung over and scratching himself. Then he looked at Jen. 'By the way, there was a photographer in the lobby, so I pulled down my shorts and showed him my wang.'

'Pardon *me*!' Jen gasped.

'Gotta scotch those rumours about the size of my package,' Theo explained, as he found the last unopened box and took off the lid. 'Oooh, leather waistcoat and diamond earrings! Ker-ching!'

42. The Aaah Moment

'Dad,' Jay gasped. 'I had no idea you were coming!'

Jay pulled his father, Chris, into a tight hug. He was backstage at the Granada Room, with the live show due on air in less than five minutes.

'Traffic wasn't great,' Chris said. 'Look at you with your make-up and your swanky watch.'

'It was a freebie,' Jay explained. 'I looked it up online and it's six hundred quid in Eldridges!'

'Cheaper to give you a watch to wear than pay for an advertisement,' Chris observed. 'Is that the leather jacket I bought you?'

'This one's from the wardrobe department,' Jay admitted. 'So how are you feeling?'

'Not bad, but it is a shock. I joined the police straight out of school, so I don't know much else.'

Jay didn't like the way his dad kept brushing it off. 'You don't have to lie. I'd rather know if you're feeling like crap.'

Chris shrugged. 'Son, it's great to know that you worry about me, but I'm not about to jump off a bridge or anything, OK? I've already spoken to a guy I know. Does a lot of special escort work. Like, driving businessmen and VIPs around. Mostly Russian and Middle Eastern. It's long hours, but the money's good.'

'Sounds decent,' Jay said encouragingly.

'Anyway, stop talking about me,' Chris said, grabbing Jay by his shoulders as a runner squeezed past carrying a tray of used coffee mugs. 'This is your big night. You up for it?'

'Slightly terrified,' Jay admitted. 'We're on second. Right after Industrial Scale Slaughter.'

Chris smiled. 'Summer Smith, my future daughter-in-law? That voice is some act to follow. Do I get to meet her?'

Jay smiled. 'Maybe, if you promise not to refer to her as *future daughter-in-law*. She's on the other side of the stage right now though.'

An announcement came over the venue's PA system. 'Live broadcast in two minutes. That is two minutes. Can all audience members please return to their seats. All mobile phones must be turned off and anyone seen using sound or visual recording equipment will be immediately removed from the venue.'

'Better go find my seat,' Chris said, as he gave Jay another hug. 'You'll do great.'

The Granada Room wasn't designed for TV, so Jay headed down a corridor beside the stage and transferred through fire doors into a huge, interconnecting marquee. Lorrie looked terrified as she waited for her cue to go out and present live for the first time.

'You'll be great,' Jay told Lorrie, as she walked past. 'You'll probably end up a bigger star than any of us.'

Lorrie gave Jay a huge smile and said, 'Thanks,' as Jay joined up with his band mates in the backstage lounge.

This part of the marquee was set up like a bar, with all the bands seated at tables. The set had been designed before Rage Cola pulled out, and silver bar trays had been crudely glued over Rage logos on the tabletops.

'You're getting pretty smooth with the ladies,' Adam noted, as he slapped Jay on the back.

Lorrie got her cue. Thirty steps from her first live TV appearance and a million miles from the student who'd turned up on the first day of boot camp, to gain unpaid experience working as a runner. A roar of cheering and applause greeted her arrival.

'Wow!' Lorrie said, as she found her mark in the middle of the stage. She looked out on a kind of mosh pit in front of the stage, packed with teens on their feet. Behind that, an older crowd, including many contestants' families, sat in chairs. 'Thanks for that amazing welcome. It's great to be here at the first ever live *Rock War*!'

The crowd erupted in another wave of cheering.

'We've got an amazing show lined up,' Lorrie said, sounding confident but feeling like she had a polar bear sitting on her chest. 'Twelve bands have spent six weeks honing their skills at boot camp. They're lean, they're mean and they're ready to rock!'

'All twelve acts will play tonight, but only ten will make it through to the *Rock War – Battle Zone* stages. Our three rock legends will mark each band out of ten, and at the end of this evening three bands with the lowest scores will go into a vote-off. Then it'll be up to *your* public votes, to save one of the three bands. And now, let's meet our *Rock War* legends!'

Lorrie gasped with relief as her piece to camera ended and the set changed, lighting up the three judges perched alongside the stage.

While a male voice-over artist introduced the three legends, Summer, Michelle, Coco and Lucy stood in their positions, while the crew plugged in guitars and wheeled in Lucy's drums. Summer felt nervous, but not puking nervous, like she'd been at Rage Rock.

After legend Jack Pepper's name sent the girls in front of stage into near hysteria, the big screen above and the viewers at home saw a brief introduction to the girls along with a few clips from their rehearsals earlier in the week.

The lights turned on the girls, ready to play. Backstage, Jay couldn't believe that the sexy rock chick at the microphone was his girlfriend. The set was cleverly designed, with the *Rock War* logo made from old-fashioned neon tubes, and a back wall made up from newspaper front pages, showing the history of rock: *Presley Banned in Bakersfield, Beatles Break Up, Cobain Dead at 27, Sex Pistols Outrage as Viewers Jam Phones.*

The effect was a kind of grungy cool, and a major contrast to the huge glitzy stage of a Karen Trim production.

'This is a Pantera song,' Summer announced softly. 'It's called "Walk".'

Boot camp had been massive fun, but the twelve bands had also been tutored by experts and spent hundreds of hours rehearsing. The results were apparent from the first smash of Lucy's drums. Michelle and Coco's guitars were sharp, and the pair faced each other with some well-choreographed flailing of long hair.

After a minute of heavy riffing, Summer's voice broke out. The crowd were expecting spectacular, but this was a hardcore metal song, and Summer had to bark rather than sing.

When the song ended, the crowd's response was lively, but not ecstatic. As the stage lights and cameras swooped in to the three legends, Earl Haart was first to speak.

'That had real balls,' Earl said, as the crowd cheered again. 'Great to see an all-girl band, that isn't afraid to mix it up with some real hardcore metal. Impressive, impressive, impressive, and it's an eight out of ten from me!'

The crowd cheered. Then there were ear-splitting screams as attention moved to Jack Pepper.

'Jack, I want your babies,' someone shouted, getting a laugh from the audience, but not picked up by the TV microphones.

'I agree with most of what Earl said,' Jack began. 'I know Michelle hasn't always been the most disciplined player, but she was great out there. And as always, Summer has *such* a voice. I just look at that fourteen-year-old girl, and it's amazing what comes out of her mouth. So it's eight out of ten from me.'

'Thanks, Jack!' Summer shouted, as Coco blew him a kiss.

But Summer's heart sank when she saw Beth Winder's sour expression. 'I'm sorry, but I just don't agree,' Beth said, as the crowd gave a soft boo. 'For me, that was the wrong song. Summer's voice is the heart of this band. Playing a song like that is like having Lionel Messi in your football team and putting him in goal. So I'm sorry, girls, but it's a three from me.'

A scoreboard at the side of the stage flashed up *Industrial Scale Slaughter – 19pts*.

Michelle gave Beth the finger as she led her band off stage. As the stage hands dived in to set up for Jet, the four girls walked into the backstage lounge where a former kids' TV presenter who'd been drafted in for the evening stuck a microphone in Summer's face.

'How are you feeling?' he asked.

'I think it went great,' Summer said.

'What about Beth Winder's comments?'

Summer shrugged. 'I'm not a solo artist. Industrial Scale Slaughter is a band and I'm totally behind the decision to play something a bit different. If we get through, I'm sure we'll play all kinds of tracks over the coming weeks.'

'Lucy,' the presenter asked, deliberately ignoring Michelle

because she was too volatile for live TV. 'Nineteen out of thirty – do you think that'll be enough to carry you through?'

'I guess it's too early to tell,' Lucy said. 'I'd be more chilled right now if we'd got a top score from all three judges.'

'Thanks, Lucy,' the presenter said. 'Now Summer, we've got a surprise for you.'

A curtain opened at the back of the set and Summer's nan was wheeled into the lounge.

'Oh my god!' Summer yelled, as she charged across and gave her nan a tearful hug. 'I'm so glad you're here! Why didn't you tell me you were coming?'

The audience in the Granada Room had seen Summer's reunion on the big screen and was making a collective *ahhh* sound as the director cut back to Lorrie on the main stage.

'I hope we'll get to hear more from Summer and her nan later,' Lorrie said. 'But we've got a lot to squeeze in tonight. So it's time to meet our second band. It's Jet!'

Once a brief intro vid had been shown, the stage lights came up, showing Adam looking like he'd stepped out of a slasher movie with his nose protector, Babatunde behind his drums in hoodie and sunglasses and Jay on lead guitar. There was some confusion about Theo's absence, but then there was a squeaking noise.

Dressed in ragged surf shorts and a black vest, Theo was being wheeled on to the stage, rattling the bars of a metal cage.

'They said I can't swear on live TV,' Theo said, as he

kicked open the doors of the cage and jumped out. 'Well I say BLEEP that.'

The live broadcast was actually on a thirty-second delay, so unlike the Granada Room audience, nobody watching at home heard the actual swearing. The standees in front of stage were going mental as Theo threw his vest to the crowd, revealing a muscular torso with JET scrawled across it in purple lipstick that was melting in the heat.

The audience was in a frenzy and Jet hadn't played a note.

'This one's written by John Bull, via the Sex Pistols,' Theo roared. 'It's called "God Save The Queen"!'

43. Oh So Dramatic

'Let's take a look at the scores,' Lorrie said. She'd gained confidence as the two-hour show wore on, but her voice was getting croaky.

1ST	Half Term Haircut	29 points
2ND=	Jet	27 points
	Dead Cat Bounce	27 points
4TH	Pandas of Doom	23 points
5TH	Crafty Canard	22 points
6TH	I Heart Death	20 points
7TH	Industrial Scale Slaughter	19 points
8TH	Delayed Gratification	18 points
9TH	Brontobyte	16 points
10TH	The Messengers	15 points
11TH	The Reluctant Readers	04 points

'So, with one band to play, The Messengers and The

Reluctant Readers will definitely face the survival vote. Brontobyte will join them, unless our final band scores sixteen points or less. And in case you're wondering, if there's a tie, the matter will be decided by a coin toss. Now, a few moments ago we spoke to Noah from Frosty Vader backstage.'

The screen above the stage cut to Noah being filmed with the guy from kids' TV.

'Noah,' the presenter asked. 'You're targeting seventeen points to guarantee your place in the next phase of *Rock War*. How confident do you feel?'

Noah shrugged. 'We've been practising for weeks. All we can do now is get out on the stage and play our balls off!'

Lorrie soothed her throat with iced water as Frosty Vader lit up on stage. Besides Sadie and Noah, Frosty had Cal on drums and stocky blond-haired Otis on keyboards. This was a contrast to the guitar and drum set-up favoured by most *Rock War* bands.

The band's quirky sound was emphasised as they started by playing forty-five seconds from the intro of Air's genteel classic 'La Femme d'Argent'. The mosh pit swayed gently, while parents in the seats seemed to enjoy the more gentle pace.

Then, just as people were starting to wonder if this was actually rock music, Sadie ripped a microphone off its stand and roared the opening line of 'Teenage Whore' by Hole. Noah's guitar and Cal's drums were proper rock, but Otis the keyboard player kept going with a weird Hammondorgan sound effect. It was either exotic or irritating, depending on your taste.

The crowd seemed quite muted as the song wound down, but Noah surprised the audience by charging off in his chair. It wasn't a huge stage so it only took a few seconds for him to go flying off the front.

The Granada Room gasped and there were a few yelps of *help him* and *oh god*.

Then the big screen showed the viewers at home that the whole thing was a stunt. Noah had thrown himself out of his wheelchair and landed harmlessly on a crash-mat down in the orchestra pit.

Everyone laughed and cheered as Noah wheeled up a ramp to rejoin his band mates, and attention turned on the three rock legends.

'I honestly don't know what to make of that,' Earl Haart began. 'Those of us who watched the *Rock War* auditions online will know that Frosty Vader was made up of two kids from Belfast, and two from the North-east who'd never previously met each other. They've been playing together for six weeks, but to me it still felt like I was watching two separate bands. So I'm *really* sorry, guys, but it's only three out of ten from me.'

Noah felt sick as he pulled up alongside Sadie and saw Earl holding up a number three.

'Three out of ten seems harsh,' Jack Pepper said, getting some claps and murmurs of agreement from the crowd. 'This was a good band, with a lot of talent and potential.

The problem is, you're competing against other bands who are just as talented, but already have a much clearer sense of their identity. For that reason, I can only award you six out of ten.'

Sadie's nails dug into Noah's arm as he worked the maths in his head. They had nine points, and needed an eight from Beth Winder to stay in the competition. Seven would pitch them into a coin toss with Brontobyte.

Noah felt sick as Beth sat shaking her head. It didn't look good.

'I just don't know,' Beth sighed, as the crowd sounded sad. But then she cracked a huge smile. 'I don't know what Earl and Jack saw. Because what I saw there was massive *potential*. There are thousands of teen bands all over the country, with talented youngsters playing rock music.

'But what I'm looking for here isn't the band that plays the best Led Zep or Sex Pistols cover. I'm looking for the band with potential to be the *next* Led Zeppelin, or the *new* Sex Pistols. Maybe some of Frosty Vader's stuff didn't gel tonight. But I saw a heap of creativity and bold ideas. So, Frosty Vader, I'm giving you . . .'

The crowd went quiet and Beth made a dramatic pause before raising a number. 'Nine out of ten.'

Sadie jumped in the air and Noah yelled his head off. The crowd went crazy as Beth left her desk and stepped up to shake hands and hug Frosty Vader.

'And there we have it!' Lorrie croaked, as she stood under the big scoreboard. 'Frosty Vader score eighteen points, which leaves them in joint eighth place with Delayed Gratification. Our bottom three remain unchanged, and now it's over to you.

'Lines are open. If you want to vote to save Brontobyte, dial the number you see on your screen followed by a one. If you want to save The Messengers, dial two. And add a three if you want to save The Reluctant Readers.

'I'm afraid that's all we have time for here on Channel Six. But we'll be back later with the results of the vote-off. And if you switch over to 6point2 in just a couple of minutes, you can hear interviews and reactions with all the bands and their families, plus a fantastic blooper reel showing some of the things that didn't go so well at boot camp over the past six weeks.

'Our young contestants take a break next week while they settle back into school. But Channel Six will be showing a three-hour special to introduce the new series of Karen Trim's *Hit Machine*. And I'll be back with all-new *Rock War – Battle Zone* the week after that. I hope you've enjoyed watching as much as we've enjoyed making tonight's show. Don't forget to call or text, and we'll see you back at ten fifteen for the results!'

*

It was eight thirty, but they'd just completed a live two-hour show and it felt way later to *Rock War*'s emotionally-drained contestants.

As the public filed out of the Granada Room, thinking up how to kill nearly two hours before they returned for the results, bands and families gathered in the backstage marquee. Nine bands were relieved. Brontobyte and The Reluctant Readers were being hugged by their families, while Christian rock band The Messengers formed a prayer circle.

Tristan's iffy drumming had probably made the difference between definite survival and the vote-off for Brontobyte. Jay was tempted to say *I told you so*, but his mates Alfie and Salman were also in Brontobyte, and with cameras all over he realised he'd just make himself look mean.

Instead he found Summer, and introduced himself to her nan.

'Did you enjoy it, Mrs Smith?' Jay asked politely.

'It wasn't bad,' she said. 'I listened to Summer, but I had my earplugs in for the other bands. And call me Eileen, for goodness' sake!'

Karolina came into the marquee and made an announcement from an upturned beer crate. 'We just got the IAB figures,' she yelled. 'Seven point nine million viewers. That puts us ahead of BBC and ITV, and it's the highest rating ever achieved for any Channel Six show apart from *Hit Machine*.'

There were a few claps and cheers. Meantime, Jen had approached Summer and her nan.

'There's a crew from *News Twenty-four* outside,' Jen said, having to yell over a room full of voices. 'They'd like to do a live on-air interview.'

'Now?' Summer said.

Jen nodded. 'If that's all right with both of you.'

Eileen looked a little anxious, but also excited by the idea of being on the news.

'Are you OK?' Summer asked, as she wheeled her nan out of the marquee. 'Do you need your oxygen for a bit?'

'I'm absolutely great,' Eileen said. 'Who'd have dreamed anything like this could happen to us?'

About fifty fans screamed as Summer stepped out of the marquee. The back of the Granada Room had a large concrete concourse, with shuttered shops along either side and the twelve matching black limousines parked in a line.

The area between the limousines and the back of the Granada Room had been fenced off with metal barriers, and a dozen security goons were ready to grab any fans or press who tried to breach the perimeter.

Jen took over wheelchair duty as Summer signed a bunch of autographs. When she'd finished, Summer looked around and took a second to spot Jen pushing her nan between two limousines. Because of the noise from the crowd, the BBC had set their cameras up on the pavement beyond the perimeter. They'd attracted a small, well-behaved crowd, some of whom lined up to shake Eileen's hand and tell her how great they thought Summer was.

A woman with a voice recorder jumped out as Summer walked between the limousines. 'Do you agree that your singing was poor tonight?' the journalist asked.

'No comment,' Summer said, remembering her media training. 'Speak to *Rock War* publicity if you want an interview.'

'How's it going with Jay?' the journalist persisted. 'Is it serious or just a summer fling?'

Summer was intrigued herself, because she didn't know the answer to that. 'No comment,' she said firmly.

The journalist finally let Summer out from between the limos when one of the security guards saw what was happening. But almost as soon as she'd stepped out, a photographer who'd been crouching between the next two limos shot up with his Canon and rattled off four photographs.

'You want that camera up your arse?' a security guard shouted, as he came charging over.

Still seeing white squares from the flashgun, Summer could just about make out Jen and a BBC person anxiously waving her towards the waiting news camera.

'Thirty seconds,' Jen shouted. 'Get over here.'

Summer broke into a jog as she moved beyond the limos, stepping off a kerb with a burly guard just a couple of paces behind.

'Careful,' the guard yelled anxiously.

Half blind from the flashes, and unaware that the limos marked the end of the fenced-off perimeter, Summer heard a motorbike engine and caught its headlight beam straight in the face as she glanced around.

The guard tried to grab Summer, but the motorbike was too fast. It hit Summer dead-on, handlebars smashing into her hip as the side of her skull hit the rider's helmet. As the bike skidded up the kerb and smashed a limo's tail-light, its rider rolled over and over.

Summer pirouetted, going completely upside down and landing on her side. Her hip and shoulder took most of the shock of landing, but her head hit the pavement, knocking her unconscious. *BBC News* switched their camera on and came running, while a couple of fans had caught the accident itself as they filmed Summer on their phones.

Leathered and helmeted, the motorbike rider held his back as he stood up. He reached Summer moments before Jen and the BBC cameraman. She was unconscious, gashed shoulder, jeans shredded and a leg twisted in a way that it shouldn't be.

'She just stepped out without looking,' the rider said defensively, as more people gathered. 'There was nothing I could do.'

While Jen called an ambulance, Eileen had been abandoned in her wheelchair on the other side of the street. She fought for breath as she wheeled herself off a steep kerb and towards her stricken granddaughter.

'Heavenly father,' Eileen gasped, when she got a glimpse through a growing crowd.

'I think she's breathing,' the rider said, as he crouched down. 'But I can't see where all this blood's coming from.'

Will Summer live?

Will Brontobyte survive?

Will Tristan sue?

Will Karolina Kundt die in a freak photocopier accident?

Will Jay get his heart broken?

And which band will win *Rock War*?

Find out in *Rock War – Battle Zone*, coming soon!

FREE! The perfect introduction to the world of ROCK WAR

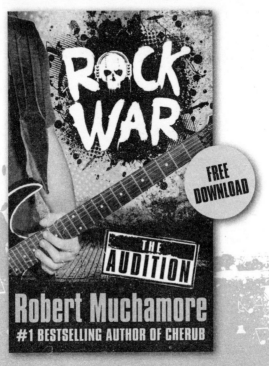

Noah's a natural on the guitar, and he'd give anything to get through the Rock War audition. But when he betrays his best friend to join another band, he knows he's crossed the line.

Will he risk their friendship for the sake of musical stardom?

Introducing new characters, a never-before-seen band, and a behind-the-scenes look at the Rock War auditions!

Go to www.rockwar.com to download now

Are you a CHERUB fan?
Read on for an exclusive extract
from chapter 27 of the last ever
CHERUB book, *New Guard*
– coming soon

27. DRAWL

'G'day,' Capstick shouted, in his annoying Aussie drawl. 'I've got good news.'

The squat instructor stood by the summer hostel swimming pool. Ning, Ryan, Leon, Daniel and Alfie faced him in their CHERUB uniform, while two assistant instructors stood at a console nearby, working out how to retract the electric pool cover.

'Normally, my job is to persecute you kids and get you into the best shape possible,' Capstick continued. 'But this is a different situation. I have twenty-eight days to prepare former CHERUB agents for a highly dangerous mission. They left CHERUB more than five years ago, and most of them now spend their days sat on fat lazy asses behind a desk. Your job is to motivate the grown-ups by showing them how far they've fallen off the pace. You're gonna go on training runs with them. You'll spar with them, play sport with them and study with them. It's old CHERUB versus new and I want you to show no mercy.'

'Current versus Crusty,' Ryan suggested.

Capstick wagged a finger and laughed. 'I like those names. So go get your swimmers on, 'cos we're gonna start with some fun in the pool.'